Mrs. Morris
and the
Vampire

TRACI WILTON

D0187970

KENSINGTON
PUBLISHING CORP.

www.kensingtonbooks.com

KENSINGTON BOOKS are published by

Kensington Publishing Corp.
119 West 40th Street
New York, NY 10018

All Kensington titles, imprints, and distributed lines are available at special quantity discounts for bulk purchases for sales promotion, premiums, fund-raising, educational, or institutional use.

Special book excerpts or customized printings can also be created to fit specific needs. For details, write or phone the office of the Kensington Sales Manager: Attn.: Sales Department. Kensington Publishing Corp., 119 West 40th Street, New York, NY 10018. Phone: 1-800-221-2647.

The K logo is a trademark of Kensington Publishing Corp.

First Printing: September 2021
ISBN-13: 978-1-4967-3304-7
ISBN-10: 1-4967-3304-5

ISBN-13: 978-1-4967-3307-8 (ebook)
ISBN-10: 1-4967-3307-X (ebook)

10 9 8 7 6 5 4 3 2 1

Printed in the United States of America

At midnight, the lights cut off and the ballroom plunged into darkness. The door slammed closed. A woman giggled in fear. Charlene, next to the exit, tried to open it but the knob wouldn't turn. Her pulse skipped.

Stephanos pounded on the wooden door.

Apprehension raced through Charlene as her sight grew accustomed to the shadows. "Is it locked?"

"Yes." Stephanos slammed his fist hard against it.

The door opened from the lobby side and a man in a gorilla costume asked, "What happened?"

Stephanos flipped on the switch and light bathed the ballroom. Charlene's gaze went to where Alaric had made his stand—his black-and-purple cloak was flat on the ground. Where was Alaric?

Serenity, one hand to her lips, raised the cloak to reveal a wooden stake with red on the tip . . .

Books by Traci Wilton

MRS. MORRIS AND THE GHOST

MRS. MORRIS AND THE WITCH

MRS. MORRIS AND THE GHOST
OF CHRISTMAS PAST

MRS. MORRIS AND THE SORCERESS

MRS. MORRIS AND THE VAMPIRE

Published by Kensington Publishing Corp.

CHAPTER 1

Hawthorne Hotel
The Witch Ball

Rock and roll music shook the brick walls of the Hawthorne Hotel. Charlene Morris left her costumed guests from the B and B boogying on the dance floor to see why Brandy Flint glared from the partially open door separating the ballroom and lobby. Why wasn't she shaking her groove thing at the biggest party of the year?

"Boo!" Charlene said into Brandy's ear. Cool air wafted toward her—a break from the hot crush at her back.

Brandy, stunning as ever, wore a sexy Little Red Riding Hood number that made Charlene's Southern belle seem very overdressed. "See them?"

"Who?"

"My daughter and her new boyfriend. Alaric."

Charlene squinted across the Victorian upholstered furniture and spied Serenity Flint in intimate conversation with a striking man. Ebony hair, dark brows, chiseled jaw, full, sensuous mouth. He had his fingers on her wrist, caressing. Black-and-purple velvet capes cloaked their bodies.

"Is it wrong that I hate him?" Brandy whispered.

Charlene hid her smile behind her antebellum-era lace fan. Unlike last Halloween when she'd worn jeans and cat earrings, this year she'd gotten into the Salem Samhain spirit. She was even a judge at the annual witch ball.

"*Hate* might be a strong word," Charlene temporized. She and Brandy stood shoulder to shoulder. They'd become friends in the past year since Charlene had moved to Salem to run her bed-and-breakfast. Flint's Vineyard supplied her house wine.

"It's not just the age difference—he's at least fifteen years older, though gorgeous. I'll give him his due." Brandy, her auburn hair a hint darker than her daughter's, scrutinized the couple on the couch. "He's a fraud. A liar. Yet Serenity is blind to it."

"A liar?" Charlene tightened her grip on her fan.

"He claims to be a vampire."

Charlene chuckled but stopped when she realized that her friend was serious. "Oh." She eyed Alaric over her lace. His face, hands, and throat were moon-white. "He's certainly pale enough."

"It's not the least bit amusing. My daughter is an intelligent witch and should be able to penetrate his illusion." Brandy sniffed and drank the wicked brew punch created in the hotel bar that smelled like sangria, served in a plastic pumpkin. "I wish she and Dru had never broken up. He really cared for her." She laughed at herself. "To be fair, I never dated anybody that my mother approved of either."

"Jared had my father's stamp of approval and he eventually won Mom over—but we loved each other from the start." Charlene turned from Serenity and Alaric to the ballroom of dancers. The clock on the wall read ten, and the king and queen of the witch ball would be announced at midnight. "How long have they been dating?"

"Alaric moved here from New Orleans two weeks ago and they've been inseparable. He told her that he wants her to be at his side for eternity. Can you believe that romantic nonsense? Serenity's eating it up with a spoon. *None* of my husbands made me that starry-eyed." She swirled the frozen-grape eyeballs in her drink. "I know they're up to something, but Serenity's being very secretive. It's not like her."

"Are you close?" Charlene folded her fan.

"Of my three kids, we're the tightest." Brandy bopped her black heel to the music. "I caught her going through our family's books on the craft from the nineteenth century. She hasn't cared about that since she was a tween and decided to be a modern witch. It's *his* doing."

"Have you spent time with him?"

"He refuses invitations to the house."

That didn't sound good. "Why did he move? New Orleans seems like a better fit with the constant nightlife."

"Alaric claims Serenity drew him to Salem—she's his soul mate and they're destined for each other. He wants to build a select vampire coven here with Serenity as his queen." Brandy rolled her emerald eyes.

"I thought *witches* had covens."

"Vampires too, according to the movies. I remain unconvinced."

Charlene lived with a ghost for a roommate, so she wasn't so quick to judge. She couldn't wait to discuss vampires with Jack once she got home. "I've seen *Dracula*—the one with Anthony Hopkins." She'd been fourteen and it had scared her so much she'd avoided the *Interview with the Vampire* craze a few years later.

"Do you see how she stares into his eyes?" Brandy's nostrils flared and her body tensed. "She's practically sitting on his lap, for Goddess's sake."

Serenity *was* very, very close to Alaric. "Aren't vampires supposed to have alluring powers?" The pair smoldered with sensuality.

Brandy gestured toward the ballroom, waving her pumpkin. "There are two hundred people at this ball tonight, and a quarter of them are dressed as vampires. He's as real as they are. Plastic teeth and all."

Charlene swayed her hips to the beat and studied the throng of costumed dancers as "Black Magic Woman" by Santana played—the cover band kept to the Halloween theme. "Makes it easier to pick a winner for best costume. What do you think of the Dalmatians over there by the punch bowl?" Chloe and Braydon Chesterfield had flown in from New York yesterday with their elaborate costumes in special luggage.

Brandy sucked the last of her drink through a green straw. "Cute. Guests of yours?"

"Yeah . . . this has been on their bucket list." Charlene watched over all of her guests to ensure they had fun. But how could they not? This was Halloween in Salem.

"You have to be impartial, Charlene." Brandy tapped her toes, dancing in place.

"I will! They went all out, though." Charlene realized that Brandy was by herself. "Where's Theo?"

Shadows crossed Brandy's face. "We parted ways, romantically. We're still friends and business partners in the vineyard."

"Are you all right?"

"My choice. Listen, I can't watch that train wreck on the love seat anymore—if they start taking their clothes off, would you dump some cold punch over them?" Brandy, slender body rocking, moved into the gyrating mass of dancers, pumpkin cup high.

A tall man with dark hair in a bright-yellow zoot suit immediately swung her toward him. Brandy tossed her head back and reveled in the attention.

Charlene was tempted to get a drink—a nice glass of red from the bar—and stepped away from the door, when Stephanos Landis, the second of three judges for the ball, joined her.

"There you are! I had some thoughts . . ." Stephanos trailed off as he noticed Alaric and Serenity on the love seat, exchanging a passionate kiss. He raised his brow. "Tantric energy shines bright around them. Good mojo for a witch. That's not Dru, is it?"

"No. Serenity's new boyfriend. Alaric." She didn't mention his claim to be a real vampire or that Brandy heartily disapproved. "Thanks for asking me to judge tonight. I can't believe all the different costumes! My favorite so far is the eight-foot alien."

Stephanos held up his palm. "Don't tell me. We need to be impartial."

"Sorry." She covered her face with her open fan.

"Your costume's lovely. Too bad judges can't enter, or you'd rack up some votes."

"Minnie helped me with the curls"—Charlene patted her elaborate do—"and Avery with the dress." She never would have managed without her housekeeper or her teenage employee. "Yours is amazing too."

Stephanos was decked out in seventeenth-century Pilgrim attire, complete with brass buckles on his shoes. In his seventies, he was very handsome and also a member of the local witch community with Brandy, and Brandy's mother, Evelyn.

"My thanks." Stephanos bowed. "What are your thoughts of the band? This is the first year we've had them. Now that you're part of the Halloween committee, we'll discuss whether or not to hire them again."

She warmed at being included. "So far, they've kept to the theme while ensuring everybody's groovin' on the dance floor." The Santana song segued into "Love Potion No. 9" by the Clovers.

"I agree." Stephanos snuck a glance at Serenity and Alaric. Serenity snuggled on Alaric's lap, her arm around his shoulders, nose to nose. He ducked his head to hide a smile. "Lucas does too."

"Where is he?" Lucas Evergreen was the third judge and also a witch, though not as powerful as Stephanos or the Flints. He owned a bookstore by the wharf that specialized in witchcraft and local talent.

"Over by the photo booth."

Charlene craned her head across the partiers to where a pirate with a parrot was getting his picture taken at the photo station with two fairies as Lucas untangled their wings. He wore a ninja costume.

There were as many witches as vampires and the other half was a mix. Some folks had gone to a lot of effort to win one of two five-hundred-dollar prizes and the king and queen of the witch ball title.

"How can we possibly pick the winners?"

"It's our solemn duty to choose the best." Stephanos winked at her. "You'll do fine. Now, I'm off to ask Evelyn to dance."

"She's here?" Charlene searched the crowd for Evelyn's steel-gray hair.

"The rowan tree," he said.

"Oh!" Silver-green leaves swayed from a sturdy brown trunk as she twisted her hips with rhythmic grace. "Who's she dancing with?"

"Don't know, but I'm going to cut in. That woman could write a book on tantric energy exchange."

Charlene didn't want to know more, so she waved at Stephanos with her fan and turned back to Serenity and Alaric.

In the past two minutes, they'd gone from canoodling to arguing. Serenity tossed Alaric's pale hand from her knee and said in a raised tone, "For tonight? I told you, Alaric. I don't share."

Charlene took a single step closer to intervene if Serenity needed her help.

"Darling," Alaric said smoothly, "it is a coven. We *all* share. Don't be a child about this. Elisabeta has been with me a long time."

Charlene's ears perked. Elisabeta?

"I refuse to come in second!" Serenity stood, her auburn locks flowing down the black velvet cape.

"Nobody can be second to you, my love." Alaric tugged her down to sit on his knee and stared into her eyes. "My queen. Trust me."

"I don't want to. *No*."

Charlene could feel his magnetism as he poured it over

Serenity—an invisible, yet powerful force. The young woman wilted beneath his kiss and he tucked her close to his body.

Was he mesmerizing her in some fashion? She bristled and agreed with Brandy that this man was no good.

Charlene left her post by the door and sashayed (thanks to the hooped skirt) over to the couple on the sofa, saying brightly, "Serenity! How are you?"

Serenity's green eyes focused on Charlene and she smiled in recognition. They'd met a few times at the winery.

"Hi, Charlene. You could be Scarlett O'Hara."

"Why fiddle-dee-dee—that was the idea, but don't look too closely." Charlene laughed and coyly fluttered her fan. "Lace and a glue gun cover a lot of mistakes."

Serenity's smile widened. "I won't tell. Have you met Alaric? He's just moved from New Orleans."

Alaric schooled his features as he realized Charlene had disrupted his enchanted hold on Serenity. "Hello." He offered his hand and his fingers were cold as ice. She dredged up what she remembered of vampires from watching *Dracula*. Cool skin—check. Pale, yep. Did he drink blood? Yuck. There were no musty castles here in Salem, so maybe he wouldn't stay.

She released his grip before he noticed her shudder of distaste. "This is my first witch ball too. I moved from Chicago to operate a B and B." Chuckling, she said, "I sure don't miss the heavy snow."

His full mouth firmed—no smile, no warmth in his gaze. His black velvet cloak with deep purple trim went perfectly over his fitted black slacks and a long-sleeved black shirt. Black leather boots encased his feet. "The old city has its charms, but I was ready for somewhere new."

She understood and wondered what reason he had for needing a change. She'd lost her husband in a terrible accident and wanted a fresh start away from all their memories. Had he lost someone too?

Alaric clasped Serenity's thigh in a possessive action. Her form-fitting silk dress had a plunging décolletage and a gem hung by a gold chain between her breasts.

"What a gorgeous piece." Charlene pointed to the necklace. The dark-blue stone was round with a white center, framed in gold. "What is it?"

Serenity lifted the pendant. "A star sapphire." She glanced at Alaric shyly. "A family heirloom. I love it."

Charlene couldn't even begin to imagine what such a gem might cost. And Alaric had only known Serenity two weeks? The hair on her arms rose in alarm.

Serenity tilted her head toward Alaric, as if seeking his approval.

Touching Serenity's shoulder, Charlene drew her attention with a low laugh. "I saw your grandmother's tree costume—she can really shake her leaves!"

Serenity rose in a swift motion. "Grandma's dancing? Let's go, Alaric. Less than two hours until midnight and your surprise." She moved toward the ballroom.

Alaric winced and shot Charlene a glare. "Love, that was for your ears alone."

"Ooops!" Serenity giggled like the twenty-five-year-old young lady she was and brushed her plum-and-black cape off her slender body. "I want to dance. Come on."

She disappeared into the crowd, leaving Charlene with Alaric. He had no choice but to get up and follow his "soul mate" to the dance floor. This close, Charlene could see that his skin was porcelain smooth. No makeup.

"Pardon me," he said, passing Charlene.

"Have fun. And good luck in the costume contest. Vampire suits you."

He stopped and whirled, his cape settling at his sides. "This is no costume. I *am* a vampire."

"Yes, I heard. From a coven in New Orleans." Charlene refused to blink as he pinned her with his dark eyes—he needed to know that Serenity had friends and loved ones around her.

"Do not mock what you don't understand." He dove into the crowd.

Charlene rubbed her bare arms, a little spooked by his adamant declaration.

Salem on October 31 was famous for its parties, witches, and supposed paranormal activities. She had friends who believed it to be the most haunted city in the world. She lived with Dr. Jack Strathmore, spectral resident of her mansion, where he'd been murdered. Who was she to say that vampires weren't real?

She followed Alaric into the room. Music boomed around them as the party raved. Her guests, Gabriel and Emma LaFleur from Georgia, were Raggedy Andy and Raggedy Ann. Olivia and Andrew Patterson had gone the witch route, as had her single female guest, Celeste Devries. Malena and Judd Hernandez decided not to match—Malena was a naughty nurse, and Judd, a pretty scary Frankenstein. Tommy Ramirez and Joey Tuft, both friends with Celeste, wore baseball costumes. Celeste ignored her guys in favor of a lanky vampire with sharp features and sexy steps.

Charlene chatted for a second with Chloe, wishing she could nominate their Dalmatian costumes, then passed Brandy as she headed toward the photo booth and the punch bowl. She never had gotten her drink.

"Hey!" Brandy called. "Charlene. Meet Orpheus."

Orpheus? Brandy was still cutting a rug with the beautiful guy in the zoot suit. He had swarthy skin, thick dark hair, and a thousand-watt smile. "Hello."

"He swears it's his real name." Brandy teased the man, who took it with good graces—as he should. Brandy was his visual equal in every way. "Let's get more punch. That's where you were headed, right?"

Charlene nodded and maneuvered through the crowd to the long table with a large punch bowl surrounded by plastic pumpkins.

"May I?" Orpheus asked in a Southern drawl that made Charlene think of the bayou, swamps, and crocodiles. He ladled punch into cups and handed one to Brandy, and then Charlene, before serving himself.

"Thank you." Charlene drank, the tart sangria quenching her thirst.

Brandy emptied her pumpkin and held it out to Orpheus for a refill. He laughingly obliged. "I have a flask, if you'd like somethin' stronger."

"Now, where are you from with manners like that?" Brandy flirted.

"New Orleans." He half bowed.

Brandy scowled and searched the crowd. "Do you know Alaric?" She pointed her pumpkin toward Alaric and Serenity. A pretty woman of about thirty-five, also pale, with black curly hair, moved like a succubus around Alaric, touching him, kissing him.

Charlene's heart sank as Serenity allowed the other woman into the circle.

Brandy's eyes blazed. "Who is that tramp?"

Orpheus offered Brandy the flask, which she accepted,

downing a quick shot, her focus on her daughter, the woman, and Alaric.

Charlene figured now was not the time to explain the scene she'd witnessed in the lobby. "Let's have lunch tomorrow, Brandy."

Brandy arched her brow but gave a nod. The ballroom door smacked open hard enough to shake the wall.

"Oh no. Dru." Brandy stepped into the multitude, dragging Charlene by the hand. Orpheus remained by the punch.

Dru Ormand, Serenity's ex-boyfriend, swayed and grasped the wall to steady himself, searching the room. He wore jeans, a black T-shirt, and no jacket, though it was chilly fall weather outside. His brown hair was rumpled and he smelled like whiskey.

Dru spied the rowan tree and headed in that direction. He halted abruptly when he saw Alaric, Serenity, and the other woman dancing provocatively. "Serenity!" Charging into the middle of the trio, he shoved Alaric backward and stood protectively in front of Serenity.

"What are you doing, Dru?" Serenity tugged on his shoulder.

Dru shook her off. "Stay away from her!" he yelled at Alaric.

"She's mine, *boy*," Alaric said with a sneer.

Dru hauled back his clenched fist and punched Alaric in the face. Alaric righted himself and brought his finger to his lip. His eyes smoldered. "That was a mistake."

Serenity jumped between them, pulling Dru toward the exit. "You're drunk!" she shouted. "Stop it."

"He's a freak, Serenity. I went to his place."

Alaric lunged for Dru. "You broke into my *home*? You'll pay for that transgression."

"You're not a vampire," Dru told Alaric, then turned to Serenity, pleading, "He's just a dude. Bleeds the same as the rest of us. I busted his lip."

Alaric flicked his tongue to the corner of his mouth.

"He's going to prove it, Dru. You'll see." Serenity left Dru to stand by Alaric. Alaric kissed her deeply.

Dru groaned and allowed Stephanos to lead him toward the door. "Let's go, son. I'll call you a cab."

Evelyn removed the mask of bark from her face. "Sleep it off, Dru. Things will be brighter in the morning."

"How can you take his side, Grandma?" Serenity put her hands on her hips. "You don't understand. I love Alaric. I *love* him." Her voice tripped.

"I love him too," the other woman said, putting her arm through Serenity's.

Lucas urged the band to play and the partiers danced like Dru's interruption never happened. Stephanos brushed by Charlene, ushering the ex-boyfriend to the lobby.

Charlene had met him once with Serenity at the vineyard. Whiskey wafted off the kid like he'd slept in a keg.

"I've called a ride for you." Stephanos clapped Dru on the shoulder.

"I love Serenity," Dru slurred. "That guy's an old creeper. Ain't no such thing as vampires. I went into his house, Stephanos, and he has blood in the fridge. No lie. Where did it come from? If he's a real vamp, why does he have it stored like that?"

Charlene tensed, thinking she must have heard wrong.

"We'll straighten it out later, Dru." Stephanos's jaw clenched with concern and he glanced into the ballroom.

Dru bowed his head. "He's rich and promised to take

her traveling all over the world. How can I compete with that? I'll kill him for stealing her away!"

"Hush, now." Stephanos led Dru out to the street.

"Charlene!" Celeste, flanked by Tommy and Joey, called for her. "Come take a picture in the photo booth with us. I want to remember this night forever."

Charlene allowed herself to be pulled toward the picture station, noting the time when Stephanos returned to speak with Evelyn. Eleven o'clock. Only one hour left to choose a king and queen.

Halfway to the booth, Celeste released Charlene to dance to "Zombie" by the Cranberries. "My favorite!" Celeste screeched.

Laughing, Charlene let her go and spent the next half hour studying the dancers and their costumes. A whoopee cushion, a serial killer, and the pirate with the stuffed parrot were a few of her faves. At eleven-thirty, Lucas, Stephanos, and Charlene escaped to the hotel bar to cast their votes for king and queen.

"I say the alien as king and the Aphrodite for queen. She's six feet of stunning." Lucas tapped the bar top. "Charlene?"

"The alien is phenomenal. The pirate's really great too," Charlene said. "That parrot on his shoulder seems real."

"The pirate is a local author who's won before." Lucas drank his beer. "Patrick."

"Oh." Charlene set her fan down. "Aphrodite is good too, but what about the rowan tree?"

"What a tree!" Stephanos reflected.

"Evelyn has also won before—maybe we should give others a chance to wear the crown?" Lucas suggested.

Charlene sipped her glass of red she'd finally had time

to order. "Let me look again." She brought her wine and peeked into the ballroom.

There were the Dalmatians, Raggedy Ann and Raggedy Andy. Witchy Celeste, dancing with the baseball players, and her lanky vampire, the naughty nurse spanking her Frankenstein. Charlene hoped they didn't regret *that* in the morning.

Brandy and Orpheus were skilled dance partners. Serenity and Alaric remained chest to chest as if it were a slow number and not rock and roll. Elisabeta pirouetted in their periphery, her gaze locked on them in a way that gave Charlene the creeps.

Aphrodite had long blond hair and a shield that she'd put just a touch more work into compared to the silvery leaves on the rowan tree. The alien definitely had more detail to his costume than the pirate.

Charlene returned to the bar, knowing they were making the right choices. "I vote for Aphrodite and the alien."

"What a king and queen!" Lucas rubbed his hands together.

The three judges went into the ballroom at ten minutes till midnight. Lucas joined the band to borrow the microphone, and Stephanos stood with Charlene just a few feet away, near the door.

The music stopped and people booed at the interruption of getting their groove on.

"It's time to announce our king and queen," Lucas said. "Each will win five hundred dollars."

Alaric and his female friend, Elisabeta, took advantage of the quiet to clear the center of the ballroom. The vampire who had danced with Celeste used a wooden stake to form a shape on the floor around Alaric.

"A pentagram," Brandy whispered, clutching Charlene's arm. Orpheus was across the room by the band, his gaze intent on Alaric. Had he ever answered Brandy about knowing him?

"What's going on?" Lucas rattled the microphone.

"Some of you doubt my power!" Alaric's voice echoed theatrically around the room. "I will prove that I am *Alaric*. Vampire. Eternal. I am death, reborn."

He reached toward Serenity, who watched, bright-eyed, with the pretty woman at her side. She grasped the star sapphire with slender fingers. "You will join me, Serenity, my necromancer, my witch, my love. We will reign the underworld together. Forever."

Orpheus stepped toward Alaric with an expression of outrage.

Brandy straightened in horror. "What did he just say?"

"I believe you, Alaric. My king." Serenity lifted the pendant. "Is it time?"

"Two minutes till the stroke of midnight!" He had the whole crowd enthralled, waiting for what would happen next. "I am Alaric."

"Alaric," the woman next to Serenity chanted. "Alaric." The lanky vampire had gathered other people to chant as well; Celeste, Tommy, and Joey. "Alaric."

Charlene's skin had goose bumps from the electric energy in the air. The band joined in the countdown to midnight like New Year's Eve. What would Alaric do?

At midnight, the lights cut off and the ballroom plunged into darkness. The door slammed closed. A woman giggled in fear. Charlene, next to the exit, tried to open it but the knob wouldn't turn. Her pulse skipped.

Stephanos pounded on the wooden door.

Apprehension raced through Charlene as her sight grew accustomed to the shadows. "Is it locked?"

"Yes." Stephanos slammed his fist hard against it.

The door opened from the lobby side and a man in a gorilla costume asked, "What happened?"

Stephanos flipped on the switch and light bathed the ballroom. Charlene's gaze went to where Alaric had made his stand—his black-and-purple cloak was flat on the ground. Where was Alaric?

Serenity, one hand to her lips, raised the cloak to reveal a wooden stake with red on the tip. The young witch fainted.

CHAPTER 2

Charlene froze where she stood near the door as Brandy cut through the restless crowd toward Serenity. "Stephanos, where is Alaric?"

"I have no idea. Come on. Let's help the Flints."

Stephanos was a big man with snow-white hair and a powerful presence. Folks yielded for them as he tugged her through the clustered mass to reach Brandy.

Brandy knelt at Serenity's side. She shook her daughter's shoulders to rouse her, then lightly smacked her cheeks.

A woman in a white-gauze mummy costume hustled toward them. "I'm a doctor. Give her room."

Chloe, her voice muffled by her Dalmatian mask, said, "What an amazing performance! This just made the night go from great to unforgettable. Where's Alaric?"

Her husband touched the dog tag at his collar. "He'll

come through the door any minute. There's really nothing under that cloak? Why a stake? Oh." Braydon laughed. "'Cause stakes are supposed to kill vampires."

Charlene eyed the red tip on the wood stick in alarm. Could that actually be blood? What was the point of Alaric's trick?

Evelyn arrived with her handbag and got between Serenity and the mummy, not an easy task to kneel in her tree trunk. She took a little jar out of her bag and put the scent under Serenity's nose.

Serenity's eyes slowly opened and she lifted her head. "What happened?"

Brandy drew her close. "Oh, my baby, you scared me to death."

"Where's Alaric? He was right here." Serenity's voice rose in panic and she struggled free of her mother's embrace. "It worked, then. The spell. Why is there a stick next to me with—with—is that blood?"

The mummy retreated. "If you need anything else, I'll be at my table."

Evelyn and Brandy helped Serenity to her feet. They clung together until Serenity pushed away. "Who was that woman?"

"She was somebody's mummy," Evelyn said, deadpan.

The crowd close enough to hear laughed nervously.

"What did you mean, spell?" Brandy asked Serenity.

Serenity clutched her star sapphire pendant with shaky fingers. "It's nothing, Mom. I need to use the restroom. I'll be right back." She hurried out of the ballroom.

Charlene noticed that Alaric's friend Elisabeta followed her. Celeste and the lanky vampire were in a loud discussion by the door.

"What did he say to you?" Celeste demanded. "Tell me how he did it."

"I can't. It's magic." He swung her into his arms. "Come on, let's dance."

"There's no music," Celeste said, giggling.

The band had taken a break while waiting for the winners of the contest to be announced. Lucas tapped the microphone to get people's attention, and feedback screeched through the speakers.

Charlene winced.

Stephanos, Evelyn, and Brandy made a triangle around the cloak. Charlene, not very mobile thanks to her hooped skirts, peered down at the hardwood floor. The rumpled cloak. The wooden stake.

She straightened and searched the room for the vampire. Beneath the fluorescent lights it was easy to see faces and hair. None, however, matched Alaric.

"Where could he have disappeared to?" Charlene whispered. She stepped on the floorboards around where he'd lain. Intact. She looked up and made out the shadows of folks peering down from the mezzanine.

"It's an act!" Tommy declared. "He's a magician—you know, like that Angel dude."

"Darnedest thing I've ever seen," the mummy said. "I hope he comes back now that it's after midnight."

"It was very clever." Celeste gave a side-glance to her new best friend. In the light, the tall, skinny vampire with sharp features had pale-blue eyes lined with black. Dark-brown hair had loosened from its slicked-back coif.

Charlene kept her voice low and directed her question to Brandy and Stephanos. "Why hasn't Alaric returned, if it was an act? And what about that stake?"

"Don't touch it," Stephanos advised. "You think the blood is real?"

"Yes. Technically, there's been no crime. I still think I should call Sam. Detective Holden. Just in case." Those instincts she listened to more often than she should were screaming that something wasn't right.

Maybe for once she'd earn some brownie points. "The blood is probably fake, Charlene," Brandy said defensively.

"It's Samhain, the Wiccan festival celebrating the end of the harvest and abundance." Evelyn's concerned gaze flicked toward the stake. "Which somehow translates into fake blood and gore you can get at any store."

Charlene studied the sticky red tip and drew her phone from her lace reticule hanging from her wrist. "I'll text. If it turns out to be nothing, then I'll take the ribbing."

Stephanos glanced around, arms crossed. "I wish the vampire wannabe would fly down from the ceiling about now, with an explanation."

She scrolled through her phone for Sam's number. "Alaric's attempting to lure Serenity to the dark side and promised her a lifetime with him—as long as she accepted this other woman as his partner too. Elisabeta, I think her name is." Charlene scanned the room for either woman, but they must not have returned from the restroom yet.

Stephanos combed his fingers through his thick white hair. "What kind of names are those, anyway?"

Odd. Dramatic. Charlene couldn't see Orpheus in the horde either. "Lucas is waving at us. Guess the party must go on." She nudged the cloak near the stake and stood in front of it so nobody stepped on it.

"It's time," Stephanos agreed. "Let's announce our king and queen before the suspense kills them." He gestured to where Lucas waited. "Coming?"

"Be right there. I'm going to text Sam first. I mean, Detective Holden."

He pulled on his brocade vest. "The whole town knows you two are chummy; you sure can't hide it from me."

She drew her exquisite lace fan to cover her face, leaving her eyes—made up in silver sparkles—unveiled. "Why, sir, Southern belles don't get chummy, not even with dashing detectives."

Stephanos laughed and rushed toward Lucas. Charlene eyed the cloak.

"I'll guard the stake," Brandy offered. "You do your thing, Judge."

"Thanks." Charlene flounced away in her hooped dress, texting her detective. **Sam. Any chance you can drop by the witch ball at the Hawthorne? Bring one of those plastic bags. It's probably nothing.**

Raggedy Ann and Raggedy Andy, aka Emma and Gabriel, rested at a table with fresh cocktails before them.

"The sangria is gone," Emma lamented, gesturing to the long table. Someone had knocked the picture booth over.

"The bar across the lobby is great, though." Gabriel raised his glass to Charlene.

"I'll visit after we announce the king and queen." Her feet were pinched in her low heels and she'd love to sit a while.

She left them chatting and joined Stephanos and Lucas at the podium. Lucas handed her the card to reveal the winners, and the men held the checks.

Charlene took the mike. "Happy Halloween! What a

festive night it's been—and the fun isn't over. It's time for us to announce the winners for the grand title of king and queen of the witch ball. Trust me, the costumes tonight were outstanding and this was not an easy decision to make."

She cleared her throat and smiled at the two hundred participants who'd gone all out for this event. Evelyn hadn't put her headdress back on. Where was the pirate? Could they give honorable mentions? "Each of you looks splendid. How about a round of applause?"

After some loud hollers and whoops, the room quieted again. "It is with great pleasure that we name our witch ball winners." She paused dramatically as the band played a few notes. "The winners are . . . The alien! Our worthy king. His queen is none other than the beautiful Aphrodite—come on up and take the stage!"

Her last words were drowned out by the roar of cheering and clapping. The eight-foot alien stepped up and assisted his lovely six-foot queen. He swept her into his arms and planted a big one right on her mouth as she struggled playfully to get away.

"Congratulations to you both." Charlene hurried off the stage, leaving room for Lucas and Stephanos to present the checks.

Lucas bowed formally in his ninja costume. "There were so many creative ensembles tonight that it was a very difficult decision. Yet, somehow," he smiled charmingly, "we unanimously agreed that the titles belong to both of you."

Stephanos motioned to the winners. "Since we only know you as the alien and Aphrodite, would you please give us your names? Then kneel so our judges can crown you. Our king might be a challenge if he were to stand straight." Stephanos put an arm up and only reached the big man's shoulder.

Everyone laughed. Lucas pulled Aphrodite forward. "Your name?"

"Cassandra, who once was a Trojan princess." She beamed and pounded her armored shield. "Tonight, thanks to you, I am now a queen!" Lowering her eyes, she said, "My parents are from the island of Santorini and my surname is Angelos. That means 'angel' in Greek. Trust me, my parents got that one wrong!"

The crowd whistled and clapped. She knelt and Stephanos centered the crown on her head, pulling silky strands of long blond hair over her shoulders as he helped her up.

The alien gave an awkward bow to his audience. "I am seven foot four." He spoke with a heavy accent. "I have had bit parts in movies and was a wrestler in the Soviet Union. My name is Dima, for fighter, last name is Smirnoff because I like to drink."

More cheering accompanied his speech. Dima fell to his knees, back straight, and removed the horned hat from his head, ready to be crowned. Lucas struggled with the alien's massive bulk, but after a little maneuvering he managed and stepped back.

With great pride the alien stood—holding his crown in place—wearing a very large grin on his bullish face.

The band began to play, and Charlene took that as her cue to check on the cloak and stake. Had Sam arrived, or had he ignored her text? He was probably very busy on this crazy Halloween night.

She reached Brandy and Evelyn just as Sam entered the ballroom. He strode through the dancers as if he had invisible armor that made him untouchable.

"Charlene, I got your cryptic message. What's going

on? Nice dress, by the way." He turned to Brandy, then Evelyn, brow arched. Evelyn only wore her brown trunk body suit.

"I was a rowan tree," Evelyn explained. "But it got too hot."

"Huh." Sam's focus returned to Charlene and she fluttered her lace fan. "You mentioned I should bring a plastic bag? I assume you meant evidence bag. For what?"

Charlene pointed to the ground behind Evelyn and Brandy, where the cloak lay, and the stake. The red tip was turning a brick color as it dried. Her stomach churned. That had to be the real deal.

"I think that stake has blood on it."

Couples danced well beyond the pentagram drawn on the floor, probably subconsciously afraid they might disappear too.

"What is that?" Sam bent to examine the wooden stick.

She braced herself for him to tease her about it being a gag or joke, but he didn't.

He straightened and rocked back on his boot heels. "Ladies, what happened here? One of you attacked a vampire?"

Brandy bowed her head. "Don't be ridiculous. I'm going to see what's keeping my daughter . . ."

"I'll go with you." Evelyn and Brandy exited the ballroom.

"That doesn't look guilty or anything." Sam placed his palm under her arm and dragged her close. "Now will you explain?" They stayed near the cloak.

She described the scene in clarity, and how Alaric kept repeating his name, then others chanted it too. "One minute he was bigger than Moses, then in dramatic style, he tossed his cape over his face, and the room went dark. Stephanos and I were at the door, but it wouldn't open!"

"And then?" Sam didn't release her upper arm.

"A gorilla opened the door from the other side. Stephanos turned the lights back on—Alaric was gone, but he'd left his cape. And when Serenity moved the fabric, the stake was there. With the"—she swallowed hard—"blood."

"He was supposed to return?"

"I think that was the plan, but Serenity never said. Just that the spell worked. So he's either a very good magician who had his fun tonight, or something else happened."

Sam let her go in contemplation. "What do you think?"

"I think Alaric wanted to impress Serenity. In my humble opinion, he had an elaborate plan to prove to everyone who doubted him that he was a 'real' vampire."

He studied her for a long moment and at last a hint of a smile lifted the corners of his mouth, partially hidden by his glorious Sam Elliott mustache.

She cocked her head. "What?"

"Charlene, you have never since I've known you had a humble opinion. You're always forthright, sometimes to a fault." He removed a bag from the inside of his canvas jacket. "You're more beautiful than Scarlett tonight. A Southern belle suits you—maybe you should try wearing dresses more often?"

She huffed but was secretly pleased that he found her attractive.

He opened the bag with a snap, which folded out to be large enough for the three-foot stake. "I'm not sure what I want to do with you."

She simpered behind her lace and batted her eyes. "I

have a few ideas of what you might like to do, but after taking me to jail, I don't think so."

"Are you ever going to forgive me for that?"

"Not until I'm good and ready." Her pride when he'd dragged her to the station to teach her a lesson about interfering in a case had suffered a direct hit. She turned to leave and he tugged her elbow.

His eyes were burning bright, and she knew that if there weren't a crowd of people around he just might kiss her.

She gave him a brief smile. "Good luck finding Alaric. Hopefully he's just at a bar somewhere waiting to surprise Serenity." But her whirling tummy didn't think so. "Want to come over in the morning and give us all the good news?"

"You're incorrigible. Maybe. Minnie makes much better coffee than the drudge at the station."

He carefully bagged the stake, and for good measure, used a second bag for the cloak.

"Where is Serenity?" Sam stiffened. "Hell, the whole Flint family is gone."

Charlene noticed that a lot of people were gone as it was almost one in the morning. The band would play until two. Aphrodite and Alien were going strong on the dance floor.

"I don't know—poor Serenity had a shock, so they no doubt rushed her home to bed. Thanks for coming, Sam." She bit her lower lip. "It's probably nothing."

"Hope you're right." He dipped his head and left.

Orpheus sidled up to her, long body loose with alcohol. Thick platinum hoops flashed in his ears. "Where'd your sexy friend go?"

"Home."

"Is she single?" Orpheus winked at her, his dark eyes beautifully lashed.

"You will have to ask her." Charlene chided him with a tap of her fan on his forearm. He'd unbuttoned the jacket of his zoot suit so it hung open, revealing a broad chest, covered in a snug black tee.

His gaze smoldered. "I hear she's a witch, in truth. I'm staying at the Longmire Hotel off Elton, if you'll let her know."

"How did you hear that? That she's a witch?"

"People talk." He shrugged. "I think it's hot."

"How long are you in town? I'll give her your message." Which was better than giving out Brandy's information to a stranger, no matter how gorgeous.

He half-smiled. "I'd planned on leaving tomorrow, but now . . . it might be a few more days."

Interesting. Before she could talk to him some more, Celeste called her name. "Charlene! We never got our picture, and now it's ruined."

Celeste, Tommy, and Joey tried to right the cardboard booth. Props of all kinds, from feather boas to a plastic machine gun, were scattered around.

"Hey!" The lanky vampire with blue eyes carried four beers from the bar. "I thought we were blowing this joint?"

"Where ya headed, kids?" Orpheus asked the group who'd surrounded the tall one like locusts on a ripe stalk of wheat.

"Calm down, calm down." He handed out the beers and sneered toward Orpheus. "Friends only, mate."

"Are you all right for the night?" Charlene asked her young guests. Well, not too young, but early twenties.

This was their first Halloween in Salem and it could be dangerous. "I'm headed back if you want to share a cab."

"We're going to hang out with Asher," Celeste said. They followed their new friend to the lobby. When Charlene turned back to talk to Orpheus, he'd left.

"Well." She said her goodbyes to Lucas and Stephanos, who assured her that she'd done a wonderful job her first time as judge, then caught a cab home to Jack and Silva at her bed and breakfast, Charlene's.

Her brightly-lit mansion brought a spark of pride. Leaving the cab, she climbed the front porch. Mums and fall flowers were arranged in baskets, some hanging, others stacked along the steps. She unlocked her door and went in.

Minnie had left the under-counter lights on in the kitchen, and a lamp lit in the main living room. She removed her coat and hung it on the coat-tree, then followed the scent from the kitchen.

She jumped as a giant fur ball pounced on her from the windowsill. "Silva! Why aren't you snuggled in your bed?"

Silva meowed and darted beneath her large hooped skirts to rub against Charlene's ankles. "That tickles! Come out of there and let's see what Minnie's left for us."

Charlene gave a shake of her skirt and Silva paraded over to her silver dish where she waited as she licked her paws. The clever cat liked to keep herself clean.

She heard a chuckle and a shadowy figure solidified at the darkened kitchen table. Black hair, turquoise eyes, an elegant figure in his black tux, Jack waved at her from his customary chair. "Welcome home."

Pleasure filled her heart. "Hello, Jack."

Charlene, Silva, and her charming resident ghost had a

unique relationship. No one else knew that the previous owner, Dr. Jonathan Strathmore IV, remained in his home and couldn't leave the boundary of the property. She'd been terrified the first night she'd met him, but now they were the best of friends, and she couldn't imagine running this place without him.

He'd chosen to stay with her, but neither knew the rules of his time as a ghost and she feared one day he'd just be gone.

"Let me feed our spoiled Silva and take a smidgen of this delicious carrot cake. I'm starving. I wish you could join me."

"I enjoy watching you." Jack stood and crowded next to her, blowing on a ringlet. "Your pleasure in food, or drink, makes me feel like I get to taste it too."

Less than a foot apart, his chilly essence doused her with cold. She moved slightly, not wanting to offend him—although in truth they were beyond that. They'd shared so much in the past year that they understood one another.

She took a tin of tuna from the cupboard and poured half in Silva's dish. After washing her hands, she sliced a piece of her favorite cake and put it on a fancy plate Minnie had left out. "Why don't you wait for me in my suite? I'll be there in a second."

Jack disappeared in a crackle of brisk air.

Next to the cake, Charlene set out a platter of crackers and cheese, and a selection of wine, leaving a note on the counter for her guests to help themselves.

She headed for her room and Jack, leaving her door open a crack so Silva could join them. The beautiful Persian had a soft silvery coat, luminous golden eyes, a fancy red bling collar, and a whole lot of attitude.

Jack lounged in the armchair across from her love seat. "You weren't long."

"No, I just put out a little something to welcome our guests home." She liked to include him since they shared the house now. It *had* been his first.

"I can't stand the suspense. Who won king and queen? Did you like being a judge?" A slow smile lifted the corners of his mouth.

"I really did." Her upbeat mood faltered as she recalled how the night had ended—with the stake and Alaric missing.

He soundlessly drummed his fingers against the armrest. "What happened?"

"Why do you think anything happened?" she asked her closest companion. Charlene studied his strong features and the touch of gray at his temples.

"You never go anywhere without collecting a story to tell." He searched her face as intently as she'd just done his. "Something out of the ordinary. Considering this is Halloween in Salem . . ."

She laughed and put her cake aside. "Let me get out of this costume and into something more comfortable. You know me all too well."

CHAPTER 3

Fifteen minutes later, Charlene had traded her hooped skirts for flannel pajamas with black cats and returned to her love seat. She quickly filled her intelligent sidekick in on the key points of Alaric's disappearance right at midnight. "He claimed his act would prove to Serenity that he was a real vampire. You should see this guy, Jack! He had smooth, pale skin, black hair, and dark eyes." She shuddered. "Quite good-looking, if you like the ghoulish type."

"And you don't?" Jack raised his hand next to a lamp and she could see right through it.

"No. And don't do that." Chilled, she wrapped a cozy blanket around herself and reached for her plate of cake.

"You're no fun. Heck, I could've made Alaric look like an amateur with some of my tricks." He floated the remote control across her line of sight.

"You're a talented ghost," she acknowledged, "but how did Alaric do it?" She and Jack loved to solve the occasional mystery. "Serenity woke up from her faint, alarmed at the bloody stake. I'm pretty sure the blood was real. She said the spell must've worked."

"Spell?" Jack cradled his chin in his hand and leaned forward. "It's the perfect night to cast spells, I suppose. Halloween. The witching hour at midnight. The Flints are a powerful Wiccan family. How did Alaric get them on board with whatever his plan was?"

"Oh, they weren't on board." Charlene swallowed a bite of cake. "Brandy said flat-out that she hated him."

"Can't blame her. She's a protective mother, that's all. What did Alaric want again—to prove he was a vampire?"

"Yes. To have Serenity be his queen. They had really strong chemistry, Jack. Could hardly keep their hands off one another."

"New relationships are like that, though. The flush of desire." He winked at her and she blushed.

"I guess you're right. Ardor will cool in time. Brandy needs to be patient." She wrinkled her nose. "I would feel better about everything if I knew where he went. That he's okay."

Jack zeroed in on her with bright eyes. "I trust your instincts. If you think something's off, then let's talk about it."

A rush of affection for Jack filled her and her adrenaline kicked in. "It's going on two, are you sure?"

"I don't sleep, Charlene." He chuckled. "What's bothering you?"

She put her empty plate on the coffee table and closed her eyes to picture all the people at the witch ball. Opening them, she said, "Alaric wanted Serenity to be part of his vampire coven, his queen, but she was to share him with another woman. I heard Serenity refuse but later, they were all dancing together."

"Who is this?"

"Elisabeta. She's probably ten years older than Serenity." Elisabeta had followed Serenity to the bathroom and hadn't returned.

"Was Serenity worried when Alaric didn't come back?"

"She was alarmed by the stick. The thing is, Elisabeta and Serenity left the ballroom and I didn't see them again." Charlene sat back and curled her legs under her rear. "Do you mind getting my notepad and pen, Jack?"

He levitated them to her, and she was able to actually think as she doodled. Old habit, and nothing that could ever be replaced by a smartphone.

"Thanks."

"My pleasure. What else?"

Charlene tapped the end of her pen to her lower lip. "You should have seen our guests, Jack. They all dressed up amazing. Dalmatians, Raggedy Ann and Andy, and our singles upstairs had such a good time they're out partying with a new friend—also a vampire, but I think this one knows he's not real."

They shared a laugh.

"Brandy and Theo split up," she said, glancing at Jack to see how he'd take the news of his deceased wife's lover, Theo Rowlings.

He shrugged.

"Brandy made a new conquest tonight—a guy named Orpheus."

"What's with these names? It's like they searched vampire names on Google and chose from a list."

"That's hysterical." She shook her head. "But Orpheus isn't a vampire, or vampire wannabe, though he does come from New Orleans."

"Like Alaric. Coincidence?"

"I don't know." Charlene adjusted the blanket around her lap. "We've learned that the world is a strange place. Do you believe in vampires, Jack?"

He scoffed. "No. But I didn't believe in ghosts either, and look where that got me."

She laughed and leaned back against the cushion. She'd been the same way, coming from Chicago. If she could touch it, taste it, smell it—then it was real. Her life had changed a lot in the last year.

"I have a message from Orpheus for Brandy; he wants to meet her again. We're supposed to do lunch tomorrow and I'll relay it then."

"So how does Brandy feel about all of this? She's very intuitive."

Charlene played with one of her ringlets, winding her finger around a soft coil. "Brandy despised Alaric and his manipulation of her daughter. She was like a mama bear, ready to attack."

"Protective, as you said. I see dark circles under your eyes—should we continue this tomorrow?"

Sweet. "Sam is coming over for coffee, and to hopefully tell us that Alaric is at home safe and sound."

Jack snugged the blanket tighter around her legs, always taking care of her. "Sam. Breakfast. Fine . . . I hope you're right; otherwise, Brandy and Serenity might have some questions to answer."

She smacked her palm to her forehead. "Serenity's ex-boyfriend, Dru Ormond, showed up around ten. He was furious that Alaric had stolen her away from him and punched him in the face. Drunk as a skunk. Ranting and raving, he said something about killing Alaric."

The yummy cake in her belly soured.

"*Punched* him?"

"I don't think we should take it seriously. Dru was very, very intoxicated. Stephanos called a cab for him."

Jack stood and moved about the small room. "Alaric angered quite a few people for only being in town two weeks."

"I know." She set her tablet and pen on the table. "He wants to make Salem his forever home." What had seemed amusing earlier no longer did and she blamed the late, or rather early, hour.

She stretched and put the back of her hand against her mouth to cover a yawn. "Do you mind if I say good night?" Friday had become Saturday and she suddenly felt the pull of sleep.

"Of course not." Jack bathed her in a warm smile. "We'll talk again tomorrow. Oh, who won the contest?"

"An eight-foot alien and a six-foot Aphrodite won. Their costumes were out of this world."

"Ha. Funny." Jack snapped off the television, which had been running in the background. "Go to sleep, Charlene. Things will be clearer in the morning."

She was reminded of Evelyn saying something similar to Dru.

As she walked to her bedroom door, the cold receded. Jack had shed his fabricated body and was back in the ether.

Was it possible that Alaric could do the same, with a spell from Serenity?

Too tired to think, she washed her face and undid her curls, then climbed into bed, covering herself with her plush duvet. Sleep arrived instantly.

When Charlene awoke, she knew she'd overslept. The autumn sun shone through the window and she heard voices filling the kitchen. She didn't have to worry, as she knew that Minnie and Avery, her precocious teenage helper, were already at work and keeping her guests happy. Saturdays Avery usually worked all day.

Charlene showered and dressed in a cheerful orange sweater and faded jeans.

"Good morning," she said to them, barely stopping as she focused on the scent of dark roast. Her mission was the fresh brewed coffee Minnie kept in the kitchen and the clarity a new day was supposed to bring. "Are the guests up yet?"

"In the dining room," Minnie said.

"Let me drink this java and I'll be human in a few minutes."

She poured a steaming mug and the smell let her brain know help was on the way. Now that she was over forty, her body required more than five hours of sleep. "Morning," she greeted Minnie and Avery at last.

"Happy Day of the Dead!" Avery shouted, giving her a big hug. The teenager's face was fresh-scrubbed from the green Martian makeup she'd worn last night when she'd gone out with her friends.

"What?" Charlene smiled over Avery's shoulder to Minnie. When she was free from the warm embrace, she hugged Minnie next. "Day of the Dead sounds terrible."

Minnie grinned and shrugged. "I didn't name it. Happy November?"

"That's got a nicer ring." Charlene sipped her coffee and sighed.

Avery hitched her butt on a counter stool, taking a banana from the fruit bowl. Fruit and pastries were always available on the countertop, and the teen had long lost her shyness over helping herself.

"Are you hungover?" Avery peeled back the yellow skin. "Some of the older kids at the center showed up drunk, and man, does that make Janet mad." Janet was the house mom where Avery lived with the other teens. "She wakes them up extra-early for chores."

"No, young lady, I'm not hungover." Charlene slurped some coffee, knowing she'd better drink it fast if she wanted to be at her best. "I didn't get in till very late."

"Did everyone like your costume?" Avery bit into the soft fruit. "I was hoping to borrow it for next year. We did a lot of work and it shouldn't go to waste."

"You're welcome to it, sweetheart." Charlene sipped again, her eyes widening as caffeine surged through her system. "I got tons of compliments." She cherished the one from Sam, especially.

Minnie placed her hands on her hips. "Who won? I love all the costumes. Should be pictures of the witch ball in the paper this morning."

"Really? That's great." Charlene took another drink, then ate a few grapes. "Alien for king and Aphrodite for queen. But that's not the coolest story of the night." Alaric and the cape came to mind. "Don't rush me now."

Their eyes rounded as they looked at each other. Charlene deliberately helped herself to more grapes and a healthy slice of a banana-walnut cake before she met their expectant gazes.

"Are you done now, missy?" Minnie asked peevishly, refilling Charlene's cup. "Can we get you anything else before you tell us?"

Avery bowed before her like royalty. "Yes, madam, it is our pleasure to serve you."

Charlene snickered, covered her lips with a napkin, then sputtered, "No wonder I love you guys. Here goes." She lowered her tones in a storyteller's cadence. "A vampire and a witch fell in love. The vampire disappeared at midnight with a promise to return, but he didn't."

"For real?" Avery's mouth dropped open.

Charlene nodded. "The clock struck twelve, and there was his cape and a bloody stake. No vampire. The witch claimed her spell had worked." She leaned closer to them in a singsong voice. "Where oh where did the vampire go?"

Minnie burst out laughing. "Charlene, I hope you're joking."

"Nope. Detective Sam should be over soon to tell us if he found our missing vampire."

"The detective, huh? No wonder your cheeks are pink," Minnie said, winking at Avery.

"Hey now." Charlene got up and topped off her coffee mug.

"He's superhot. If you don't want him, maybe somebody with a spider tattoo on her neck and a stud in her nose has a shot."

"If you were ten years older, I might be worried." Charlene was so happy that she'd taken a chance on this girl from Felicity House—a home for children with nowhere to go. She'd hired her with a little apprehension, but Avery had won over Minnie and herself, and even Jack.

"I'm just kidding." Avery's eyes glistened. "He might be my boss one day."

One of Sam's officers had given Avery a ride in a police car, and Avery was now considering joining the Salem police department . . .after college, thank you. Charlene had won that battle at least, and Avery would attend Salem State University for her bachelor's degree.

"His job is very important. Now, I think I hear our guests?" Charlene put her plate in the sink.

"Oh-la-de-da." Minnie flipped her apron. "We have some very fine people here this week."

"So fine, they don't even say *please* and *thank-you* half the time." Avery put her finger under her nose and lifted it in the air.

Shaking her head, Charlene left the two joking around in the kitchen and sat down at the end seat of the dining table. "How is everyone this morning?"

Gabriel, out of his Raggedy Andy costume, had brown thinning hair and a round face. She'd learned yesterday that he was a curator for a museum in Georgia. He slung an arm affectionately over his wife's shoulders. "Too late is all I know. We danced our feet off and consumed a little too much of that sangria, but it was certainly the best Halloween we've ever had."

Emma rubbed the crease between her brows—was that a hint of red makeup from her Raggedy Ann costume? "I have a deplorable headache—my own fault, of course. After the Hawthorne, we went to another few bars on Essex." She gave Charlene an apologetic look. "I managed toast and black coffee, but Gabriel devoured the frittatas and ham."

Chloe put down her apple juice and winked at her green-tinged husband. "We'll have to get our Dalmatian costumes dry-cleaned from all of our dancing, but it's worth every penny. The wine when we got here was just the right touch, Charlene."

"For you, Chloe," Braydon moaned. They were in their mid-thirties, no children. Both worked at a Manhattan publishing house. "Wine!" He made a sour face. "After the sangria? And mixed drinks? My undoing, I'm afraid."

Charlene chuckled sympathetically. "What about you, Olivia and Andrew? Did you overindulge?" The black-on-black they wore this morning was similar to their witch costumes yesterday.

Andrew ran a hand over his shadowed face. "Oh, man. Big-time."

Olivia shook her head. "Not me. Guess I'm the last one standing. But I could barely sleep all night. My mind was whirling, trying to figure out how that vampire escaped right in front of us! I wonder if he's a professional illusionist. Has anyone Googled him?"

Celeste Devries was at breakfast without Tommy or Joey. The bartenders from Jersey City had the three single rooms at the top floor. "No, but me and my boys partied with a friend of his, Asher." She blinked her eyes and grinned. "So cute. Anyway, we were out until four this morning when most of the bars closed. I guess Asher's renting a house with friends and we couldn't crash there, so he's staying in my room. I hope we didn't wake anyone coming in?"

They all shook their heads.

"We tried to be quiet," she said with a giggle.

"Did you see Alaric then?" Charlene asked. "Since Asher and Alaric are friends."

"Nope." Celeste bit into her toast. "Salem is the coolest city I've ever been to. I may not want to leave."

Judd Hernandez raised a brow. "It's incredible—but I like the witches better than the vampires."

"Alaric wasn't really a vampire, though," Malena said.

"Asher thinks so." Celeste swallowed her toast with some orange juice.

"I have my doubts, but it was part of the fun." Judd's tone let them know he wanted to deal with reality on his terms during breakfast. Charlene could hardly take him seriously, recalling how Malena had spanked Franken-stein on the dance floor.

"Speaking of fun, it's going to be a lovely fall Saturday." Charlene stood. "Might be nice to walk into town and get some fresh air. I can't recommend the tours enough. If you want to stay in and nurse your head, we have plenty of games in the den and a stocked bookshelf with local Salem interests."

"Thanks, Charlene." Celeste wiped her fingers on her napkin. "I'm going to wake up the sleepyheads and me-ander downtown."

"The wharf is a nice place to visit. Check out their har-bor cruise. You have a map and lists of tours with phone numbers in the welcome package we put in your rooms. If you need any more information, just ask us."

Avery entered the dining room. "Coffee or tea?"

Some ignored her, Charlene noticed, while others held their cups up and said, "Yes, please."

Avery put her hands in the pockets of her apron and

did a little curtsy that almost made Charlene laugh. She caught her eye and smiled.

Just then the doorbell rang and Minnie called out, "Want to answer that? I bet it's your handsome detective."

"Excuse me." Ducking her head, Charlene went to the door. She opened it invitingly. "Good morning, Detective. What brings you here? Good news or the scent of coffee and pastries?"

"Can it be both?" He ambled past her, removed his overcoat, and hung it on the coat-tree in the foyer. "I do have something to tell you, but privately. The information hasn't been officially released yet."

"Let's go into the parlor and we'll light the fire. I'll rustle up some of your favorites that Minnie makes special for you."

"At least one person in the house likes me," he said, tugging at his mustache. His brown eyes warmed.

She smiled. "Not the only one. Avery adores you. Silva too."

"Anyone else?" Sam moved a step closer, crowding her space. There were times when she wished she liked him more, and plenty of moments when she wished she liked him less. He disturbed her senses.

"On occasion I'm very fond of you too." Charlene took a step back, lips twitching. "Light the fire. I'll be right there." She felt a chill and gave a cold shoulder to her jealous ghost. Jack didn't like other men's attentions focused on her and made it quite clear. One of the conditions of his remaining in the house was that he behaved and didn't frighten the guests—or reveal his presence.

The last thing she wanted was to be overrun with ghost hunters. After giving Jack a stern look and tilting her chin in the air, she marched into the kitchen to prepare a tray for Sam.

His coffee, black. A pecan-and-cranberry butter tart that Minnie laced with warm orange juice and brandy. Greek baklava with phyllo dough, stacked with honey and nuts. This should sweeten Sam up enough to tell her things he probably shouldn't.

"Going overboard, aren't you, Charlene?" Jack's whisper in her ear made her cheeks flame.

"Do not create a scene, Jack, please." She peered into his deep-blue eyes. "Take a back seat and let's hear what Sam has to say—then I don't need to repeat it, correct?"

"Fine." He crossed his arms. "You left Silva in your suite and she kept pouncing on me to play. I finally opened your door and she went straight to her bowl in the kitchen, very put out with you."

"You opened the door?" What if someone had seen it!

Avery cleared her throat from the end of the hall.

Charlene turned her back to Jack. "Hi, Avery. Did you need something?"

"No, I'm still clearing the dining room." Avery squinted her eyes. "Were you talking to someone?"

"Just myself." She brushed some crumbs from the counter to the trash can. "If you need me, I'll be answering questions from Sam. We'll need a little privacy, okay?"

"Mm-hmm. Did you see what I meant about . . ." Avery cocked her head toward the dining room and lowered her voice. "Those people?"

Charlene had found them pleasant enough, but they weren't overly friendly with the hired help. "The way of the world," she told her. "Some good and bad everywhere."

"You want me to take that to Sam? You can tell your

guests goodbye." Avery had a silver stud in her nose and purple tips in her highlighted hair. It might put off some people, but she'd never apologize for Avery. She was streetwise and sharp—and adorable in a million different ways.

"That's okay." Charlene went to step past Avery but found herself blocked instead.

"I was wondering what time you'd like me to leave today?"

"Around three, the usual. Unless you've got something else going on?"

Avery shrugged her thin shoulders. "No, it's not important."

"What is it, hon?"

"Well . . . Some kids I know are going ice-skating today in the park. They asked me to come."

"You totally should! As much as we love you, you're not completely indispensable," she teased. "This is your senior year in high school and you should have some fun. Minnie and I can take care of the guests. What time are you thinking?"

"In about an hour? Is that okay?"

"Of course. Tell Minnie that I said yes."

"Will do!" Avery pranced off and Charlene carried the tray toward the glowing fireplace and Sam. Jack was smoldering a few feet behind the velvet wingback chair where Sam sat—it was his chair when they were alone.

"Here you go. Everything is still warm." Charlene sat across from him and rested her feet on the fancy ottoman she'd bought at Vintage Treasures, one of her favorite shops in town. Other prizes were the large ornate mirror centered over the fireplace, a mid-century solid brass shell for the entranceway, and also a gleaming brass telescope for the widow's walk to view Salem's historical sights.

"You didn't need to put all my favorites on one plate," Sam said. "How am I supposed to choose?"

"You don't have to. Take a moment and enjoy everything. I know how busy Halloween is for you." She relaxed against the backrest. "What did you discover on the stake? Did you ever find Alaric?"

"You were right about that being real blood on the stick. The stake was a prop—it came from the photo booth last night."

Alarm filled her. "Alaric's blood?"

"Don't know yet." Sam picked up the tart and took two quick bites, then leaned back in the chair with his coffee. "A body washed up on shore this morning. Male. Dark hair. Dark eyes." He stared at her over the rim of his cup. "Naked. With a hole punched through his chest."

She covered her mouth with her hand. "Staked to death."

"Like a real vampire," Jack said.

"I don't know the cause. Just that the man is dead. Can't imagine anyone being able to do that to themselves." Sam drank his coffee and bit into the baklava, then wiped his mouth.

Murder.

Alaric had been murdered. Charlene's head spun.

"You were there. What did you see? I'm especially interested in Serenity's relationship with Alaric. Be honest with me, Charlene."

Charlene glanced at Jack, who nodded encouragement.

She sipped the water she'd poured for herself. As Jack

had surmised last night, if Alaric didn't turn up, Serenity would be in trouble. "Sam, I don't think—"

"You can't protect your friends." Sam held her gaze fast. "The Flints are involved up to their witch brooms."

"Have you talked to them?"

"I sent two officers out already." Sam shrugged. "You didn't mention last night that Dru Ormand had shown up, threatening to kill Alaric."

Blood drained from her face and she swallowed hard.

Jack whooshed the embers of the fire. "He wants your help to solve this case."

Charlene focused on the detective. "It slipped my mind since Alaric had disappeared. You're sure that the body is him . . ."

"I want you to identify it."

"Oh!"

Sam showed her a picture of a man, obviously dead, on his back. In a morgue? She nodded slowly. "Yes." The man was beautiful even in death.

"Serenity said the same. We're waiting on his prints to come back to get his personal information."

Charlene bowed her head. "Poor Serenity."

"Poor Serenity? Charlene, she could be guilty." Sam steepled his fingers and stared into the flames.

"She isn't!"

"From all accounts, Alaric was coming on too strong." Sam eyed her and sat back. "A sexual predator. What if she fought him?"

Charlene had seen Alaric's hold on Serenity for herself. Still, would Serenity have killed Alaric? Even in self-defense? Serenity said she loved him. "That can't be right, Sam."

"Brandy, Evelyn, Dru . . ." Sam continued. "They'd all protect her if need be. But if she is guilty, I'll find out."

Her stomach churned.

Jack watched her from his position by the mantel. "We must discuss what happened. Find out how Alaric left the Hawthorne Hotel and ended up dead, washed up on shore, with a hole in his heart."

Sam polished off the baklava, took his water bottle in hand, and stood up. "I appreciate the information and Minnie's cooking. Thank her for me."

"You can thank her yourself if you don't run off." Charlene gestured behind her. "She's changing sheets upstairs."

"I will next time." He gave her a long look that she couldn't decipher.

"I just don't think that Serenity is guilty."

"We need facts. There are a lot of unanswered questions about this case."

"Sam needs to be on top of this," Jack said.

"I understand." Charlene cleared her throat. "I hope you figure it out soon. You know he's from New Orleans?"

"Yes. Be careful. If you hear anything, call me."

"I will. And I'd appreciate it if you do the same."

Jack snorted.

Sam opened his mouth, then slammed it shut. Straightening his shoulders, he appeared all of his six-foot-six self. He was a handsome devil. If only he could be a teensy bit more understanding.

CHAPTER 4

Around eleven, with her guests all out and the cleaning done, Charlene took her phone to her back porch and sat on the step. Jack had disappeared on her when she'd told him to be nice, so they hadn't gone over what had happened since Sam left.

She dialed Brandy's cell phone number, concerned for Serenity and how she was taking the news of Alaric's death.

"Hello?" Brandy's melodic voice held a hint of heat.

"Hi, Brandy. It's Charlene."

"I know."

Magic?

"Caller ID." Brandy scoffed. "You are so easy to read, even across the phone line."

Charlene shook her head and laughed. "Got me. You probably know why I'm calling, then."

"Serenity is devastated about Alaric," Brandy confirmed. "She acts like her soul mate was murdered . . . and that can't be right. They hardly knew each other."

Charlene understood losing the love of your life, but she and Jared had years together—not mere weeks. Still. "I'm sorry for her pain."

"I didn't like him, but it's killing me to hear her sobbing her heart out."

"Should we reschedule lunch?" She'd wanted to tell Brandy about Elisabeta and the lover's triangle, but it didn't matter now with Alaric dead.

Brandy hesitated, then asked, "Would you like to come over to the house? I'll put together some pasta."

Charlene had been to the winery a million times in the past year to pick up cases for her home and business, but she'd never been inside the historic mansion where Brandy and Evelyn lived. The place had been in the family for two hundred years.

"Sure. You need a distraction?"

"I was hoping you could help, actually."

Hair rose on her nape and she asked warily, "Help?"

"The police have been here already to ask questions, hard questions, about my daughter's relationship with Alaric. They took Serenity's statement and warned her not to leave town."

"Oh no." Should she still mention what she'd seen? It could be relevant. If their situations were reversed, she'd want to know. "I overheard Serenity and Alaric arguing last night."

"What about?"

"Alaric wanted her to be one of many women; at least one other—the woman he was dancing with before he disappeared, Elisabeta."

"That sleazy bast—"

"Serenity said no."

Brandy sucked in a breath. "That's my girl."

"But then they were dancing . . ."

"I saw. I saw. Light porn on the dance floor. He had her in thrall and I just don't understand it. My daughter is strong and powerful in her own right. She doesn't need a man, especially one so controlling."

"Have you asked her about it?"

"I'm her mother. She's not talking to me or her grandmother. That's why I thought you could maybe reach her."

"I'd be happy to try."

"You're a lifesaver. How soon can you be here? I'll shove her in the shower—she's been sobbing all morning. She didn't have anything to do with Alaric's death, but that officer suggested Serenity's tears could be guilt, not pain. Took all I had not to spell him with herpes."

Charlene snapped her jaw shut before she questioned Brandy about whether she could really do that or not.

She hung up and went to the living room. "Hey, Minnie. I'll be out for a few hours. Call me if you need anything."

"We'll be fine," her housekeeper said, singing as she watered the plants.

Charlene drove the fifteen minutes toward the winery, stopping at the two-story stone building before the shop. She was greeted by two large German shepherds on the stone porch and she scratched their heads. Brandy opened the door, in an emerald sweater and jeans, and ushered her inside.

Breathing deep of the unusual scent, Charlene asked, "What's that smell?"

"Juniper candles and sprays. It's part of the spiritual new year for Wiccans."

"It's really nice—kind of piney. Did you say *new year*? But it's November first."

"Samhain is the end of harvest, and today we celebrate the new year as well as honor the dead who have gone before us." An opal glinted off her forefinger. "It's known as the Day of the Dead."

"That's what Avery said, but I didn't get it. Is it a day of reverence for you?"

Brandy showed her into a living area with a fireplace, cozy couches in dark-brown leather, and assorted tables. A side table in dark wood held more sprays of juniper tied with forest-green bows. Short candles flickered before an array of photographs, some in old frames.

"Yes. My grandmothers," Brandy explained. "Each a talented witch and healer. Come meet them."

Charlene admired the rows of beautiful women, including the black-and-white pictures. How wonderful to be so connected to your ancestors.

Brandy picked up a photo dated 1920. "This is Amara—she started the grapes for our pinot noir wine."

"She looks like you, or I guess, you look like her."

Brandy smiled, pleased, and replaced the photo.

"Someday my picture will be there too," Evelyn said, joining them. "And Brandy's and Serenity's, and so on."

"Not for a long time, Goddess willing. Where is the child?" Brandy asked her mother.

"On her way down." Evelyn clasped her hands together. Her ivory linen dress was loose, yet stylish. "Thanks for coming, Charlene."

Serenity entered the living room and plopped on the couch. The lovely young lady had splotchy cheeks and wore a robe over fluffy pajamas—dressed for bed despite the hour.

"I'm going to make an altar for Alaric. Mom said you know what it's like to lose your heart?" Serenity dabbed at her eyes with a paper tissue, her nose red.

Charlene sat next to her and patted her arm. "I do. I was married to the love of my life, and then he was killed in a car accident. It isn't fair."

Serenity peeked up at Charlene in sheer misery. "I can't live without Alaric."

Her heart ached. "I remember how difficult it was to find a reason to get up in the morning. I think I spent an entire week in bed, not speaking to anyone."

"See?" Serenity glared at her mother.

Brandy eyed the ceiling, her thick auburn braid over her shoulder.

Evelyn took a chair across from the sofa. "Darling, we understand love and loss very much. We just don't understand how you came to be so close in so short a time with Alaric. Help us."

Serenity clutched the tissue in her palm, fresh tears streaming from her eyes. "He said that we would be together for eternity."

Brandy gritted her teeth. "He was playing you."

"He was a real vampire, Mom."

"Did you do drugs together?" Brandy demanded.

"No. Mom! You just don't understand our connection."

Charlene stroked the girl's forearm to keep her calm. Her emotions were dramatic, yes, but very real. She was only twenty-five and hadn't yet learned the cruel twists of fate. "Tell me about him. I never got a chance to know him like you."

Serenity sniffed and sank back to the couch, drawing her feet up. Black polish dotted her bare toes. "Well, he was amazing, that's all. Sexy, deep, a real heavy thinker. He loved to philosophize about the world. We were going to bring peace."

"Did you believe that he was a vampire right away?" Charlene couldn't forget how he'd had Serenity under his thumb.

"No." She blushed. "We never went out in the day, since he sleeps, but even at night he kept his skin covered. One early morning he showed me the effect the sun had—his skin blistered in seconds. It was very painful for him. He needed blood to heal."

"You gave him your blood?" Brandy shrieked. "Do you know how much power is in your veins? You're a witch that can trace her ancestry back to the 1600s! What were you thinking?"

"Chill out, Mom! This is why I can't talk to you." Serenity buried her head against Charlene's side.

"Serenity, love, did you give him your blood?" Evelyn asked in a measured tone.

"Only once." Serenity lifted her sleeve to show a faint red line on her wrist. "We were saving it to be most potent, after midnight."

"When was this?" Evelyn sat forward.

Serenity lifted her auburn head. "Yesterday—before the ball. To help with his immortality. He was going to make us all immortal."

"Who?" Brandy asked.

"Me, his queen, and Elisabeta. There were supposed to be two others, but I never met them." She cried fresh tears.

Charlene rubbed Serenity's back, angry on the girl's behalf. Sam had been right to call Alaric a predator. "How was he going to do it? Did he drink from you?"

Serenity turned beet red and clasped her wrist. "This was just a taste. I don't know for sure how, but he said my blood was pure and would aid in the transition."

"Transition from human to vampire." Evelyn's posture exuded steel and it was a good thing for Alaric that he was already dead, or the Flint women might take matters into their own hands. Charlene would drive the getaway car.

"He called you his necromancer," Brandy said. "You planned on raising him from the dead—he was already supposed to *be* dead."

"Well, sort of. He'd been preparing his entire life for this moment, he said. He needed me." Serenity brushed a tear from her cheek.

Charlene recalled Alaric's midnight performance. "What was he trying to prove by disappearing from the ball last night?"

"I guess he wanted to show the doubters, like that Orpheus dude Mom was dancing with"—she curled her lip at her mother—"that he was a true vampire at the height of his powers."

"Why would Orpheus care?" Brandy asked.

"He leads the vampire coven in New Orleans—he and Alaric had a big fight and Alaric left with hard feelings between them."

Brandy recoiled. "Orpheus is not a vampire."

Charlene sucked in a breath and stared at her friend. He'd wanted to get in touch with Brandy and Charlene was never more glad that she hadn't given Orpheus any personal information.

"Alaric agrees with you." Serenity sniffed. "He thinks Orpheus was using him to gain power and knowledge."

"That's ridiculous." Brandy crossed her arms. "I suppose Alaric had an aversion to garlic too?"

Serenity lifted her chin, but the defiance was heartbreaking as a teardrop fell to her lap. "He said it made him physically ill."

"Well," Charlene said in a nonjudgmental way, "his skin blisters in the sun and garlic makes him sick. Like the vampire lore we are familiar with. Did you ever see him drink blood, like, with fangs?"

Serenity shook her head. "He licked my wrist."

"Oh." Evelyn perched on the edge of her chair, ruddy-cheeked as she listened to her granddaughter.

"He drank it from a cup."

"What?" Evelyn rose and stood next to Brandy, the ladies standing united.

Charlene patted Serenity's back. "Where did he get the blood?"

"Don't know. He stored it in the refrigerator and warmed it up on the stove, then drank from a mug." Serenity smirked at her mom and grandmother. "He explained that it isn't any different than bone broth."

"Human blood?" Brandy's brow arched and her slender nostrils flared. "A great deal different and you know it."

"He said he has—*had*—willing donors." Her chin wobbled. "Elisabeta for sure, and another guy."

Charlene shuddered. Dru had said that Alaric had a fridge full of blood too. "Did he eat any actual food?"

"Not that I ever saw." Serenity glanced at Charlene. "I understand that it sounds far-fetched, but I believed him."

"Shouldn't his body have evaporated, then, once he'd been killed?" Evelyn asked. "Straight to ash."

"Mother!" Brandy said.

"What? I happen to like a good horror movie."

Serenity burst into more tears. "Alaric was unique—he suffered his whole life, he said. He wanted to live in peace. We were going to travel the world and—"

"Just you, Alaric, and his other woman?" Brandy jabbed.

Serenity winced. "Elisabeta. I didn't want to share, but . . ."

"He convinced you?"

"He died, Mom. Alaric wanted to prove to everyone that he was exactly as he claimed by vanishing. He was supposed to be at his rental house at midnight, but he wasn't there. Something went horribly wrong."

"Is that where you disappeared to after the ball? His house?" Brandy asked hotly. "We were worried sick about you."

Serenity tightened her lips and didn't admit to anything.

"Why midnight, exactly?" Evelyn asked in a calmer tone.

"He was drawing the supernatural power from the Day of the Dead with me, a witch with exceptional skills in contacting the other side. I can raise the dead."

Charlene's eyes widened at the young woman's claim—she wasn't boastful, just truthful and confident.

Brandy bristled with emotion. "It is never good to toy with spirits, Serenity. That is Witchcraft 101."

"We were going to use my heightened magic and rise again—both of us immortal."

Brandy's mouth was an angry red seam. "You realize that means he was going to kill you, to raise you up?"

Charlene gasped.

Serenity turned pale but nodded.

"And you agreed to this?" Evelyn said.

"He was going to make me immortal, Grandma. I was going to live forever with him, at his side. Bringing peace."

"If there was a spell for immortality, we would know about it. Longer life, yes, not eternal." Brandy crossed the room to drop to her knees and grip Serenity's hands. "Sweetheart, it scares me that you would even consider death."

"A momentary pain, then rebirth," Serenity whispered, not looking at her mother.

"According to Alaric, who is now dead. Dead-dead. Like you would have been, our angels have mercy." Brandy tucked a lock of Serenity's hair back. "Who else did you meet besides Elisabeta?"

"I only met her a few times, Mom. Mostly it was just the two of us."

"So he could convince you to do his bidding without outside interference." Brandy raged.

"Did you have doubts?" Charlene asked.

Serenity shrugged slightly. "He sensed that I had . . . reservations."

"As you should have!" Brandy said, standing again.

"Is that why he gave you the star sapphire?" An expensive gift with a hint that her life would be full of such treasures.

"He said it was his mother's. Star sapphires are a powerful talisman for a necromancer."

"What is that?" Charlene had never heard the word before.

"Someone who can raise the dead," Evelyn answered. "Serenity has the gift, like me and Amara. We used to hold séances in this house."

"So last night's disappearance was about convincing you of his power so that you could both be immortal. Not Elisabeta or anybody else," Charlene said.

"He promised. Just us two."

"But then he was killed instead." What had the plan been and who had interfered? The lights had gone out at midnight. Had that been part of the plan? Who had shut and locked the door?

"Yes." Serenity brought the damp tissue to her nose.

"And the fact that his dead body was just a dead body, and didn't turn to dust, doesn't make you doubt his story in the light of day?" Evelyn asked.

Serenity sighed deeply. "I don't know for sure how he died. The officer said a hole in the heart. Was it given by the stake that I woke up next to on the floor?" She sobbed in fear. "Maybe something went wrong with the spell I did."

Evelyn was across the room in four strides. "What spell?"

"He'd had a taste of my blood so that his spirit could find mine in the universe. If we lost each other during the transition." Serenity's fingers shook. "I don't know vampire lore—what was supposed to happen?"

"Poof," Evelyn snapped. "Dust to ancient dust. It's called *lore* because it's mostly make-believe. Serenity, he wasn't a vampire. He needed you to become immortal and was going to risk your life."

"Alaric loved me." She hiccupped. "He said he knew it the instant he saw me."

"When was that?" Charlene asked.

"At the coffee shop, two weeks ago. I'd ordered a soy latte and had a seat inside. He chatted me up, saying he was new in town. The rest is history."

"He was trifling with your life," Evelyn said. "He is no more a vampire than I am."

Brandy raised a clenched fist. "It's a good thing that somebody already killed him, or I would do it myself."

CHAPTER 5

Charlene accepted a glass of wine with grateful fingers from Brandy. Serenity had fled the room in tears and Evelyn had followed.

"What a nightmare," Charlene declared. "Is there a way to break her free from whatever he's done to her?"

"I'll do a spiritual cleansing for her and pour sage tea down her throat. She wants to make an altar for him!" Brandy took a large drink of the crisp white wine. "How could he have deceived her like that?"

"Serenity is young, and the idea of eternal love is romantic." Charlene sipped and set her glass down on the coffee table.

"My daughter was going to let Alaric kill her to bring them both back. There are no white light spells or magick for that, only dark." Brandy shivered. "I'm glad he's dead."

"You have to stop being so emphatic about that or

you'll attract the wrong attention," Charlene only half-teased, thinking of Sam.

"I want to talk to this Elisabeta first, and then Orpheus. Head of the vampire coven in New Orleans? That—argh." Brandy shook her fist in the air. "He played me and I don't like it."

"Well, he's staying at the Longmire Hotel."

"How do you know that?"

"He asked me about you—said you were sexy. I wouldn't give him your number, so he told me where he was staying if you wanted to look him up."

"Oh, I sure do." Brandy's eyes glinted with malice.

"He was supposed to check out today, but is hanging around a few days."

"Perfect. To hell with lunch. Let's go." Brandy stood.

"Hang on a sec. I'll go home and you run your errands. Do you know where Elisabeta lives?"

"Probably the house Alaric rented. The tramp."

Charlene agreed with that assessment. "Did Orpheus say last night whether or not he knew Alaric?"

"No. He evaded the question. But Orpheus is not the one I want to confront first."

Confront? Charlene drank her wine, dread a knot in her stomach. Brandy was on edge.

"I want to have a heart-to-heart with Elisabeta to see if she believed Alaric was a real vampire. What if Alaric duped her too somehow? And you, Charlene, are coming with me."

"What?" Charlene shook her head immediately. "I can't!" She'd promised Sam not to get involved.

"You have a knack for getting people to open up to you, and I need you to save Serenity. Not only from jail, but who knows what dark ties that animal may still have her bound by." Brandy tapped her fingernail to her glass, the opal twinkling. "How did Alaric find her to 'bump' into her at the coffee shop? That was no accident."

Charlene wondered if the act had been a deliberate pickup by a predator. He called himself a vampire, but who was Alaric Mayar really?

"We can't just barge into Alaric's house," she said.

"He's dead."

"But Elisabeta still lives there, unless she's fled."

Brandy rose abruptly, plucked Charlene's glass from her fingers, and placed them both on the table. "Let's go. I'll drive."

"Brandy!"

"You owe me for all the times you've wrongfully suspected me. I'm calling in what's due." Brandy speared Charlene with her bright-green eyes.

Charlene wished she could forget the instances where Brandy had appeared guilty, but wasn't, and her shoulders slumped. "Fine. But we can't just break into the house. We have to knock, and if nobody answers, we go home."

Brandy speed-walked from the living area to the foyer. "Get your jacket. After the rental house, we'll give Orpheus a surprise visit at his hotel. I can't believe he claims to be a vampire too. He mocked Alaric the entire night."

Charlene swallowed the words "I can't" and asked, "How so? We should definitely tell the police about that."

"Calling him a fake. A poser. I'm going to blame the copious amount of sangria for my lowered guard."

Charlene shrugged into her lightweight coat and grabbed her purse, following Brandy out of the house and into her sporty red Porsche.

"Great car."

"It's fun in the fall, crunching through the leaves. She goes in the garage over the winter." Brandy patted the dash and revved the engine, peeling out of the driveway with the dogs barking at them excitedly from behind.

The streets were relatively quiet for a fall Saturday and they made good time, though Charlene was in no hurry to get to Alaric's rental house.

Serenity had reluctantly given them the address, which was on the historic square around the Commons.

Brandy glanced at her. "You should see yourself! You're white as a ghost," she exclaimed. "This should be a piece of cake for you. Sticking your nose into other people's business is second nature."

"Very funny. I promised Detective Holden that I'd stay out of trouble. He'll have a fit if he finds out."

"Dear Sam, your champion. Well, he doesn't have to know, and if he catches wind of this, you can always say I forced you to come."

"I can take responsibility for my own actions, thank you." Charlene opened the door after Brandy parked before the house. "Are you sure about this?"

"I have to know what was going on here." Brandy grabbed something from her hobo bag and stuffed it into her coat pocket, slinging the strap over her shoulder.

"What was that?" Charlene closed the passenger door and waited on the sidewalk. "You're not bringing a gun, are you?"

"No! Just some special herbs in the event we need to temporarily immobilize her until we're gone." Brandy slammed the car door and they both jumped guiltily at the noise.

"And here I left my pepper spray at home." Charlene

recalled an anti-bad-spirit sachet Evelyn had once brought to the B and B. "Guess being a witch gives you a few more options."

"Stick with me, kid," Brandy said in all seriousness. "Seriously. We stick together."

The historic home had two levels and a shingle roof. Two red brick chimneys rose on either side of the house. The curtains were drawn tight over the front windows. The bright fall day had turned gray with clouds, adding to the gloomy atmosphere. The small yard was overgrown with weeds. The tiny wooden porch had a broken light and two ghoulish pumpkins next to the door.

Not exactly welcoming. Charlene kept Serenity's tearstained face in mind as she straightened her back and gave a firm knock.

"Holy crow." Brandy glanced around nervously. "What are you doing?"

Charlene glared at her friend. "Seeing if anyone's home. You want to talk with Elisabeta, correct?"

"I was kind of hoping we'd be able to break in and snoop, actually," Brandy confessed.

A flap of curtain informed her there was someone home. Charlene's pulse skipped. "Did you see that?"

"Yep." Brandy sighed. "The curtain moved. Some-one's inside."

"Good, our trip wasn't wasted." It was clear that Brandy needed direction, so Charlene hit the door again with the flat of her fist. "Elisabeta, please open the door. We just want to ask a few questions, that's all. We know you're there."

"You're good," Brandy murmured at her back.

The click of the door being unlocked sounded, then it opened a crack. A delicate pale chin stuck out, followed by a wan face, cheeks streaked with black makeup. "What do you want? This is a house in mourning."

"We just want to talk about Alaric," Charlene said.

"Who killed him? Do you know?" Brandy asked in outrage over Charlene's shoulder.

Elisabeta tried to close the door.

Charlene stuck her foot into the opening and Brandy pushed through.

Elisabeta breathed heavily as she confronted them in her front foyer. She was wrapped in a black silk robe too big for her body—probably Alaric's. "Have you no respect for the dead?"

"Oh, I do. More than you can ever know." Brandy's voice was steely. "You know who I am?"

Elisabeta drew herself up. "You're the mother witch. I noticed you and the crone's auras last night at the ball, along with Serenity's youthful gold glow. Not that Serenity was any *maiden*."

"Watch yourself," Brandy warned.

Charlene stepped a few feet inside the dark and gloomy place. There was a fireplace in the living area in the center of the house, though no fire burned. A leather couch took up one wall and there were shelves crammed with gold and porcelain knickknacks. A small chest of jewels was open on the coffee table, filled with gold chains and gemstones. How had Alaric earned his living? Though this house was small, it was in the historic district and had to cost a pretty penny.

"Or you'll do what?" Elisabeta sneered. "Our lover, our *master*, is dead. You can't do anything to me." She pounded her palm to her heart.

Vision adjusting to the dark interior, Charlene got a

better view of Elisabeta. Without all the fancy clothes and makeup, she seemed older than she had last night. Course, years of donating blood to a wannabe vampire could age any girl.

"My daughter is also grieving. What did Alaric do to her?" Brandy demanded. "She wouldn't have gone along with some elaborate scheme to be immortal. Did you know about the spell?"

Elisabeta belted the large robe around her skinny body tightly, her long neck showing red marks. Not from fangs, but hickeys. Her cheeks were hollow, her blue eyes luminous with golden flecks. She got into Brandy's face. "Of course I knew—I helped him plan. Your baby slut was all over him, eager to be his eternal love."

Before Charlene could defuse the situation, Brandy smacked the woman so hard that Elisabeta's knees buckled and she clasped her hand to her face. When she straightened, Charlene saw the hint of tears clouding her eyes.

"Get out of here," she hissed. "Or I'll call the police."

Charlene cringed, imagining an irate Sam. "Let's all sit down. Calmly. We'll ask a few questions and then be gone." She spoke as pleasantly as possible though the tension in the room was off the charts.

"Why should I?" Elisabeta lifted her nose. "I've been assaulted."

"You asked for it," Brandy countered.

Charlene reached for Elisabeta, palm up. "We want to find who killed Alaric. You can help us." If you didn't do it, she thought. "Bring him justice."

Keeping a safe distance from Brandy, Elisabeta led them to the couch. The only light came from candles on the fireplace mantel. Pictures in ornate frames crowded the walls. Wealthy objects appeared to have been scattered around without particular care.

Elisabeta, trembling with anger, took one side of the sofa, and Brandy the other. Charlene perched on an antique chair. She had to calm their hostess down. "We're sorry to barge in on you this way."

"Got any wine?" Brandy eyed the room and looked down a hall that led to a kitchen. "What do you serve your guests—blood?"

Elisabeta ignored her, shifted against the rolled arm of the sofa, then turned her attention to Charlene. "Ask your questions, and then leave me alone."

"Happy to do so." Charlene unbuttoned her coat. The heat in the room was stuffy and making her light-headed. "What was Alaric's plan last night? Was it an elaborate hoax?"

"He couldn't even get that right," Brandy taunted. "What a fool you were to believe in him."

Elisabeta kept her shoulder to Brandy. "He wanted to do something spectacular to prove his immortality to Serenity. And now—" she glared at Brandy—"he is dead. You have a lot of nerve coming to our home like the injured party!"

"Did he really believe he was a vampire?" Charlene asked, interrupting the ladies staring at each other with fury. "Did you?"

"Alaric was human," the woman admitted, "but he believed with the right power he could transition to vampire."

"Serenity. Her supernatural power. You used my daughter." Brandy's voice quaked. "You should have warned Serenity that he wasn't real. Don't you have any heart?"

"Go to hell." Elisabeta tucked her legs under her, un-concerned.

"Had nothing gone wrong, my daughter would also be dead." Brandy shivered. "There is no spell for immortal-ity."

Elisabeta rubbed the sleeve of the silk robe. "We'd di-vined that two in the morning would be the best time to perform the necromancy ritual. But . . . I came home after the ball and he wasn't here. He was supposed to be waiting for us downstairs. Serenity should have told you this already. She was here."

Brandy seethed. "Now that he's dead, what do you be-lieve?"

Her shoulders bowed. "I don't know what to think. It hasn't sunk in yet that he's actually gone. Alaric wasn't supposed to die."

Charlene fanned her face for air. "Who might want him dead? Do you know Orpheus?"

Elisabeta's mouth twisted. "Orpheus and Alaric were pretty tight when we lived in New Orleans."

"Together?" Charlene scanned the room for evidence of roommates, but it was tidy besides the clutter of stuff. Nothing personal.

"In the same coven, yes. All of us. NOLA has an amazing vampire scene with parties and festivals." Elisa-beta smoothed the end of the belt, tying and untying it. "They were really close but had a falling-out—I can't say why. Orpheus followed him here."

"How many of you moved here to Salem?" Not even shoes left by the door for a clue.

"Just the three of us. Alaric wanted to start over and do it better—that really pissed off Orpheus. It's no coinci-dence that he'd be in Salem at the ball the very night

Alaric died." Her eyes narrowed as they lasered on Brandy. "I don't believe in coincidences." She tapped her bottom lip, then suddenly sat forward.

"What?" Brandy asked.

Like an actress, Elisabeta paused, holding her audience enthralled until she delivered the final line. "If Alaric wasn't a real vampire, then why did his skin blister in the sun and why did he hate garlic so much? It physically made him ill." She sighed. "I wanted to believe in him . . . is that so bad? I loved him, through all the craziness, and now he's gone."

"It didn't bother you that he wanted you to share him with Serenity, a powerful witch?" Charlene rested her hand on her knee—nonthreatening.

Elisabeta jumped to her feet. "What are you suggesting? That *I* killed him? I think it's time for you to go."

Charlene stood up. "If I loved someone, I wouldn't want to share, that's all." She grabbed her jacket and purse.

"Listen, the whole vampire scene is one orgy after another." Elisabeta's voice lowered. "No room for jealousy. Ask Orpheus."

Brandy also rose, hobo bag over her arm. "What do you mean?"

"Orpheus was jealous of Alaric. I wouldn't be surprised if he jammed that stake through my lover's heart."

"Is your roommate home?" Charlene asked. "So you don't have to be alone in your grief."

"I am alone." She raised her chin like gothic royalty.

They moved toward the front door when a loud noise erupted from upstairs. Elisabeta appeared startled by the sound.

If she lived alone, that meant someone was there, possibly the killer. "Call the police," she told Elisabeta.

Brandy pulled out her herbs and dashed up the stairs—Charlene had no choice but to follow her friend.

"It's fine!" Elisabeta called from the foyer. "Come back down."

"What if they have an innocent girl up here? A victim to their stupid games?" Brandy stopped at the top of the stairs, winded.

It was so dark upstairs that it was hard to believe it was two in the afternoon. Charlene used her phone's flashlight to show the switch in the hall.

Brandy flicked it on, but the hall stayed dark. No bulb. "We have to check, Charlene."

Charlene nodded. "All right."

The first room smelled musty, the linens dirty and rumpled. Charlene noticed the window was partially open and peeked outside. A tall man ran full-out from the house, down the street, his black cape flying behind him.

Brandy pulled Charlene to the second room and jerked open the curtain to allow in some natural light. "Charlene, that's a coffin. Alaric slept in a coffin?"

Charlene gulped, her heart racing. "This is scary. I think someone jumped from the first room to the street. A man." She patted her chest to calm her heart. "Let's go."

"It's time for you to leave. If you value your life the way it is, you won't come back."

They turned in unison to see Elisabeta standing in the doorway with a wicked grin and a baseball bat in her hand. She smacked the fat end against her open palm.

"We're going now," Charlene said. "Brandy." She

yanked on her friend's sleeve, passing Elisabeta to the stairs. They raced down them.

In the brick foyer once more, Charlene shrieked when her cell phone buzzed. She and Brandy exchanged a glance, then Brandy opened the front door.

She accidentally hit the *answer* button rather than *mute*. Shoot. "Hi, Sam. Uh, did you learn anything new?" Why else would he be calling?

"Hello, Charlene. Wanted to tell you that we got a— what are you doing?"

"What am I doing? Oh, just chatting with Brandy." She pushed her friend to the front porch. Elisabeta practically flew down the interior stairs after them. Brandy tossed her sachet just as Charlene slammed the door in Elisabeta's face, keeping the woman inside and them outside, holding the knob.

"About the case?" Sam rumbled.

She breathed in deep and did her best to sound normal. "Brandy wanted me to console Serenity. She's in a bad way after Alaric's death. I'll call you when I get home." She cut off any further conversation with Sam and panted with Brandy on the front porch of Alaric's house.

"Sam is so not going to be happy with me."

CHAPTER 6

Brandy's not-so gentle shove had Charlene down the porch steps to the driveway. A black cat on the bottom stair arched its back and hissed—Brandy hissed right back.

"I thought witches liked cats," Charlene said once they were both in the car and the engine started. Elisabeta stood in the threshold of the open front door, the bat in hand. She didn't chase them. Was that due to Brandy's magick herbs?

"There is dark and light—that one was dark." Brandy sped down the street.

"Should we just call it a day?" Charlene would rather go home and regroup than head to the next person Brandy wanted to "talk" to.

"No." Brandy partially braked at a turn, then stepped on the gas. "Elisabeta is a nut. Orpheus seemed rational."

"What?" Charlene gripped the strap of her seat belt. "He lied to you. He runs a vampire coven in New Orleans."

Brandy didn't respond to Charlene's logic. "Where's he staying again?"

"The Longmire Hotel off Elton."

Brandy spoke into her GPS and the route popped up toward the historic hotel. "Orpheus will help us. He's a smooth liar, but I can get him to talk."

"What if he's the killer? What if Elisabeta did it? What if they're working together?" She cringed hearing the panic in her voice. "We need to be careful."

Brandy exhaled. "I had no idea that vampire covens existed outside of the movies. Have you ever been to New Orleans? It's very magickal."

"Jared and I fell in love with the French Quarter and history when we vacationed there for a week. Lots of spook factor in the dark alleys and cemeteries." She preferred the daylight, beignets, and creamy chicory coffee.

"Salem has old magic too, as you know. So does St. Augustine in Florida. There are thousands of other places with ancient power." Brandy strummed her finger against the wheel. "Alaric needed power that he didn't have, and he locked on to Serenity. Why her, in particular?"

"She's a young witch," Charlene said immediately. "Beautiful."

"Serenity keeps her Wiccan heritage on the quiet. She isn't flashy about it—she just is."

"What about social media? Everybody has Instagram and Facebook."

Brandy shrugged a single shoulder, focused on the road. "She doesn't post anything about the craft. It's very personal." Her nose turned red and she sniffed back tears. "She's torn up right now."

"Give her time," Charlene said. "She's strong."

They arrived at the old hotel and Brandy parked. Four stories of red brick, white trim, and chimneys on four sides. "I thank the Goddess that she is. She's descended from a long line of strong women, as you saw earlier on the altar."

"She's very fortunate." They got out of the car and Charlene tightened her jacket against the chill of the November air. Halloween decorations were still up everywhere. Salem was all about Halloween and witches—they didn't need vampires moving in. "What's the plan? I have to keep this short so Minnie can go home. My guests . . ."

"I know. We'll just . . . talk to him." Brandy opened the door and they both walked in.

"You can't simply ask if he killed Alaric."

Brandy gave her a stink eye.

The female clerk behind the desk greeted them with a chipper, "Afternoon! May I help you?"

"I'd like to speak with a guest of yours that goes by the name Orpheus." Brandy leaned against the tall counter.

"Last name? Room number?" She kept her fingers poised over her keyboard.

"I was hoping you could tell me."

"It's against hotel policy. Sorry, ma'am."

Brandy waited until the woman looked up, then she held the clerk's gaze for thirty seconds, saying softly, "Give us the room number for Orpheus."

"Orpheus?"

Brandy didn't blink as she kept the clerk on the visual

line. "You remember a handsome man with dark hair and eyes. A melodic Southern accent."

Charlene couldn't believe it when the clerk nodded. "Orpheus Landon. He's from New Orleans, that's where his accent comes from. Room three-twelve. Shall I ring him for you?"

"No need. We'll go up." Brandy didn't release the clerk. "Is he alone?"

The woman hummed as she drew on her memory. "Yes. He's checking out tomorrow morning."

"Thank you."

Brandy blinked and the clerk was free from her intangible grip.

The clerk raised her hand as they walked toward the elevator. "Have a nice day."

Charlene, stunned, murmured, "That is a very useful trick."

"That's nothing. Child's play." Brandy pressed the button.

They got into the car and rode to the third floor. If Brandy wanted to, she could get away with anything, including murder. Thank heaven she was a good witch, Charlene thought. "So we're going to wing it?"

"Though sloppy, it worked with Elisabeta." Brandy shrugged. "Thank you for taking the lead there. I was too emotionally involved. Anger tainted my intentions for answers. I can't believe Serenity would want to live in such a dark place."

"Did you see all the jewels and goodies? They weren't poor."

"Spiritually dark. But yes, you're right." Brandy left the elevator first and turned to Charlene as she walked out. "Heirlooms?"

"Like the star sapphire Serenity was wearing last night." Charlene adjusted her purse over her shoulder.

"It's all she has of Alaric now." Brandy strode down the hall, Charlene at her side, and they stopped before room 312.

Brandy nodded once at Charlene, then knocked.

Orpheus, dressed for the day in jeans and a partially buttoned silk shirt, boots laced and tied, answered the door. He grinned at Brandy, then Charlene—happy, but not surprised to see them. How often did strange females take him up on his offer for a playdate?

"How're ya doin' this afternoon, Brandy? You brought your friend. Sharon." He widened the door, light prisming off of the diamond studs in both ears. "Come on in, dahlins."

"Charlene," she corrected. "Charlene Morris."

"You were quite lovely as a Southern belle. Still are. I have wine in the room. Would y'all care for somethin' to drink?"

"No, thank you," Charlene said as Brandy countered with, "Yes, please. Our last place we visited was too rich in iron."

Orpheus laughed from deep in his chest and gestured to the sideboard where a bottle of red was open. He was using the water tumblers for glasses.

"Is this about Alaric's death?" His tone was cordial, like a man with nothing to hide. Leather bracelets were stacked on his pale wrist, catching on thin dark hair. Masculine rings were on multiple fingers. He exuded sex appeal. Wealth.

"Yes." Brandy sauntered fully into the room.

"Elisabeta called to give me the news but I don't know many of the details."

Brandy shucked her jacket and tossed it on the made bed, on the offense as she'd been with Elisabeta. "Last night you were very vocal in your dislike for Alaric."

"You were no fan, either," Orpheus said. "We had that in common." He flashed his white teeth as he handed Brandy a glass of red wine. Were his eyeteeth a little bit longer than normal? "Among other things."

Curling her nose after a sniff of the liquid, Brandy set it down without taking a drink. "We did."

Charlene hid a smile—was the wine truly that awful or was Brandy regretting their flirtation in the light of day? Orpheus was very attractive, but also arrogant; he knew he was sexy and used it to his advantage.

"What brings ya here," Orpheus drawled, "so upset? You should be thrilled that Alaric's gone and no longer a threat to your sweet daughter."

"A man is dead." Brandy crossed her arms, not amused. "You said that Alaric was a fraud. Why?"

"He claimed to be a vampire. As for me callin' him a fraud, well, I'm hardly wrong, am I? His death proved it." Orpheus's grin was unrepentant.

Charlene didn't care for his smug attitude. "Alaric had physical symptoms—his skin blistered in the sun, and he had an aversion to garlic. Did you witness that? It wasn't made up, from what Serenity and Elisabeta both said."

"Psychosomatic," Orpheus decreed. "His mother was a wack job and raised him to think he was 'special.'"

He thought Alaric brought on the symptoms himself. Charlene would have to ask Jack if that was even possible.

"Why didn't you mention that you're part of a vampire coven in New Orleans?" Brandy huffed. "Do you think you're a vampire too?"

Orpheus's eyes darkened to black and Charlene shivered. "You profess to be a witch," he purred wickedly, brushing his knuckle across Brandy's cheek.

Brandy smacked his hand away. "I *am* a witch." Her energy seemed to grow before their eyes and Charlene stepped back, bumping into the mirrored closet door. "You are just as much a fake as Alaric."

"I beg your pardon?" Orpheus's skin flushed with anger. "We are nothin' alike."

Charlene cleared her throat to get his focus off of Brandy. "Your disdain for Alaric is like the pot calling the kettle black."

The last of his easy manner disappeared. "Careful, now, ladies." Orpheus straightened and got in Brandy's face. "Alaric and I go way back. There are things about him of which you have no clue."

"Everybody has secrets." Brandy shrugged. "They don't matter in the end."

Orpheus gave an ugly laugh. "I wouldn't be so sure."

"Tell us, then," Charlene said. "It might help find his killer."

"The police will sort it out." Orpheus lifted the water tumbler of wine he'd poured for Brandy and drank it, never taking his eyes off of her.

Brandy bristled. "Did you know my daughter before last night?"

"I never *officially* met her at all. I'd be happy to rectify that. Why don't you invite her over to the hotel? We can have our own private party. I've never had two witches in bed."

"You're a pig. Stay away from her." Brandy glared at Orpheus, unintimidated by his larger frame and muscles.

Charlene, back against the closet, scanned the room

for anything she might use to protect her and Brandy if Orpheus went crazy.

The historic hotel had a small balcony and modern updates—but nothing too fancy. The walls were papered in white-and-cream stripes, the wood trim oak. There was a queen-sized bed with a maroon comforter, a maroon and ivory upholstered armchair, with an oval table and a reading lamp.

He had a Gucci suitcase wheeled by the front door. Wallet and keys on the nightstand. Black leather shoes with reddish dirt on the heels by the closet—the double doors were closed, the mirrors reflecting the furniture to make the space appear larger.

The bed was made, an open book on the comforter.

Charlene stepped to the side of the bed to skim the title—what did bad-boy vampire wannabes read for pleasure? A paperback on Salem's bootlegging history. Nothing nefarious or obvious in intent, like, how to kill a vampire.

"What're ya doin', love?" Orpheus asked.

Charlene jumped back. "Sorry. I'm always curious about books on Salem—for my guests. It is any good?"

He shrugged, his gaze hard. "A bit academic for my tastes. Secret societies and hidden tunnels that lead nowhere."

"But isn't that what you have in New Orleans?" she asked. "A secret club?"

Orpheus ushered her away from his bed toward the armchair. Charlene sidestepped, not wanting to sit. She glanced out the partially open curtain of the closed balcony. Orpheus was very tall. The man leaving Elisabeta's in a cloak from her second story had also been tall.

She swallowed hard. How well did the two know each other?

"It's a very private organization," Orpheus murmured. "I could put a word in for you, but it comes to a vote. Care to submit your application?"

"Uh, no. Thank you."

Brandy stepped between her and Orpheus, maneuvering him closer to the wine. "Did you know that Alaric slept in a coffin?"

"Everybody is different—as you can see, I prefer a bed. The only rule is that you're not supposed to draw attention to yourself or the vampire coven, or other members. Alaric broke the rules."

"Did you punish him? Stake him?" Brandy asked fearlessly. "Drown him?"

He chuckled as if Brandy wasn't a powerful witch who could crush him in an instant. "I did not."

"Elisabeta told us that you were jealous of Alaric. That's why you fought, and Alaric left New Orleans for Salem."

"Elisabeta's loyalty is suspect as she is always out for herself and not the good of the coven." His upper lip curled. "I was not jealous of Alaric. Talk about the pot and the kettle and all that. Elisabeta wanted his full attention, but as *you* know, he wasn't faithful."

"Who else moved here with Elisabeta and Alaric?" Charlene asked. "Serenity said there were others he had promised to turn into vampires, but she only met Elisabeta."

Orpheus scrubbed his jaw in frustration. "Others? Alaric was a fool who deserved what he got. I sit in judgment, but I was not his executioner."

"What will Elisabeta do without Alaric?" Brandy tossed her long braid.

"She'll find her own way," Orpheus said. "El's got more lives than a cat."

Charlene's gaze was drawn toward the mirrored closet. Was that black fabric, like a cloak, visible at the edge of the door where it met the carpet? Her nape tickled. Orpheus really wanted to be a vampire and that spooked her more than all of the costumes of vampires last night. "We should get going, Brandy." She picked up Brandy's coat and walked toward the room door.

Brandy nodded, but held up a finger. "Orpheus, I want you to look into my eyes and tell me the truth about your vampire coven."

He smirked.

Brandy held his gaze. "How many members are there? Do any have actual powers?"

"I'm not telling you anything. It's top secret."

Brandy didn't release him from her emerald gaze. "Tell me, Orpheus. How many are in your coven?"

He stepped back until his calves hit the bed, knocking the book to the floor. Sweat formed on his brow. Charlene picked it up as he gritted out, "Fifty."

"Do you have special powers?"

"No."

Charlene read the author, Dr. Patrick Steel, and put the book on the sideboard by the wine. Maybe the secret societies part was what had tempted Orpheus to buy it. It had an Evergreen Bookstore tag.

"Did Alaric have supernatural powers?" Brandy asked.

Perspiration dotted his lip. "No."

Brandy continued, calm but relentless. "What did Alaric want?"

His jaw clenched as he struggled not to answer, and yet he said at last . . . "To be immortal."

"Is that what you want too?"

His face darkened with anger as he admitted, "Yes."

"There is no such thing as immortality," Brandy chided, as if Orpheus were a child.

Charlene had new respect for the witch-vineyard owner as Brandy coaxed answers from a twisted man.

"You're wrong," Orpheus declared. "There are ancient texts."

"Fiction. Next time try Anne Rice."

Orpheus glared at Brandy. "I feel your power and know you're a true witch. Alaric said he would find one. Serenity. He claimed a witch's blood would make him immortal."

Brandy tsked. "I bet you wanted to be part of the new coven, if it had worked. You were waiting on the sidelines last night, uninvited. Pathetic."

His face flamed with unhealthy color.

That might make a man mad enough to kill, Charlene thought.

Brandy walked backward from where he sat, keeping eye contact. Charlene opened the door. "Stay on the bed until we leave," Brandy said.

Orpheus clenched his jaw but remained seated.

"Wait!" Charlene turned back into the room. "Did Alaric know Serenity before he left New Orleans?"

Orpheus, no longer in Brandy's sight line, leaped from the edge of his mattress and shoved both women to the hall, slamming the door.

The chain lock slid shut behind them.

Charlene and Brandy stared at one another, then

Brandy pounded on the door. "Let me in. Answer the question."

"I'm calling the cops if you don't leave. Now," Orpheus shouted.

"We have to go," Charlene said, pulling Brandy down the hall. "We can ask more questions later, but right now he's probably a little ticked off at your show of witch power."

"Why did you ask him that?" Brandy demanded.

"It was how he said that Alaric had told him he'd find a witch. Serenity. I could be completely wrong, but it made me wonder."

Brandy glared back at room 312, then pressed the elevator button. "You're right. We'll have to question him later. At least we have confirmation that Alaric had a 'witch blood' plan for immortality—not a thing, by the way. What an idiot. Desperate, or deluded, people will believe the strangest things."

"You're pretty amazing, with your ability to get information like that. I've never seen you use your powers before."

"Why would I?" Brandy's gaze hardened. "In a normal day, I believe in live and let live. Alaric messed with the wrong witch, and now Orpheus. Serenity must be cleared of any hint of responsibility in Alaric's death."

"Do you believe Orpheus didn't do it, as he said?"

"Yes. Unfortunately."

"What about Elisabeta?"

"Possibly her, that I believe."

The ladies reached the hotel lobby and went outside of the Longmire Hotel. The clerk acted as if she didn't see them.

Charlene zipped up her jacket as the afternoon had gotten colder. Gray clouds covered any hint of sun. "I have to be getting back to the B and B. What's next for you?"

"Pots full of cleansing sage tea for Serenity. Hopefully Mom and I can find out how Alaric found her."

They heard the sound of balcony doors opening above them on the third floor.

"Isn't that Orpheus's room? Maybe he wants to tell us that secret about Alaric," Charlene said, peering up through the elm trees.

Brandy pushed her out of the way just as Orpheus hit the sidewalk next to them. "Orpheus?"

Charlene gasped. He lay still and she knew in her bones that he was dead.

CHAPTER 7

Charlene shrieked when Orpheus's hand twitched. His eyes were open, his jaw slack, his head at an odd angle. His legs were splayed, his dark curls snagged on the one visible diamond earring.

Brandy tossed her long braid. "Let's just leave him and call the cops on the way home, anonymously."

"We can't do that!" Oh, but Charlene so didn't want to be involved. Sam would give her hell for sure. She knelt down and bent her ear over Orpheus's mouth, her gaze on his unmoving chest in the open black silk shirt. "He's not breathing." She put a finger to his wrist but found no pulse.

The clerk raced outside. "What was that?" she asked, wide-eyed.

"Is he dead?" Brandy snapped nervously.

"Yes." Charlene cringed at being so close to another death. They'd just been talking five minutes before when he'd been angry, but alive. "Call the police right away."

The clerk lifted her phone. "I'm doing it right now."

Oh, Sam. If only I could call you. But I know you'd never forgive me this time.

Brandy unlocked her car with a beep of the fob in her hand. "Let's go. Hanging around here won't bring Orpheus back to life. Do you think he jumped because he's guilty?"

Blood pounded between Charlene's temples and she winced. "I can't leave. Isn't it against the law to leave the scene of a crime?"

"No crime, Charlene. It was a clear suicide brought on by intense guilt. You can call Sam on the way, but I want to get home to Serenity."

"I thought you believed him when he said he didn't kill Alaric."

"You are such a goody-goody, aren't you?" Brandy pulled at her sleeve and nudged her toward the passenger side of the Porsche. "Maybe I was wrong. It happens."

Charlene gritted her teeth. "I'm waiting for the police. Go on ahead and I'll take a cab to your house to get my car."

Brandy blew out a breath. "Have it your way, then. But I'm not saying a word that will tie me to this wannabe vamp, got it? I have to protect Serenity until we find out more."

"I understand." Charlene turned to Orpheus and studied his lax and broken body. His mouth had pulled back to reveal his elongated eyeteeth. "Brandy, check this out. Are those real, you think?"

Brandy peered over at Orpheus. "He said he didn't have supernatural powers—I'm assuming that means he didn't have fangs."

The ambulance and police car arrived with blazing lights and loud sirens. Charlene was grateful that Sam's blue SUV didn't show up too.

Brandy's mouth was pinched, but she stayed by Charlene's side.

Officer Jimenez got out of the car and skewered her with stony gray eyes. The policewoman didn't much care for Charlene and the last time they'd met, the officer had wanted to arrest Charlene and throw her in the slammer.

"Ms. Morris. What's going on?" Officer Jimenez asked.

Charlene smiled politely, knowing she was screwed. Sam would find out about this before she had a chance to call him and her story about errands would go up in smoke.

"Hi. We were just leaving when this man jumped from his window. We think."

Brandy stuffed her hands in her jacket pockets and gave her Porsche a longing look.

The EMTs surrounded Orpheus and immediately loaded his body into the back of the ambulance. The driver murmured something to Officer Jimenez, and then the vehicle sped off toward Salem Hospital.

"Can we go?" Brandy shuffled her feet to convey that she was chilled.

The officer ignored Brandy and asked Charlene, "Did you know this man?"

"I think his name is Orpheus, and I met him last night at the witch ball."

"What were you doing at his hotel?" The officer lifted a suspicious brow. "Spend the night?"

"No, I did not." Charlene bristled.

The clerk waved to the officer, falling apart in tears. "I have all his information, Officer. I can show you."

Jimenez glared at Charlene, then Brandy. "I know where to reach you. I'll be in touch later this afternoon. I suggest you go home and stay there."

She sauntered inside the hotel to deal with the clerk.

Brandy clasped Charlene's arm. "That woman loathes you."

"Yeah. It's a long story. But for now? Let's get out of here before she tries to toss me in jail again."

They hurried into the Porsche and Brandy put the pedal to the metal. Charlene gave Brandy a watered-down version of what had happened that summer, gasping as Brandy took a corner like a professional NASCAR driver. "Hey!"

Normally having trees fly by in blurs would make Charlene sicker than a dog, but she clung to the seat and prayed to be delivered safely as they sped down narrow county roads at eighty miles an hour. No hurling. She pointed to the speedometer and stuttered, "You—trying—to—kill us?"

Brandy laughed and pressed the pedal harder. "Witches fly and that's what we're doing now."

"I'd like to get to your house in one piece."

"You're actually a bit green, so I'll slow down." Brandy glanced at Charlene. "That wasn't the first time you've seen a dead body?"

"No. It doesn't get easier." Charlene closed her eyes and rubbed the crease between her brow. "What about you?"

"Not my first time either." Brandy didn't elaborate but inserted a CD into the player. Soothing music sounded from the speakers—New Age stuff that actually calmed Charlene down.

They reached the vineyard and the Flint home. "Here we are, in one piece as requested. Try some chamomile tea for your stomach, and a lavender sachet for ten minutes over your eyes in a dark room for your head. Trust me." Brandy slipped out of the car and grabbed her bag and keys.

"I won't come in, but give my regards to Evelyn and Serenity. Thanks for an insane afternoon. Now to call Sam and confess everything, hopefully before that officer rats me out."

Charlene slid behind the wheel of her Pilot and waved goodbye to Brandy. She'd learned a lot about her friend this afternoon. Witches were real. Vampires, to her knowledge, were not.

She arrived at Charlene's after a slow, easy drive where her call to Sam went to voice mail—but she'd tried.

"I'm home!" she called, entering the kitchen full of delicious smells—spice and sugar both.

Minnie took one look at her and gave her a hug. "Are you all right?"

"I'm much better now, thank you," Charlene said. "Sorry that I was late. My errands ran over."

Minnie indicated the platter of happy hour treats she'd created. "It was nice and quiet. I got to sit down and watch a little telly with my feet up. Lovely, I must admit."

Charlene eyed the almond-covered brie. The spinach tarts. "These look amazing." She and Brandy never had eaten—no wonder she was starving. "I'm sure the guests will enjoy them. I know I will."

"The LaFleurs returned about a half hour ago. They're upstairs resting, but will be down soon, I expect. The Chesterfield, Patterson, and Hernandez couples aren't back yet, or the singles."

That eased the guilt Charlene had been feeling at leaving Minnie without Avery to assist while she'd been gone.

Minnie grabbed her coat from the corner coat-tree, put it on, and then a hat with squirrel ears and tail. "Gift from the grandkids." She shrugged, a good sport.

Charlene laughed, her headache receding now that she was home. "Say 'hello' to that charming husband of yours."

"Will? I wouldn't call him a charmer—he barely mumbles two words at dinnertime, then either works on a puzzle or watches TV until he falls asleep. My hero." With a sunny smile, Minnie headed out the door. It was only half past four, but it would be dark by five now that it was fall.

Charlene dashed off to take a quick shower and change her clothes, feeling dirty after the day she'd had.

Jack was waiting for her when she made it to her sitting room, striding back and forth before the television he had on low. "Thank God you're home!"

"What?" Charlene sat at her desk, noting his alarm.

"I was worried about you." He gave her a sheepish look. "After our argument earlier concerning Sam, I wanted to apologize. I shouldn't have sulked off. I waited, watching the clock. Then it was after four . . . You're always home for happy hour with the guests." He knelt and peered into her eyes. "You're all right?"

"I am, of course." If she'd been in a better mood, she might have thought it was amusing—explaining herself to a ghost. But he cared about her, as she did him.

"You had lunch with Brandy?"

"Not exactly." She folded her hands in front of her. "I know I'm going to get ambushed by Sam later, and I really can't take it from you too."

He relaxed enough to give her a quick smile. "Tell me what you can."

"It's complicated." She pointed to the kitchen. "Minnie made snacks and I'll need to get drinks for our guests."

"Fine. I know the drill." He stood up. "I can follow you."

"And have everyone think I'm talking to myself?" She shook her head. "I'll have to give you the short version."

"I'm all ears."

Charlene's stomach rumbled. "As you know, I had a date with Brandy for lunch, but when I called, she asked me to come to their house instead and console Serenity."

"Oh?"

"Serenity was a wreck. She loves Alaric, like, completely brokenhearted."

"Odd!" Jack tilted his head. "She's only known him for such a brief time."

"Yes, well, she really fell for his spiel. You'd think an intelligent, beautiful girl with centuries of witches to lean on wouldn't succumb to a self-proclaimed vampire." She shivered, remembering the coffin at Elisabeta's dark house. "Just the thought of spending an eternity with a man who sucks blood, or in his case drinks it from a cup, and sleeps in a coffin, makes my head spin."

Jack raised his arm to his side. "Vampires have a romantic reputation—maybe that appealed to her."

"Imagine never seeing daylight again, or going to a beach, hanging out with good friends and sharing a laugh or two—gone forever. That would be terrible. Surely you can concede that being a ghost is better than dead?"

He chuckled. "You have a valid point."

"Well, after calming Serenity down, I was ready to come home, but Brandy said that I owed her for all the times I'd suspected her of nebulous misdoings and she insisted that I accompany her to Alaric's rental house to ask Elisabeta about Alaric." She gulped, recalling how Orpheus had died. "And Orpheus . . . he—"

"Were they together?"

"No, and that Elisabeta is a dingbat. Orpheus." She clasped her fingers together tightly. "He's dead, Jack."

"Oh no."

"We'd stopped by his hotel to ask him about Alaric, and he tossed himself off the balcony after answering Brandy's questions." Her headache returned and she stood up. "We were on the sidewalk, ready to leave. Bam." She glanced to the kitchen. "I hear folks moving around. It was awful, and I know Sam is going to be furious that we were there."

Jack escorted her to the door. "Have fun if you're able."

Charlene passed through the kitchen to the living room, where her guests were all accounted for, even the lanky guy with Celeste. Everyone seemed to be at ease. "Glad to see you found the wine. I'll be right back with a platter of apps that Minnie made."

She returned to the kitchen, where the tray was already

made and covered in Saran Wrap. All she had to do was remove the plastic and serve. Minnie was a certified angel.

A few almonds helped tide her over as Charlene popped open another bottle of red and left it on the counter. She gathered together small plates, forks, and napkins, placed them on top of the heavy platter, and carried it to her guests.

"Hey, Charlene? Need any help?" Celeste rose from her spot by the fire where she'd been talking to Tommy, Joey, and Asher. What was he still doing here?

Joey and Tommy had been on either side of Celeste, and she wondered if the guys had competition for Celeste's affections.

"Thanks." Charlene set the heavy dish on a sideboard. "If one of you bartenders would grab the open cabernet on the counter, that would be a big help."

"I'll get it," Tommy said.

"And pour a glass for me, please?" She'd earned it after her rough day.

Tommy gave her a thumbs-up and headed for the kitchen.

Celeste went to the open bottle of white on the sideboard. "Anybody need a refill?" Emma and Malena raised their hands.

What a sweetheart. Charlene put the plates and napkins on both sides and the two platters in the middle. "Help yourself, everyone. I apologize for the late start and hope it doesn't interrupt your dinner plans."

The warm brie, baked in phyllo, was covered in almonds and berries with fancy crackers and small chunks of artisan bread on the side. Spinach tarts and pumpkin bread were on the other. Bean dip and chips. Her stomach rumbled, but she would wait until her guests had all eaten first.

Tommy returned with the red and gave Charlene a wonderfully full glass. "Thank you—now get in line." She sipped.

Celeste brought the bottle to the sideboard and gestured for Charlene to come to the foyer, where she murmured, "I hope it's okay that Asher is staying with me in my room? I mean, I can pay more, if you want." Her cheeks were pink. "Since there's two of us."

The room had a full-sized bed, but if the girl wanted to share it, it made no difference to Charlene. "It's fine. Will he be leaving with you on Wednesday?"

Her pretty eyes glittered with infatuation. "I've been talking up Jersey City, but I don't know that Tommy and Joey are quite as on board."

Charlene nodded but kept quiet. She'd seen how Tommy stole peeks at Celeste. Celeste might think they were all just friends, but she'd bet Tommy thought differently.

Young love.

"What's his name? For my records, is all."

"Asher Torrance. Isn't he cute?"

"He is," Charlene said. "Love his blue eyes."

"Me too." Celeste sighed.

Charlene bit her tongue before she warned the girl to be careful. It wasn't her place. "Is he from around here?"

Celeste shrugged. "I haven't asked. Hard to believe we just met last night, but it was instant chemistry. Even if it's only for a few more days, no regrets. Life is short, right? I mean, that Alaric guy is dead. Just like that."

"Life is short." Charlene agreed wholeheartedly. "Where'd you hear about Alaric?"

Celeste waved at Asher, distracted. "Dunno. Talk to you later?" But the young lady was already crossing to Asher, practically floating on air.

Her skin dotted with a chill, then Jack said, "Celeste is besotted, but I'm not sure about her guy. Asher seems a little jumpy. Constantly looking over his shoulder." Silva joined them, squeezing between Jack's legs—or what should be his legs.

Annoyed, the Persian's tail shot up in the air, and she took off to the fourth step of the staircase, licking her paws.

Charlene chuckled at Jack and Silva's antics. "I'll keep my eye on him."

The line for the buffet had shortened, and she got behind Tommy and Joey as they scooped up treats. She chose a plate, not too concerned about Asher. In the past year her business had hosted strangers week after week, but Charlene had an unseen protector. She never had to worry as long as she had Jack.

Charlene helped herself to a few crackers, brie, and a spinach tart, then topped off her glass of red. She found an empty seat next to Olivia and Andrew. She'd liked this dynamic couple the moment she'd met them.

"So how was your day? What did you do?" Charlene leaned back in her chair and sipped her wine. Next, a bite of spinach tart.

"We took a harbor cruise," they both answered at once, sharing a look and a laugh. Just as she'd have done with her husband, Jared, when he was alive.

"Great! I still haven't done that. I seem to have so little free time." Running a large B and B kept her very busy. "Which cruise line did you take?"

"The *Schooner Fame*. We heard they were all good, but we were having lunch down at the wharf, and it was right there, so . . ." Andrew told her with a shrug.

"I want to hear all about it. Where does it take you; what did you see?" Charlene piled warm brie on a cracker. "Sorry to sound nosy, but if you really enjoyed it, I'll add it to my 'things to do' for my guests."

"Definitely add it," Olivia said. "We had the best time. The staff on board were excellent, happy to answer all our questions."

Andrew put down his empty wineglass. "I'll refill our drinks and tell you the highlights. I know we can't monopolize your time."

"I wish you could," she answered truthfully. They were an easy couple to chat with, and after the day she'd had? She deserved a break.

A rumbling voice sounded behind her and she gave a guilty start. "Here you are. I've been trying to reach you all afternoon."

She stood up and put her glass and plate on the floor at her feet. "Sorry, Sam. It's been one of those days."

His eyes narrowed and his mustache quivered. "So I've heard. In private, please?"

She glanced at Andrew and Olivia, who looked at him with interest. Sam was dressed in casual jeans and a denim jacket—they probably wondered who this guy was, and if they should intervene.

"Sorry I can't hear about your adventure right now, but

Detective Holden needs to ask me a few questions." She shrugged. "Later, maybe?"

She didn't hear their answer as Sam had taken her arm and was leading her to the dining room. Like she might try to escape. Once again treating her like a criminal, when all she wanted was to catch the real bad guys or girls.

She gritted her teeth. "Unhand me."

CHAPTER 8

Always the gentleman, Sam dropped his hands and backed up a few steps.

"Thank you," Charlene said coldly, crossing her arms in defensive mode. "I'm guessing this has to do with Officer Jimenez?"

"Please take a seat." He pointed to a dining room chair. "I want an explanation before I—"

"Wring my neck?" She sat down quickly, propping her elbows on the table.

"Pretty much." He turned his seat around and leaned on the back.

His brown eyes searched her face, and she knew he was seething by the twitch at his clamped jaw.

She averted her gaze, ashamed to be in this position where he was disappointed in her actions. Again.

"You can't even look me in the eye right now, can you?"

He had a strong voice normally, but it came out low and throaty. How long would he continue to forgive what he viewed as her shortcomings?

She raised her eyes and half-smiled. The truth was, given the circumstances, she would do the same thing all over. "Sam," she said gently, "what is it?"

"I'll need you to go to the station tomorrow. Office will be open on Sunday because of the murder investigation. Talk to Officer Jimenez and give her a statement."

"Okay." Charlene nodded right away—happy to comply.

Sam tipped the chair forward, then snapped it back. "I called you earlier to tell you that the blood on the stake was O negative—the most common blood type."

"You did?" Surely this was progress in their relationship.

"And then I find out that you were at the Longmire Hotel. On the scene when a man fell to his death. A man that is connected to the victim in the morgue. I was honoring our bargain, and you were not."

"I am sorry about that, you know." She didn't look away. "I had a reason."

"It better be good." He stared at her, steady. Calm.

"Brandy was angry and determined to speak with . . ." She paused. Did he know about their visit with Elisabeta too? She hedged. "I was afraid to let her go alone because she was so upset."

He was silent for a long minute, and it made her more nervous than if he'd just yell at her.

"Brandy found out that Orpheus and Alaric both

wanted immortality and thought they could get it through the Flint bloodline."

Sam frowned. "I'm not concerned right now about Brandy. It's your hide that I'm trying to keep safe."

"I know." Charlene reached across the table for his fisted hand and covered it with hers, squeezing slightly. "I do appreciate it."

"Look—we're not playing a game here. I have half a mind to take you to the station and charge you with interfering in an active police investigation. Obviously, the last time didn't make a strong enough impression."

"So why don't you?" Charlene lifted her chin, knowing that she wasn't completely in the right, but her pride won out. She wasn't totally wrong either.

"Why don't I?" He exhaled explosively. "Good question that I don't have the time to answer."

"Let's shelve this conversation." She straightened and interlaced her fingers on her lap. "How can I help you?"

"Charlene," he said in that super-soft voice he used when he was about to put the hammer down. "Please share what you were talking about with Orpheus." His gaze narrowed. "Unfortunately, we were unable to ask our questions since we didn't get to his room before he leaped to his death."

She shuddered, recalling Orpheus on the sidewalk, unseeing, broken. "As I said, we learned that Orpheus also wanted to be a vampire and believed that a witch could make that happen."

"Vampires." He scoffed.

"It's true, Sam." She swallowed and pushed ahead. "Orpheus was going to leave town today, but then something happened to change his mind and he extended his stay until tomorrow."

Sam nodded for her to continue.

"He admitted that he'd been friends with Alaric for a long time in New Orleans until they had a falling-out."

"Over what?"

"He didn't tell us."

"And?"

"He said that Alaric broke the rules of the vampire coven by telling people about it. We asked if he'd punished Alaric, but he said no."

"And then jumped to his death?" Sam shook his head in disbelief.

"He also seemed glad that Alaric was proved to be human when he died."

"Of course he was human. You don't believe this nonsense, do you?" Sam leaned forward to study her.

"No!" She exhaled, glad that she was able to answer that honestly. "I noticed that his eyeteeth were odd."

"How? Fangs?"

"No—just, bigger."

He withdrew his notepad and jotted something down. "I'll have the coroner examine his mouth. And Alaric's."

She nodded. "Brandy and I were thinking he might have jumped because he felt guilty. Maybe we'd asked a question that alerted him to getting caught, or our visit unsettled him somehow."

Sam tapped his pen on the table. "That would be the easy answer—which means I don't buy it. What else did you notice?"

"His earrings. They were huge diamonds. How does a vampire wannabe make money like that?" Charlene was torn about confessing to their trip to Elisabeta's.

"That's a good question."

"He had Gucci luggage and boots. He was dressed when we got there."

Sam's brow raised. "That sounds normal."

"I mean, he had on clean boots. His dirty boots were by the door."

He made another note. "I've got the clerk sealing the room until we're done with it." His cell phone rang and he pulled it from his jacket pocket to answer. "Oh? All right. I'll be there in ten."

"Sam, there's more." She had to tell him about Elisabeta.

He stood, placing his two large hands on the table. "Can it wait? They've got somebody in custody. Hopefully with a full confession."

"Who?"

"Can't say, Charlene." Sam patted his jacket pocket. "Stay home tonight and I'll try to come by later. If not, then you can tell me in the morning."

"I'm sorry, Sam." She was, for upsetting him. But she couldn't change who she was, either.

His face softened. "I'm sorry too. When I get so riled up it's because I can't protect you." He reached out a hand to feather her face. "I want you to be safe."

"Sam, you and I both know that there are no guarantees in this life. I can't live in a gilded cage, and I can't ignore my friends and people I care about who need my help."

He sucked in a breath and released it. "We're at an impasse. Again." His phone buzzed. "I have to go."

Sam left, not waiting for her to walk him out of the

dining room. Charlene returned to the living room, sadness in her heart.

"Hey," Andrew said. "Everything all right?"

"It's complicated." Charlene poured a little more wine, then took her seat.

"Is this about Alaric's death?" Chloe asked. "Celeste was just telling us all about it. I feel bad now for doubting his magician abilities at the breakfast table."

"Why?" Tommy asked. "He wasn't any good, obviously. Or he wouldn't have ended up dead."

Asher stood and glared down at Tommy. "You don't know jack. Shut your face before I—"

Charlene partially rose from her armchair. "Hey, now. Let's calm down."

Joey punched Tommy's arm. "He didn't mean nothin' by it, Asher. Sorry, dude."

Asher slowly sat back down, as did Charlene. Would this stressful day ever be over? It was only six.

Asher whispered to Celeste and Celeste nodded, glaring at Tommy. "What did the detective want, Charlene?" Celeste asked. "Did he find out who killed Alaric?"

Charlene shook her head. "He didn't say." And she wasn't sharing about Orpheus's death—she was already on Sam's last nerve.

"Do you think it's safe here? We were just down at the wharf." Malena reached for Judd's hand. "Where the body washed up."

"I feel perfectly safe here," she assured her guests. "Salem has a lower violent crime rate than the national average." She'd checked—relieved to discover that satisfying information.

"We were fine and out all night, partying at the wharf," Celeste said with the confidence of youth. "Asher knows everybody."

"I'm sure we'll have more information in the morning. The Sunday paper is here at six. Did you see the write-up about the ball in this morning's paper?" Charlene tried to steer the subject toward positive things.

Chloe nudged her husband. "Braydon, your dad won't believe that we're here while a murder occurred. We'll need extra copies of the paper to bring him."

Braydon gave his cabernet a twirl. "He'll be jealous. Dad used to save clippings all the time for his writing; he hoped to be the next Stephen King."

"What do you do in the publishing industry?" she asked.

Braydon lifted his wineglass. "We're both editors—met in college, freshman year, and haven't been apart since."

Charlene loved to read, but these days steered clear of the scary stuff. "How did your dad make out?"

"Tons of rejections at first, but twenty years later he's got a few books published, mostly horror." Braydon grinned. "Didn't get the fame and fortune he was looking for, but still has a legacy to be proud of."

Charlene smiled. "My husband Jared and I enjoyed thrillers. We'd cuddle on the sofa and watch them together with a huge bowl of popcorn. I miss those days."

"What happened to your husband, Charlene? We thought you might have inherited this place." Braydon helped himself to more brie. The dish was almost empty.

"Unfortunately, he died in a car accident." She squeezed

the napkin in her hand and added, "He was the love of my life and I thought I'd never recover—yet here I am."

"You're a brave woman to find a new path." Chloe touched her arm in comfort. "We lost our first child—he was stillborn, and I haven't been able to conceive again."

"I'm very sorry." Tears stung her eyes. "We couldn't have children."

Braydon glanced at Chloe. "We're considering adoption."

"I hope you do it." She thought of Avery. "There are so many wonderful kids living in government subsidized shelters who could use a good home. Here in Salem, I can recommend Felicity House personally."

Asher, Tommy, Joey, and Celeste all rose, voices high as they talked over one another. "I guess you don't want us to hang out?" Tommy shouted at Celeste. "Salem was your idea."

"I do!" she said, not letting go of Asher. "Let's all go to the beach again. Okay, Asher?"

Asher waited a minute before giving a gruff, "Yeah. Let's get another beer here, and then we can take off."

Though new to the group, he was the leader.

Charlene eyed the clock. Six-thirty. Her energy was totally depleted, but she gamely smiled and conversed as best she could. She hoped to spend the rest of her Saturday night on her love seat, relaxing until bed, and could hardly wait to escape to her room.

She picked up empty dishes and brought them into the kitchen to soak, the conversation in the other room a low murmur.

Maybe instead of television, a nice book?

Her phone rang. Sam? She hoped he wasn't planning on coming over, because she was beat.

"Charlene?"

"Hey there. What can I help you with?" She yawned. "I'm so tired I could sleep for a week."

"Hate to bother you, but I really need to talk to you."

Her long day wasn't through yet.

Then she brightened. Had his person in custody confessed?

CHAPTER 9

Charlene put on her warmest jacket and met Sam on the front porch, hoping he had wonderful news.

He parked and climbed the steps, brow arched.

"Miss me?" she teased.

"It hasn't even been an hour since I was here last," he rumbled. "I'm not allowed in the house now?"

She laughed. "I want to keep our visit short and sweet. You've got my guests wondering what's going on and if they're safe in Salem."

He tipped his hat back and smiled at her. "I'm here to apologize."

"Oh, really." She was immediately suspicious of his motives.

"I may have come on a little strong earlier. In my defense, you make me crazy, Charlene."

She stuffed her hands in her pockets and grinned at him. The crazy feeling was mutual. "Okay. Apology accepted. I'm sorry too. How did the confession go?"

"The person changed his mind. Slipped out the back door."

"Oh no!"

"Yeah. It was too good to be true." Sam glanced at her sideways. "What were you going to tell me earlier?"

She hated to ruin the good vibe between them, but it was best to be honest. "Uh, just that Brandy also talked to Elisabeta earlier."

"Brandy . . . and you?"

She braced herself for his reaction. "Yes. She was driving, remember?"

He sank against the railing on her front porch, stretching his long legs before him, his hands on his thighs. "And what did you discuss?"

"Well, that conversation is why we went to see Orpheus, so it is relevant. Elisabeta claimed that Orpheus was jealous of Alaric."

"Uh-huh."

"Maybe jealous enough to kill him."

"Huh."

She stepped closer to Sam to see his expression in the porch light. "You're not mad?"

"Nope." He spread his arms to the side. "I want to know everything that you talked about."

"I can't just spout it out like that." She paced a few steps. "It was much earlier in the day. A lot's happened since then."

"How about this: You write down everything that you remember and tell it to me in the morning at the station when you're there to give your statement to Officer Jimenez."

She whipped her head to face him, still not sure that she was hearing correctly. "That sounds very reasonable, Sam."

He nodded and stood up. "That's me. A man of reason. I figure if we have these chats from now on at the station, then it will be professional. It will remind you of how serious this is. And for me, it won't be personal. Got it?"

Charlene brought her clasped hands to her waist. "Thank you. I'll do it."

"If you happen to see Dru, let him know I'd like to talk to him." Sam had descended the stairs but now stopped, one boot on the ground, the other on the last step.

"Why would I see Serenity's ex-boyfriend?"

"I have no logical reason to suspect you would, and yet, you turn up in the least expected places."

Charlene sniffed at his tone but could hardly fault the man. She wrapped her arms around her waist, her jacket not cutting the chill of the fall evening. "I haven't seen him since last night when Stephanos sent him home in a cab."

"He didn't go home. Got plenty of witnesses that place him at the pier after midnight, which is a problem."

Oh no. Dru had left the Hawthorne Hotel at ten, with his threat to kill Alaric. Then Alaric washed up near the pier. Not good for Dru unless he had a solid alibi.

Was that who had walked out of the station?

Charlene sighed. "If for some very strange reason I see Dru before you do, I will relay your message."

"Night." Sam climbed into his SUV and left her house with a stern, "Stay home."

Charlene had no plans to do anything other than sleep and try not to obsess over why Orpheus had jumped from the window. Like Sam, she'd learned that the obvious answer was not always the correct answer.

Shivering, she watched Sam until he drove out of sight and then returned to her guests inside.

Celeste, Asher, Joey, and Tommy had switched from wine to a pumpkin beer she got through Brews and Broomsticks where her friend Kevin worked.

Celeste sauntered over with a raised brow. "Are you in hot water with the cops? Two visits in an hour?"

Embarrassed, Charlene laughed off the question. "The detective and I go way back, that's all."

"Does this have anything to do with the sexy Alaric from last night's ball?" Celeste sighed dramatically and pulled her collar from her throat. "I wouldn't have minded baring my neck for him."

Tommy, Joey, and Asher joined them. "You still goin' on about that dead vamp?" Tommy asked with a sneer.

"You're just jealous." Celeste winked at him over her beer.

"Obviously." Tommy blew her a kiss.

"Celeste said that you were cool with me staying over . . . do you have another room? I'm happy to pay." Asher brought a wad of twenties from his pocket.

"Nope. Everything's full through Wednesday." Charlene's suites were booked through November and part of December, but the singles were harder to fill.

Asher stuffed the cash back and sipped his pumpkin ale. "Thanks."

Tommy nudged Celeste. "You can bunk with me, if you want."

She rolled her eyes. "You, Tommy Ramirez, snore."

"Is that what kept me from sleeping this morning?" Asher groused.

"Sorry. Deviated septum." Tommy rubbed the bridge of his nose with a shrug. He was cute in a clean-cut way while Asher had a bad-boy edge, from his bat tattoos to the titanium rings on his fingers. No earrings.

"Just busting your balls, dude." Asher half-smiled. "I'm a light sleeper."

"I don't mind," Celeste said flirtatiously, linking her arm through Asher's.

Asher lifted his beer. "Problem solved."

Celeste stepped toward the sideboard. "The brie was delish, Charlene. Do you have any more chips for the bean dip?"

"Sure do." Charlene hurried to the pantry for another bag of tortilla chips and filled the empty bowl. The topic of Alaric and his death had waned to the subject of vampires in general.

"The sexiest vampire ever was Brad Pitt in *Interview with the Vampire*," Chloe announced.

"I think Alaric was hotter. Hey, Charlene, did you know him?" Emma asked. Her husband shook his head good-naturedly.

"I didn't. Just met last night, actually. Alaric was . . ." she paused, "dating my friend's daughter." Charlene turned to Asher. "You knew him though, right? I'm sorry for your loss."

His eyes narrowed. "Not like we were close, but yeah. Thanks. Uh, you could reach Serenity, Charlene?"

"Sure, but I'm more friends with her mom. Why?"

"Alaric spoke highly of her." He shuffled from one black leather boot to the other. "It just really sucks."

"It does." Charlene finished her wine. "She's hurting right now."

His brow furrowed, and she could tell he was struggling with what to say.

"I can pass on your condolences if you like."

"It's all right." Asher ruffled his hair. "Like I said, Alaric never introduced us."

Celeste gave him a side hug and changed the subject. "Charlene, we had a bonfire on the beach last night. Can't do that where we're from."

"That sounds like fun. But cold." Charlene straightened the napkins on the sideboard. "Was it crowded?"

"It was Halloween, so yeah, there were a ton of people not ready to go home," Tommy said.

"Most of the girls were in sexy costumes," Joey said, clinking beers with Tommy.

Charlene shook her head. "That must have been the after-after-party. Don't you agree that the alien and Aphrodite were the best choice to win?"

Celeste drank her beer. "Yeah. But that tree was amazing, and the pirate was cool too."

"The parrot on his arm actually squawked," Asher said. "The pirate knew a lot about Salem—going on about the history of the Hawthorne Hotel."

"It's supposed to be haunted." Charlene fake-shivered. Speaking of ghosts, where was Jack? She was getting a second wind.

"According to the tour we took on Thursday," Andrew said, "every building in Salem has a ghost."

On that, Charlene changed the subject. "I really wanted to vote for your Dalmatians," Charlene told Chloe and Braydon. "But I had to be impartial."

The couple high-fived.

"I thought my baseball player was pretty good," Tommy said. "And I wanted a shot at the five hundred bucks."

"Asher was a boring vampire." Celeste looked up at him. "But my witch wasn't very creative either, so I can't mock him too hard."

"Hey!" Asher stepped away from Celeste. "I had fangs special-made, but I lost them somewhere."

"We are definitely coming back next year," Chloe said.

Braydon nodded. "With more elaborate costumes than our Dalmatians. And we want to stay a full week. I had no idea that there would be so much to see in Salem. Four days isn't enough."

"Let's put in for vacation as soon as we get back home," Chloe suggested.

"Benefit of being self-employed," Asher said. "I can do what I want, whenever I want."

"What do you do?" Emma asked.

"It's classified, but all on the computer." Asher lifted a shoulder.

"These days that's the way to go!" Braydon agreed.

"Me, Celeste, and Joey bartend in Jersey," Tommy said. "Easy money."

It didn't sound near as impressive as "classified," Charlene thought. Could Celeste glow any brighter as she stared at Asher?

"That's hard work," Emma countered. "I bartended in college."

"That's how it started for me too, but then I made more money than I did with my hospitality degree." Tommy and Celeste looked at one another and shared a laugh.

"Skipped college," Asher said. "I've been making money on my own since I was sixteen."

"Entrepreneur. Good for you." Charlene wondered why he flashed his cash around. To gain friends, maybe?

"Had to. Mom died. No dad." Asher cleared his throat. "No big deal. I love being independent."

At that, Celeste melted toward Asher, and Tommy's eyes narrowed.

Jealousy was not a pretty emotion to witness, and Charlene was reminded of Dru. "Hey, did any of you happen to see the young man who caused a scene last night, about ten?"

"I thought for sure there was going to be a fight, but Alaric was chill after getting punched," Celeste said. "Remember, Asher? Tommy, you and Joey had just gone to get another round."

"Yeah. Tall, skinny dude, drunk out of his mind." Asher finished his beer and set the empty on a table. "Alaric wasn't in any danger from him." He blew out a breath.

"It was tense," Chloe said. "But the committee handled it well, escorting him out before he could actually do anything."

"That was Stephanos." Charlene had been glad he'd stepped in. "He's a leader in the Wiccan community here."

"Witches are real?" Celeste asked.

Charlene nodded. "Not in the hocus-pocus sense, but in their spiritual beliefs."

"I love Salem!" Celeste said. "What do you say, Tommy? Joey? Should we just move here?"

"Slow down, slow down." Tommy lowered his hands. "We have lives in Jersey City."

"I can put you in touch with someone if you want bartending jobs," Charlene said. "Kevin at Brews and Broomsticks."

"That would be cool." Celeste's eyes shone. "Every day living in an old town filled with magic. What do you think, Asher?"

"Witches and vampires and pirates. What's not to love? But for me personally"—he touched his chest—"I plan to travel the world, not settle in Salem. Been there, done that."

"Got the T-shirt," Joey joked.

Celeste dropped her gaze and Tommy clapped his hand over her shoulder. "You got me, babe."

But Celeste had an obvious crush on Asher. Charlene cleared her throat. "Anyway, the young man's name is Dru. Did any of you see him after the ball, maybe at a different party?"

Celeste scrunched her nose. "I wouldn't be able to pick him out of a lineup. Not to mention that by the time we were at the beach, things were a bit fuzzy."

"A lot fuzzy," Tommy agreed.

"Please tell me you took a cab home," Charlene said.

"We walked," Asher informed her. "Around four or so."

"Whew. You can always call me." She'd hate to feel responsible for one of her guests over-imbibing.

"We're fine," Celeste said. "I'm ready to do it again. Right, guys?"

Oh, to be in her twenties, Charlene thought with a smile. "Now that you've all had appetizers, what are your dinner plans?"

"We're going to Finz." Chloe gestured to Braydon. "Seven o'clock reservations."

"We're bundling up and walking around town," Emma said. "We'll find something that looks good."

"I'm thinking clam chowder." Judd patted his flat stomach.

"Sea Level is the best for that," Charlene said.

"Pizza?" Joey suggested, and the three others agreed.

Within thirty minutes, her guests were out of the house and Charlene was left alone to clean up.

"Jack?" she whispered.

"I'm here." Her ghost appeared in his full solid glory and sat at the kitchen table. "How was it?"

"Wonderful. I love my business, Jack, I really do. I can channel my curious nature into getting to know my guests."

Jack chuckled. "Does that observation have anything to do with the detective peeling off in a rush?"

"Saw that, did you? Sam wants to talk to Dru, Serenity's ex."

"Sam can't find him without you?" Jack tapped the table with ghostly fingers—no sound, just movement. "That's a low point, even for him."

"He was back a second time to apologize for coming on too strong the first time. I'm going to the station in the morning to fill out a statement for Officer Jimenez, about the Longmire Hotel." The sound of Orpheus landing on the sidewalk made her stomach knot and she swallowed hard before she could continue. "And write out what I remember of the visit with Elisabeta. I know I crossed a line."

"You didn't do it on purpose," Jack said in her defense. "You were helping a friend."

"I know. Sam knows that too. I hope."

Jack's brow rose, not necessarily in agreement. "What else did he want?"

"Dru to turn himself in for questioning. If I just so happen to run into him somewhere."

"Sam involves you even as he tells you not to be involved."

"I noticed that too, believe me." She and Jack shared a smile.

"What are you going to do about it?"

"Dru was at the pier last night, drunk, rather than home in bed after threatening Alaric. Alaric washed up on the beach this morning. Dead." Charlene eyed the house phone, knowing what had to be done. "Call Serenity, what else?"

CHAPTER 10

Charlene and Jack decided to move to her suite for more privacy—she had her legs crossed and a blanket over her lap on her love seat with Jack next to her. She picked up her cell phone, put it on speaker, and dialed the Flint residence.

Brandy answered after two rings. "Hello, Charlene."

"Hey, Brandy. I'm just calling to check in with you. How are you doing?" She didn't say *after seeing a dead body on the sidewalk*, but she didn't have to.

"Could be better. I *will* be better, once they clear up who killed Alaric. I've decided that Orpheus had to have been lying to us. Guilt made him jump. Your detective needs to hurry up and confirm that. Or that lady cop who hates you."

"I'm going in tomorrow to give a statement. Did you get a summons?"

"Yeah. I'm ignoring it. I figure the less the police see of the Flint family until this blows over the healthier it will be for us. Our family has known persecution."

Jack laughed. "Can't blame her."

"Three hundred years ago!" Charlene pointed out. "Anything in the last century that's making you nervous?"

"The way our ancestors described getting tarred and feathered before being hung keeps it fresh in my mind."

"Don't use that excuse with Sam, whatever you do. He's black-and-white in his thinking . . . no paranormal or supernatural allowed."

Jack scoffed. "Narrow-minded, in my opinion."

Charlene nodded.

"I've seen a lot of weird in my day, but this vampire thing is over-the-top. The witches I know in Salem are mostly good people—upstanding members of the community. Vampires, or the people that I've met that want to be vampires, are very dark. Can you see auras, Charlene? Halos of color around people?"

"No. But Orpheus and Elisabeta gave me bad vibes without that." Charlene blew out a breath. "I got a tongue-lashing from Sam this afternoon, twice, thanks to you. We are definitely even as far as grudges go."

"Yeah, fine." Brandy sniffed. "But you also thought my mother was involved in that nefarious business with the dead witch, so basically that's a double betrayal."

"You put us both in danger today—two times, three, including the flight home. Now we're even."

Brandy burst out laughing. "Okay. Even. You were the color of our palest green Riesling grape."

"She's funny," Jack said. "I forgot that about her."

Charlene smiled at him. "Do you mind if I talk to

Serenity for a second? It's important. Has Dru been around?"

"No." Brandy shifted the headset. "You think she's in further danger?"

"If Orpheus turns out not to be the killer, then, maybe." She recalled how Dru had slugged Alaric in the face.

"Dru would never hurt Serenity. He's a great kid with an art degree who works at the Peabody Essex Museum. Wait. Why would *anybody* want Serenity dead? I thought her only worry was getting sent to jail if the Salem police department can't find the right killer."

"It depends on why Alaric was murdered. Jealous lover—either side of the equation." Elisabeta or Dru.

"Oh." Brandy cursed softly. "I don't care for that line of reasoning at all. Do you need to speak with her now? She's upstairs, mooning over her lost love."

"Yes, please."

"Hang on. I'll get her on the phone."

Jack said, "It *would* be very helpful to know why Alaric was killed the way he was. Staked. Dumped at sea? Our currents are very strong, but you have to time it right and he ended up back in the harbor."

"Motivation, as Mom would point out." Charlene could hear her mother now, smugly deducing the killer. "Finding the reason—even if it isn't logical to anyone else but the murderer."

"Your mom loves those shows." Jack shifted awkwardly, very humanly, on the love seat. "I have a confession."

"Yeah?"

"I'm hooked." He lay back against the cushion. "I blame your mom, Brenda Woodbridge."

"Addicted to true crime?" Charlene said, appalled.

"Who is?" Brandy asked.

Jack roared with laughter.

"My mother." She shook her finger at her wayward ghost. "Mom claims to solve the mystery faster than the police."

"Well, call her up, Charlene. Fly her and your adorable father from Chicago and get her on the case." Brandy sighed. "Serenity is fast asleep, Charlene. Snuggled up with her teddy bear like she hasn't done since she was a little girl. I can't wake her. We need to find the killer. When do you need to be at the station?"

"No set time."

"Come over around ten, then. We'll have sage tea and scones for everybody." Brandy ended the call.

Charlene turned off her phone. "Well, Jack. I'm wired now—beyond exhaustion to jittery. I guess I'll spend my Saturday night writing up that report for Sam. You can go ahead and watch television if you'd like." True crime.

"I'll keep you company," Jack said. "That report combined with what you discover from Serenity tomorrow will be enough to keep Sam off your back."

She could only hope.

Sunday morning, Charlene awoke to the sound of rain against her windowpane. Not a nice day for her guests, but hopefully the weather would clear soon.

She heard voices in the kitchen and knew Minnie would be preparing coffee and breakfast. Minnie arrived early on the weekends when they had guests.

Charlene turned on her shower and while it was heating went to her closet and chose her clothes for the day. Nasty weather meant warm, cozy clothes. Going to the station and Brandy's for a visit didn't require dressing up.

She pulled out a pair of faded blue jeans, a Chicago Cubs T-shirt, and a blue cashmere cardigan.

As she showered, Charlene strategized for her busy day. The report was finished for Sam, so that was good. Writing it out like that had helped clarify the facts, as well as illuminate major questions. Had Alaric chosen Serenity specifically before leaving New Orleans?

What secret did Alaric have that Orpheus knew?

Did Orpheus kill Alaric?

Charlene toweled dry, slipped into her clothes, and then braided her thick hair on one side. She added silver skull earrings and gold glitter to enhance her hazel eyes.

Done, she went into the kitchen. At nine, it was a good chance that some of her guests were up and at the dining table.

Silva pounced on her slippered feet the moment Charlene shut her suite door behind her. Coffee, bacon, potatoes . . . "Hey, little fuzzball." She scooped Silva up and carried her in one arm. "Morning, Minnie. I think Silva must be as hungry as I am."

"Silva's food is in her dish, but she hasn't touched it." Minnie patted her gray curls. "Sweetie seemed a little off yesterday, and again this morning."

"Oh no! We don't have time for her to be sick."

"No time's the right time." Minnie chuckled. "I know that after all my kids—they pick your busiest day to get the flu. Or chicken pox. Strep throat."

"I'm sure you're right." Charlene put Silva down by her dish. "Just wanted to say that your appetizers were highly appreciated last night—the brie and the dip. I ate my way through everything as dinner. Delicious." She sat at the table.

"That's nice to hear." Minnie poured her coffee. "You going out this morning? You're all sparkly."

"Yes. Gold powder on my lids." Charlene blinked rapidly, then tossed her hair. "Like my earrings?"

"What are they?" Minnie moved closer. "Skulls?" She laughed. "Perfect. Where are you headed?"

"I'll have a quick bite with the others, then I'm going to drop by the Flints before giving a statement at the police station. Should be home around noon."

"The station?" Minnie straightened her apron, then turned on the water in the sink. Soap suds floated like bubbles and Silva leaped up to pop one. "What for?"

"Yesterday was a very long day." Charlene drank her coffee and filled her housekeeper in on the latest. "Anyway, neither stop should take too much time."

"Should I be worried?" Minnie asked. "If you need to stay later, I can fill in. Avery should be here from ten to two."

"No need to worry. I know Sam and the other police officers will find the bad guys."

"I hope sooner rather than later," Minnie said, putting a plate in the dishwasher.

"Tell me about it." She rolled her eyes. "This case is a weird one and I'll be glad when Sam wraps it up. Vampires."

"You know Sam. Thorough—makes sure he dots the i's and crosses the t's. No slipups for him."

"You're right, of course." She wished he'd do this one a little quicker, though, and get Serenity clear.

Charlene brought her coffee to the dining room and joined her guests at the table. The LaFleurs had gone to Marblehead, and Olivia and Andrew were headed for

Plymouth. That left Judd, Malena, Chloe, and Braydon—along with her singles.

Joey, Tommy, and Celeste were hunched over the table. Celeste looked like she'd had a rough night of partying. Bags under her eyes, still in the same clothes as yesterday but with a few more wrinkles.

Tommy had more scruff than usual on his chin. He kept refilling his water glass from the pitcher to help with an unquenchable thirst. A large plate of pancakes sat before him that he seemed determined to finish.

Asher, she guessed, was still upstairs in Celeste's bed.

"How's everybody this morning? Ready for more adventures?" Charlene asked.

Celeste moaned and leaned her head in her hand, her elbow on the table. "I might have overdone it. Can't eat. Feel like I'm going to puke."

"Please don't do it at the table." Charlene, who'd been across from Celeste, got up and changed her seat just as a precaution.

Joey slurped his orange juice. "Try this," he said to Celeste, "it might help."

Celeste put her hand over her mouth and nearly gagged. "I'm going back to the room. Asher better scoot over."

Silva, who'd been dozing on the windowsill, uncurled and watched Celeste leave the dining room. Charlene would love to know the cat's thoughts. Silva hadn't warmed to the millennials, or any of the guests for that matter. Was she a little put out because they had no little kids this week?

Charlene turned to Judd and Malena beside her. "So you two, what are your plans?"

"We're going to lay low this morning and wait for the rain to stop. We were hoping to take that harbor cruise, but not today." Judd slung an arm around the back of Malena's chair. "How about a game of chess? This could be your lucky day."

"Could be, you never know. But first more coffee and maybe another square of that apple spice cake."

Charlene reached for the last pancake on the platter, put it on her plate, added syrup, and took her first bite. "Oh my gosh! Minnie can turn a simple pancake into gourmet. I think she has a little pumpkin and walnuts in this mix. I should have added whipped cream."

"Not too late." Tommy nudged the bowl of topping toward her. "I've had four so far."

"Got anything in mind for the day?" Charlene drank her coffee, which perfectly melded with the sweet and savory flavors.

"We'll see how Celeste is feeling later. Her and Asher partied really hard last night. Things went off the hook." Tommy swallowed his pancake down with water. "Salem has an edge that Jersey City don't have."

Joey nodded. "Know what you mean, bud. No vampires in Jersey."

"You met vampires last night?" Charlene asked.

"Just a guy and gal who are really into it. Like, blood-drinking and everything."

"Who?" Could this be who had come from New Orleans with Alaric and Elisabeta?

"Didn't get names. It was around the bonfire." Joey shrugged. "Lots of drinking—everybody's your best friend, right? Asher bankrolls the festivities."

"What does that mean?" Charlene asked, feeling naïve at forty-three.

"He picks up the tab. Makes sure the beer is flowing."

"His job sounds lucrative." Charlene edged a fluffy bite with her fork.

"Asher's got issues." Tommy and Joey exchanged a look. "I mean, online security? What is that really?"

Charlene shrugged. She'd have to ask Sam later. "Well, if you can find out who his vampire friends are that are drinking blood, I'd be interested to know."

"It wasn't just his friends, Charlene." Joey finished his juice and lowered his voice, glancing up at the ceiling. "It was him. And he was trying to get Celeste to do it too."

"That's gross," Malena said, having listened in.

Charlene straightened in her seat. "Asher wants to be a vampire?"

"Yeah. I guess that Alaric dude told him that there was a way." Tommy ate another bite.

Charlene needed to have a serious conversation with Asher and Celeste as soon as she returned from the station.

Joey shrugged. "Alaric's dying was a real downer. Talk around the fire was that his whole vampire act should have turned out differently. With Alaric alive, forever. And not just Alaric, right? Asher and this other chick . . ."

"Which is bullsh—" Tommy cut himself off, nodding to everyone around the table. "Sorry. Vampires are *not* real. Alaric was just a regular guy."

She pushed her dish away. "The detective has several leads and is working on an explanation. Shouldn't be long until he figures it out."

"That's reassuring," Malena said. "I'd like to see this resolved before we leave."

"I'm sure it will be." Judd squeezed her shoulder. "It just takes longer than the movies."

"Very true," Charlene agreed. "Hey, did the paper come yet this morning?"

"I think it's in the living room on the sofa," Malena said.

Tommy pushed his chair back from the table, the pancakes gone. "Charlene, do you mind if we check out your shelves? I noticed some books on witchcraft and history in Salem. If the rain clears up, this guy last night was talking about a pirate tour that sounded cool."

"Help yourselves, of course. And if it continues to rain, I highly recommend the Peabody Essex Museum."

"That sounds interesting to me," Malena said.

Judd shrugged. "Let's see how the day unfolds. After I kick your butt at chess."

Charlene stood and lifted her plate. "I'm going to leave you to your own devices this morning. Got a few errands to run."

Tommy slid a croissant on his plate, loaded it with butter and jelly, and put a napkin over it. "I'll take this upstairs for Celeste in case she gets hungry. If she pukes, she'll feel better."

They all watched him leave, and Judd gave a wise old-man smile. "Kids will be kids."

Malena snorted. "That's why we never had them."

Charlene showed up at the Flint home just before ten, and Brandy let her in. "Serenity will be down in a minute. I hope you're not going to interrogate her; she's been through enough."

"I won't, I promise. She was an innocent victim in all

this, and I hate that Alaric used her the way he did." Charlene noticed Serenity at the bottom of the stairs. She was wearing a tie-dyed shirt, one shoulder exposed, leggings, no makeup, with her hair in a messy bun.

"Good morning," Charlene said cheerfully. "You're looking much better today."

Brandy turned around and smiled. "Lovely, as always."

"Yeah, well, it's an illusion." She dragged her fingers on the railing. "That's what life is, right?"

"Life is what you make it, my sweet child. Charlene, I have to do a rain check on the tea and scones. I got a big order in last night that requires my attention at the winery. Life must go on."

They watched her leave and Serenity sighed. "Can she use any more clichés?"

Charlene chuckled and clasped Serenity's cold hand. "Truthfully, how are you feeling?"

"Let's go sit in the sunroom and we can talk there." The room was all windows with a view of an enormous garden full of herbs and flowers. Today, in the downpour, the bright glory had faded.

"Even in the rain, this is a spectacular room," Charlene said. "I can imagine many beautiful afternoons sitting here and reading."

"Yeah, it's especially nice in the summertime. Like being outside, only not so hot." Serenity glanced at Charlene. "Mom said you had more questions for me. About?"

"I'm trying to piece together what we know of Alaric."

Serenity plopped down on a wingback chair and drew her legs up, hugging them. "Like?"

Charlene removed her coat and sat on the sofa facing her. "I was wondering if he ever mentioned his family.

Are his parents still alive? Does he have siblings? That kind of thing. Will there be a funeral, you think?"

"He's an only child." Serenity tucked a soft velour pillow on her side. "He said his mom was dead—died a *long* time ago."

"Was he a young boy when it happened?" Orpheus had told them that Alaric's mother had been a nut, but still, losing a parent might damage a child's psyche.

"No. He made it sound like it was hundreds of years ago. She was supposedly like him, a vampire, I guess." She sniffed, more angry tears than sad. "That wasn't nothin' but a big, fat lie."

"I'm sorry, Serenity. Some men don't know the truth if they stumble over it, but his was a whopper. Where did his fascination with being a vampire come from?"

"I've been thinking about this, like, round and round." Serenity shifted and repositioned the pillow over her lap. "It must have something to do with his blistery skin and his avoidance of the sun."

"Did your mom talk to you about where we went yesterday?"

"No." She tilted her head. "Just that you'd decided to go out to lunch rather than eat here."

"Oh. Well." That meant not bringing up Orpheus or the conversation at his hotel before he jumped. That he thought Alaric's symptoms psychosomatic. "Did he tell you his mother's name, or his dad's? Did he always live in New Orleans?"

"He was born in Memphis." Serenity patted the pillow at her side, much like Silva when trying to make her space comfy. "His dad left when he was a baby and he and his mom moved around a lot. They didn't have much money, but his mom would tell people's fortunes." Serenity glanced at Charlene with empathy for Alaric in her gaze. "She had a room set up wherever they lived. People would come to the house and pay her. He said she made it all up, but she was so good she had folks believing."

Alaric had similar qualities to make folks believe in him. "The majority of psychics are fake, but I know a few people in town who are the real thing. Kass Fortune— you probably know her."

"Oh yeah. Mom and Grandma have had her tea readings a few times."

"So some people do have a special gift—maybe his mom had something unique that he inherited too."

"Maybe."

Charlene shifted on the sofa. "Just to be clear—they moved around a lot, but she supposedly died hundreds of years ago. How could that be?"

"I don't know. Nothing makes any sense with Alaric dead." Serenity's eyes welled and shimmered like the rain against the glass in the sunroom. "I mean, even if she was a so-called vampire, doesn't that mean she'd never die? Or do they leave their earthly bodies and still exist in this world and beyond? That's kind of what he told me. I just went with it." She dabbed her nose with the back of her hand. "I don't feel Alaric around me now. Spiritually."

"Did you do an altar for him?"

"I tried but couldn't connect." Serenity shrugged in confusion. "Maybe as a vampire, he has no soul?"

"So many questions are unanswered. What if vampires *are* real? A lot of people don't believe in witches, and yet we know they exist." She hoped to lighten the tension. "They don't fly around on brooms with warts on their noses."

Serenity laughed. "I'm sure glad of that. I believe there are good witches, like our family, and bad. Some use their gifts for good and are healers, while others want power, and power corrupts." She bowed her head and wiped her eyes. "Alaric wanted peace."

Alaric wanted immortality at the cost of her young life, but if Charlene was to say so, she'd shut Serenity down. Charlene steered the conversation to his family again.

"Did his mother live in New Orleans with him?"

"No, his mom was dead-dead by then. I think he lived in New Orleans for at least ten years before he and Orpheus had a falling-out."

"Have you given any more thought to what that was about?"

She shrugged. "Orpheus was jealous of Alaric and wanted to bring him down. He mentioned a breach of trust."

Charlene recalled how Orpheus had stayed on the sidelines to watch what had happened Friday night. Had the coven leader taken things into his own hands?

She checked the time on her phone. Quarter to eleven—her errand to the police station loomed. "Have you seen Dru since Halloween night?"

Serenity stilled. "Why?"

"Well, he threatened to kill Alaric. Do you think he's dangerous?"

Serenity straightened her legs, sitting upright. "No. He wouldn't do that. No matter what people say, he'd never hurt me. Or anyone—even Alaric. He loved me and I should never have broken up with him." Serenity bowed her head as fresh tears fell to her lap.

Charlene rooted around for a clean tissue in her purse and handed one to Serenity.

"Thanks." Serenity crumpled it in her fist. "I've heard from our friends that after he was thrown out of the witch ball, he went to the pier. They said he was stinking drunk and was mouthing off about how he wanted to kill Alaric. But he didn't mean it." Her lower lip trembled. "Dru wouldn't hurt a fly. It was just the booze talking, not him."

Nodding, Charlene said, "I believe that. Your mom liked him a lot, and she's a very good judge of character, especially with men around you."

Serenity laughed through her tears. "That's for sure true!"

Charlene had to get Dru off the hook as well as keep Serenity's name clear. "Has Dru tried to contact you?"

"He called once, but I didn't stay on the line long."

"When was that?"

She twisted her mouth and wouldn't look at Charlene. "I don't remember."

An evasion. "What did he say?"

"Dru said, sorry, but I think he meant about bursting in and embarrassing me, not that he killed my boyfriend." Her brow furrowed. "I still can't figure out what happened. Someone had to have helped Alaric turn off the lights and lock the door to the ballroom. He was supposed to be in his rental house, by the fireplace in the basement. He wasn't there when I showed up." She brought her knuckles to her lower lip. "Was he already dead? What was the blood on that stick?"

"Call Detective Holden to see what he can tell you. He's bound to have answers." Answers that she couldn't give the poor girl. Like, the stake being a prop, the blood being O negative. Sam had no idea how fair she tried to be to him in this process—he only saw how she broke his rules.

"Serenity, sweetie, it would be really helpful if you happened to talk to Dru, to have him call Detective Holden."

"Why?"

"To clear his name." Charlene spoke softly but firmly. This was not a joking matter.

"He didn't do anything wrong."

"But you can admit that his actions don't look great?"

Her eyes widened and she gave a slight nod.

Charlene stood. "Thanks for chatting with me this morning. I appreciate it and hope that one day soon you'll heal from all this. Anytime you want to talk, call me. Or if you think of something useful, either call Detective Holden or me. We care about you and your well-being."

She put a hand on Serenity's shoulder as the distraught young woman cried into her pillow. "I'll see myself out."

CHAPTER 11

Charlene drove to the Salem police station, conflicted by what she'd learned that morning from Serenity.

The young lady had been in contact with Dru. She didn't believe her ex would hurt a fly and yet he'd punched Alaric in the face hard enough to draw blood.

Making a point of Alaric's humanity with his fist.

Actions spoke louder than words. Except that Dru's words matched the violence of his actions.

Even their friends had called to tell her what Dru was saying. Well, that he wanted to kill Alaric. Not that he *had* killed Alaric—that was something.

She tapped her finger on the wheel, wishing Jack could answer the telephone so she could ask him to re-search Alaric Mayar's family. A mother who told fortunes for a living was not your normal nine-to-five mom who baked cookies with a warm glass of milk for an after-school snack.

Charlene parked in front of the brick building and went inside. A harried woman sat behind the front desk, her uniform collar askew.

"Morning," Charlene said. "I'm here to see Officer Jimenez. To give a statement."

"Have a seat. It's been insane around here. I think there was a full moon last night or something." The officer waved Charlene toward a row of plastic seats. "I'll buzz her to let her know."

Charlene sat down and picked up a section of the Sunday paper that she hadn't had a chance to read yet. Alaric Mayar's face, handsome and alive, looked back at her. The photo was about five years old and taken in front of a bar on Bourbon Street.

Alaric Mayar—born Allan Mayar. Age forty-five. Washed up by the pier and the old Derby tunnel entrance across from the stone bridge. She'd passed by there a hundred times but hadn't realized there was water access. What had Jack said about tides in Salem?

She scanned the article, but there really wasn't more to learn. He'd been in Salem just two weeks. Not married. No children. Alive, and then gone.

"Ms. Morris."

Charlene hopped up and dropped the paper to the seat next to her. "Yes. Morning."

Officer Jimenez's hard jaw and pulled-back hair allowed zero softness. "Follow me." She strode down the carpeted runner on the floor, past Sam's dark office, to a warren of open cubicles.

"Take a seat."

The woman had about as much personality as a paper bag, but Charlene would not give her any trouble.

She sat, her purse balanced on her knees.

Officer Jimenez perched before a computer and pulled up a form that read *STATEMENT*.

"Name."

"Charlene Morris." Hoping to save the officer time, she said, "You know that already . . . I should be in your system."

The officer glared at Charlene. "Your cooperation will be appreciated. The sooner you answer the questions, the sooner you may go."

"All right." Feeling like a scolded child, Charlene squirmed on the hard chair.

Charlene answered readily—name, date of birth, address. Where things got interesting was when the officer stopped typing to face Charlene with flinty gray eyes.

"Tell me again how you know the victim."

"Victim? I thought Orpheus had committed suicide."

Her jaw tightened. "Until we get our report back from the coroner, we will refer to him as a victim. Understood?"

Charlene nodded, but had the feeling the officer had accidentally given something away.

"I understand. Is Orpheus his real name? We could call him that, if you'd like."

"Do not try to be my friend, Ms. Morris. I don't have friends, and if I did you are not the kind I'd pick."

"Hey!" She was a very good friend. She remembered birthdays and was an excellent gift giver. She didn't tell secrets. What was this lady's problem?

But she knew.

Officer Jimenez didn't appreciate Charlene's friendship with Sam, her superior. The robotic officer probably slept in her uniform with a gun under her pillow, counting laws rather than sheep.

Well, Charlene was very patient and would wear the woman down with kindness. With professionalism . . . maybe even Minnie's apple spice cake.

"I will ask again. How do you know the victim?"

Charlene straightened as if she had a book on her head for perfect posture and her mother was watching. "I met Orpheus the night of the witch ball. I was a judge."

"Was he in costume?"

"A zoot suit. He was dancing with my friend, Brandy; she was with me yesterday at the Longmire Hotel."

"The witch."

"Well, I don't know that she would refer to herself like that, but her family is part of the Wiccan community."

Officer Jimenez's mouth thinned. "How did you end up at his hotel?"

"Well"—this was an example of her being a wonderful friend—"he wanted Brandy's phone number but I didn't know him, and everybody had been drinking, celebrating Halloween, so I didn't give it to him."

The officer tapped her short, unpainted fingernail to the keyboard as she typed. "And?"

"Well, he asked me to give her a message, and since Brandy and I had plans for lunch the next day to talk about the other woman—"

"What other woman?"

"Well . . . to discuss her . . ." Charlene stopped being chatty. She couldn't tell this woman that Serenity was being overpowered, emotionally at least, by Alaric and having a second woman as part of their vampire coven.

Charlene personally agreed with Brandy that Serenity didn't belong with Alaric. Alaric was a bad guy. A dangerous man.

The officer would no doubt bring in Brandy for further questions, which could lead to Brandy looking guilty, or worse, add to their suspicions of Serenity.

The family *had* left the witch ball suddenly—even Sam had commented about it.

Charlene's cheeks heated and Officer Jimenez turned from the computer to study her.

"What is going on with you?"

"Nothing!"

Her heart raced. Her pulse skipped. This was not the calm and collected image she wanted to portray to this woman. It was lucky she wasn't taking a lie detector test.

"Why don't I believe you?"

"I'm—I'm just—" Charlene exhaled. "Can I have some water?"

Officer Jimenez's brow hiked. She wanted to say no, but couldn't, really. "Stay here."

Charlene stayed, fighting the temptation to run out the door like Sam's mystery person with the confession. While she waited, she processed every infraction she'd had in her mind. Running a red light, not paying a parking ticket within thirty days.

Officer Jimenez returned with a bottle of water and handed it to Charlene, narrowing her eyes.

"Thanks." Charlene uncapped it and drank two big gulps to cool down.

"Wanna tell me what has you so flustered?" Officer Jimenez peered down her slim nose.

"No. Okay, you make me nervous." There. The ball was now in the officer's court.

Officer Jimenez grinned. "Good." She sat down again. "You were telling me about how you and Brandy Flint ended up in the hotel room of the victim at the Longmire Hotel."

Forty-five minutes later, Charlene's nerves were so taut that she was about to snap. "I think that's everything."

"Thanks for coming in on a Sunday. Murder doesn't take weekends off." Officer Jimenez stood up. "Is there anything else you want to add regarding this statement? Pertaining to this case?"

"Oh! Sort of. I mean. Yes." Charlene pulled her report for Sam from her purse. "Is Sa—Detective Holden in? I saw that his office was empty when we passed, but he'd asked for this written report. I met with Elisabeta, Alaric's roommate."

Officer Jimenez snatched the paperwork from Charlene's fingers in annoyance. "We've been trying to reach her—but she's never home."

"Well." Charlene thought to how forceful she and Brandy had been, not taking *no* for an answer. As a civilian, you could do that. Not so much as an officer of the law. "Maybe she's hiding," Charlene suggested, automatically filling in why the woman might have a reason to hide. "She could have killed Alaric. She had reason to be jealous of Serenity Flint."

Officer Jimenez's mouth dropped open and she clamped it closed. "You can't help it, can you? Just talking. Being where you shouldn't be."

"I didn't know we shouldn't have been at Alaric's house." Charlene faced the officer in confusion. "Why not?"

The officer shook the report. "Oh. No reason. Other

than *he was murdered* and we don't know who did it."
Her voice couldn't be more sarcastic. "I'll give this to the
detective. You should probably go."

"All right." Charlene shouldered her bag under the
pointed glare of the officer.

"You better not get so much as a speeding ticket in this
town. Got it?"

Charlene raced out of the building without saying
goodbye.

Her hands were trembling when she reached the Pilot
and climbed in. Already one in the afternoon. Holy
smokes. What a day. Why hadn't Sam been there?

It took her a few minutes to calm down before she
started the car and drove home. She rushed inside, waved
to Avery, who was dusting the golden oak railings of the
grand staircase, and bypassed Minnie, sorting things in
the pantry.

She got into her room and turned on the television.

"Jack?" she whispered. "Jack!"

He appeared in a burst of cold air. "Yes? What's
wrong, Charlene?"

Jack ushered her in with a flourish, and she noticed the
cozy blanket he'd placed on the love seat for her. She removed her bulky jacket and he floated it to the armchair.

"Have you ever been hated before?" She scooted Silva
off her pillow to the floor, but the Persian had a mind of
her own. Using her wet nose and furry head, she rubbed
against Charlene's legs with a throaty protest. Caving in,
she picked up her majesty, settling the uppity cat on her
lap.

"I was murdered," he said dryly.

"Oh." For some reason, that set her off and she burst
out laughing. "Jack, if something happens to me, it's prob-

ably going to be Officer Jimenez that does me in. She hates me. Not just a little—Brandy could tell yesterday that she *loathed* me."

"That's a strong word."

"It's true." Charlene made Jack laugh as she replayed her moronic moments in the station giving her statement. "Her loss, Jack. I'm a good friend to have."

"I know that. Just ask the cat." Jack folded his arms as he watched them. "The day she jumped on that moving truck was her ticket to stardom. She thinks she's royalty and acts like it too."

"That's true, isn't it, little Miss Fancy-pants?" The feline lifted her head and speared her with golden eyes. Silva licked her hand and purred until Charlene stroked under her chin.

Charlene switched on the local news for Salem. "I think Officer Jimenez made a mistake, though, Jack. She kept referring to Orpheus as a victim. I thought Orpheus committed suicide, but she says they're waiting for the coroner's report."

"That's very interesting. She wouldn't want you to know that there might be another murder."

"And Orpheus's death hasn't made the paper." Charlene pet behind Silva's ears, calming down after her emotional morning. "Jimenez did perk up a bit when I said that I saw what looked like a cloak in the closet at Orpheus's hotel. I told her about the tall guy running from Elisabeta's and the dirty boots. I was trying to be as helpful as possible so they can catch who did this."

"Sam wasn't there?"

"No. I hope he'll call later after he reads my report. Hey. You think she'll give it to him?"

Jack rubbed his jaw. "You should probably text him to let him know it's there. Just in case she tries to say you never dropped it off."

Charlene sank back against the cushions of her love seat, thinking of the article in the Salem newspaper. "Jack— did you know that there used to be a bunch of waterways around Salem?"

"Sure. Filled in to make streets. The Commons had a river running through it. Farm animals even. Can you believe it? Why do you ask?"

"Alaric's body washed up by the Derby Wharf and didn't go out to sea. The paper mentioned the Derby tunnel entrance. Are there a lot of those?"

Jack gestured to the laptop on Charlene's desk. "Let's do some research. I'll man the computer and you text the detective to cover your behind."

She shot off a professional text to Sam to let him know she'd been in, then set her phone aside.

"How was Serenity this morning?" Jack sat in her office chair.

Charlene considered all that Serenity had shared, the brokenhearted girl. It had only been two days since the supposed love of her life had died tragically. "I asked her about Alaric's family, you know, in case there was a funeral. He told her his mother had been dead a long, long time. She got the impression he wanted her to believe hundreds of years."

"I doubt that."

"She does too."

"Mom's name? We can do a quick search." Jack waggled his brows. Cyber energy made him stronger.

They'd played around with trying to capture Jack's

image on film, but it hadn't worked. There'd been no
image at all. That had made Jack upset, so they'd left the
whole paranormal photography thing alone since.

Jack spent his days, when he was able to manifest himself for her, reading or watching documentaries. He was
up on world news as well as local events and was a fabulous conversationalist.

She hadn't been lonely a day since she'd moved in
with Jack. She blinked when a cool breeze of Jack's air
tugged her hair to get her attention. "Sorry. Serenity didn't
know his mother's name."

"Where was he from?"

That she knew. "Memphis."

"Do you mind me doing this and not you?" He flexed
his fingers.

"Go right ahead—you're much quicker." She reluctantly got up from her love seat.

Jack, using some sort of telepathic connection to cyber-
space, went through the articles, reading and discarding
quickly. Charlene read over his shoulder.

"The paper this morning said his name was Allan."

He scrolled and scanned. "Bingo. Here we are. Clay-
ton, Ohio. Not Memphis. Allan Joseph Mayar born to
Melissa May Mayar. How old was he?"

"I don't know for sure. Brandy was angry about the
age difference between him and Serenity . . . He appeared
to be in his late thirties. The paper said forty-five?"

"According to his birth certificate, he was forty-six."

Three years older than her. Did drinking blood give
him a youthful appearance? She winced as she recalled
the stories of Countess Elizabeth Bathory, bathing in vir-
gin's blood to maintain her youth. Charlene would keep
her crow's-feet, thank you.

Allan Joseph. How simple. "He must have changed his name for effect."

"Allan isn't very vampiric," Jack said. "If that's what he was going for. Not like Alaric, which has an ancient feel."

She wondered if Elisabeta had changed her name, as well as Orpheus. If you wanted to convey vampire, Jane didn't cut it.

"Is there a picture of Melissa? A Mr. Mayar?"

Jack brought up another server and searched Melissa Mayar. "No record of marriage on file."

Impressed, Charlene smiled at Jack. "You're getting so fast!"

"Practice makes perfect." He smiled at her with pleasure for her compliment. "Ah, here we go. Melissa died ten years ago. Her obituary was published in the small-town paper. 'She shunned the light that harmed her.'"

Charlene didn't understand—was it a poem? "What does that mean?"

"Hang on. Let me enlarge the photo." He squinted to read. "'She shunned the light that harmed her in favor of eternal darkness.'"

Eternal darkness, like her son longed for. "That sounds crazy."

"Could be. Mental illness is hereditary."

"She told fortunes for a living. Did she want to be a vampire too?"

Jack tapped something else into the search bar. A picture of a pretty woman with a pale face and pained eyes covered the screen. "It doesn't say."

"She's so sad. How did she die?"

Rubbing his hands together, his shoulders hunched over the keyboard as he typed, Jack's fingers were soundless against the keys. "Don't worry, Charlene, I'll find out, if you have something else to do."

"We need to get you your own computer," she joked.

"Not a bad idea, if you mind sharing yours?"

"No. Usually we're working on things together." Teamwork.

The rain pelted the windows with increased force. A day to stay in and watch movies or play games.

The smell of roasted chicken with rosemary potatoes for Sunday lunch snuck under her door, followed by Avery's laughter and Minnie's chuckle.

"Never mind. I'll go help Minnie and Avery. They sound like they're having fun in the kitchen without me."

"I'll try to discover how Alaric's mom died. Maybe there will be a connection."

"Thanks, Jack."

He worked on the mystery that allowed Charlene to focus on her guests, and she walked into the kitchen. "Minnie, how long until lunch?"

"Another hour or so."

"Avery, go see which of our guests might be up for a game of Clue. It's called Cluedo in other parts of the world, but the Parker Brothers, right here in Salem, designed the American version after a murder that took place in Salem."

"Where did you learn that?" Minnie asked.

"It was an article in the paper last week. Cool, huh?"

Twenty minutes later, Emma, Gabriel, Andrew, and Olivia were seated at the dining room table big enough for them all to play. Joey was there. Judd and Malena had risked the weather for the Peabody Essex Museum, Avery said, as had Chloe and Braydon.

Tommy clomped down the staircase as Charlene was entering the dining room. "Does Celeste want to join us?" she asked.

His face turned red with anger. "Her and Asher are gone. Bedroom's a mess."

And hadn't invited Tommy or Joey. She put her hand on his shoulder and squeezed. It hurt to be the one not included in love.

She reached for Avery. "Come on, Avery. Let's play."

CHAPTER 12

Tuesday morning, Charlene balanced her accounts for the week. She'd learned in her bed-and-breakfast business that most people stayed for a long weekend. Tapping into her marketing background, Charlene offered a special deal—pay for five nights and get the sixth for free. This tempted folks into booking for the entire week at such a great price, turning the average three-night stay into six.

Her gamble had worked and most of the guests who'd checked in for Halloween weren't leaving until Wednesday, giving her one more day of a full house. Just how she liked it.

Bills paid, website updated, Charlene allowed her curiosity to wander and typed *Alaric Mayar* into her search bar to see if anything new had popped up about his death overnight. Nope . . . same as yesterday. His murderer still at large. Not a thing about Orpheus either.

Allan/Alaric wasn't on any of the standard social media sites, or the second tier, suggesting he avoided an online presence.

And yet, he'd targeted Serenity. He'd needed a witch. She was reminded of a predator watching his prey from the shadows and waiting for the right victim before making a move.

She typed *modern-day vampires* into the search bar next and was appalled that there were really people living off of human blood. Worse somehow was that it was all consensual.

"What's got you so agitated?" a male voice rumbled behind her.

Her stomach leaped into her throat and she whirled toward Jack. "Just a little light reading, that's all."

Jack studied the image of a scalpel. "Tools of my old trade."

"Well, Dr. Strathmore, did you ever have someone ask you to cut them so they could feed another person?"

"No." He started to read over her shoulder, drawn in by the gruesome subject matter. "A fleshy part of the body, so as not to scar. Odd. Who would do this?"

Charlene rubbed her queasy tummy. "Not me! I don't even like to donate blood in the doctor's office."

"This is by far different." Jack glanced at Charlene. "Is the feeding sexual?"

"Not for everybody." Charlene couldn't believe she was having this conversation. With her ghost. "They have communities of real vampires living together in houses or covens. They can eat garlic and regular food but supposedly need blood to be their best self." Charlene scanned the rest of the article with trepidation. "They don't sleep in coffins and can handle the light."

"Not at all like the movies."

"No." She turned toward Jack. "Or what Alaric and Elisabeta had set up in their rental house." Charlene recalled the coffin with a shudder. "Blood and coffins, Jack."

He nodded sagely. "They were putting on a show."

"Alaric believed he was a vampire, from all accounts so far." Serenity and Elisabeta had been adamant. "Oh— I meant to tell you that Orpheus said Alaric's symptoms were psychosomatic, brought on by his crazy mother. What do you think?"

"The human brain is capable of just about anything. If he'd convinced some part of his mind that his skin blistering in the sun was essential to his survival as a vampire?" Jack spread his arms to his sides. "I wouldn't rule it out. There are Christians who believe in stigmata, the wounds of Christ appearing on the faithful."

"Maybe Orpheus was jealous of that too. Alaric believed it as much as he could, as anybody could."

"Did Alaric have pointy teeth?" Jack asked. "Do the 'real' vampires have fangs?"

"One of the articles I read said that a person could have dental pieces made to fit in their mouth if they wanted a custom set. Or you can buy plastic ones online."

Jack smoothed his chin in contemplation. "I'd want my own set. I mean, if I was going to commit to the vampire persona. No cheap plastic."

"I think Orpheus had his done permanently. Sam said he was going to check Alaric's dental work at the morgue."

Serenity would know for sure—she and Alaric had been plenty close enough, kissing and whispering on the sofa of the Hawthorne Hotel lobby.

"Jack, you're a doctor . . . is there a medical reason for Alaric's skin to blister in the sun?"

Jack's image clarified and he tilted his head. "I never dealt with anything like that in my particular practice, but that doesn't mean it doesn't exist. Here in Salem, it was the routine stuff like high blood pressure from too much butter with the lobster."

"Let's check." Charlene motioned to the laptop. "Perhaps Alaric had a physical reason to believe himself a real vampire."

She watched over Jack's shoulder as he typed *blistered skin* into the search bar.

The results at first had everything to do with sunburns or accidental burns, but by the second page, she stepped back and pressed her hand to her stomach at the photos of people with blistered skin. A father and son. Cousins. "Oh no. How unfortunate!"

"*Solar urticaria* . . . this can be inherited, poor folks." Jack sighed. "That would explain the message on his mother's obituary. She found eternal release from the light that had plagued her."

Charlene looked at Jack. "This is so sad. Does it hurt?"

"I don't know. Let me do a little more research."

She gave a half nod and another step backward.

"Any word from Sam?" Jack asked as he pulled up web pages.

"Nothing this morning. He'll be in touch when he's ready. Thanks for finding all of the waterways in Salem for me. Makes me think of pirates and bootlegging. I wish I could remember the name of the book Orpheus was reading."

"This disease boggles the mind. Even with modern medicine, there are some things just out of a doctor's reach."

Charlene turned toward the kitchen to find her phone. "I'll call Serenity about the vampire teeth before I forget."

Jack didn't look up. "Good luck."

Charlene halted in the threshold. "I think I'll go to Evergreen Bookstore. The book came from there. I can see what else they have on the subject while I have a free hour." She and Minnie planned to take down all of the Halloween decorations to replace with fall foliage, but it could be done later.

Jack shot a grin over his shoulder at her. "What for? Gonna take up bootlegging? Rum smuggling?"

Charlene laughed at the idea of being a swashbuckling pirate like the one at the witch ball. "You never know. I liked being a Southern belle."

"You can probably order the books online," Jack said.

"I know. But I also want to talk to Lucas about that night, jog his memory to see if he remembers anything odd."

Jack chuckled. "Now *that* is more believable. You're a smart woman, Charlene Morris. Just be careful."

"I will!"

Charlene dialed the Flints' house but had to be content with leaving a message. She then drove to the bookstore. Lucas carried a lot of Salem memorabilia, as well as Wiccan nonfiction and fiction.

She walked inside and greeted him. "Hi, Lucas!"

There was a picture of Lucas and his wife Martine behind the register. A year ago they'd gone through some marital problems that seemed to have sorted themselves out, if their smiles were anything to go by.

"Charlene! How have you been since the ball? Stephanos and I hope you'll judge again next year."

She patted her heart. "Of course!"

"I'm so glad that we chose Aphrodite and the alien to win." Lucas strolled around the long counter. "We may have created romance for them too—they were in to buy a few books on the area, holding hands and making moon-eyes at one another."

Charlene clapped. "Wonderful! How's your daughter? I meant to ask the other night but things got chaotic."

"As well as can be expected. She's on a new medication that she hates. Still, it could be worse."

Charlene half-smiled in commiseration. "Listen, I had a few questions about Saturday night. Did you know Alaric at all?"

"The dead vampire?" He shook his head. "Never met him."

"He moved to town two weeks ago and kept a low profile." She asked casually, "Do you believe in vampires?"

Lucas did a double take to see if she was joking. "Do you?"

"I have an open mind," Charlene said. "I've learned a lot since my move from Chicago, especially about the modern-day witches in Salem. So why not vampires? They have their own communities."

"Well, when you put it like that . . . let's just say I have never met an actual blood-sucking vampire with fangs." He bared his teeth.

Charlene laughed and set her purse down on the glass counter. Shelves of books were all around the store. Tarot cards. Writing journals. It was an inviting shop and Lucas a knowledgeable bookseller.

"Me either—but according to Serenity Flint, Alaric believed himself to be a real vampire, not just dressing up as one for Halloween. It's a lifestyle."

"Hmm. I saw them dancing together right before he did his disappearing trick."

The evening hadn't gone according to plan. Charlene tilted her head, her elbow on the counter, showing she had time to chat.

"Were they a couple?" Lucas straightened a book on a shelf. "It's hard to know these days."

"Kind of—Serenity cared for him, very much. That's why I'm asking around to see if you maybe noticed something off that night. An argument or an altercation."

"Just the one Alaric had with Dru. Can't believe the kid punched the guy." Lucas sighed. "I saw Serenity and Dru last summer after Dru got the job at the Peabody. They exuded love and unity. You don't think he had anything to do with it, do you?"

"Me?" She moved to a set of tall wooden shelves and scanned the titles. "No, no." Sam might think differently so she changed the subject. "Hey, do you happen to have any books on Salem's bootlegging days?"

Charlene hoped to visually match what she remembered of the cover on Orpheus's bed to the book in the store since she couldn't recall the title or author.

Lucas immediately turned to his left and a middle shelf with a book facing out. "We carry this nonfiction book by a local author. There are a few dryer pieces, but this is the one I recommend for sheer factual entertainment."

She reached for a copy. "*Salem Confidential: Secret Societies, Rum Smugglers, and Hidden Tunnels.*"

"Catchy title, isn't it? I know the author personally. Dr. Patrick Steel." Lucas gestured to the stacks of three or four books behind five in stock. "He poured over those documents and books for fascinating details."

Her mind put the waterways and tunnels together. "Are all of the tunnels open?"

"Goddess no." Lucas grimaced. "Most are an accident waiting to happen. But the smuggling was a real deal. Lots of treasure from the seafaring days is kept right here in Salem."

"Where?"

"The Peabody Essex Museum, of course. Did you know that it's the oldest, longest running museum in the United States?"

"That's a cool claim to fame." Charlene brought the book to the counter, opening it to the first page of maps.

Lucas joined her to read the pages. "That's the Derby Wharf there, with the lighthouse. And the old Derby tunnel."

"Such a great view those old houses had, right on the water."

"It used to be where the ships came in to unload their goods. Molasses was worth a bundle because it made rum."

Salem's inhabitants still liked their drinks. "I learned some of that on the history tour I took with Kass." Charlene traced the familiar main streets with her finger. "Old Salem Hall. Hard to believe these streets were under water once."

"Yep. Another place the boats were unloaded. I'm pretty sure there were tunnels there too."

The area today was all filled in and paved. "Did the townspeople use the tunnels back then?"

Lucas waggled his brows. "From what I understand, some were secret passageways."

She grinned. "Like the secret staircase in the House of the Seven Gables?"

"*Salem Confidential* probably touches on that too." He tapped the open pages. "It's a fun read on Salem's secrets."

"I'll buy it, please. Guests at the B and B will love it. Too bad there are no tours of the tunnels."

Lucas rung up the book and bagged it for her. "There was talk of making it into an attraction, but the city can't afford it. The liability would be through the roof! First time a tourist tripped and fell, and sued? There go Salem's coffers."

Salem was all about the tourists to make up for the loss of the glory, and profit, of their ship trading days—and Lucas sat on the city council.

"You have a point." Charlene held her bag. "You know the author, you say?"

"Patrick and I go way back. He had his first big signing here, before the town put the kibosh on the tunnel tours actually being underground."

"Thanks, Lucas." Charlene tried one more time to shake something free from his mind of the night. "You're sure you didn't notice anything odd right before the lights went out?"

"Nope. I mean, I kept waiting for him, Alaric, to pop back into the room to finish the trick, but he never did." Lucas shrugged. "It's sad."

Had Alaric been dead already by then?

"I could have introduced you to Patrick at the ball—he was the pirate you almost voted for, but he'd already won before."

"I loved his parrot."

"And I'm sure you'll love his book too."

Charlene exited the bookstore feeling very confident that Patrick Steel would know secret tunnels and ways in and out, along with a wealth of information that might lead them straight to Alaric's killer.

CHAPTER 13

Charlene took the book home, anxious to get started, but there was work to be done so it would be a treat for later. Her phone rang as she prepped for Tuesday afternoon's happy hour.

"Hi, Charlene, it's Serenity. Mom said you called this morning?"

Charlene put her earbuds in so that she could have her hands free and still talk. "I did."

Serenity's exhale held a tinge of annoyance. "Listen, I complained to Mom—four phone calls in two days? Right? But she explained that she asked you to help out so I don't go to jail."

Charlene bit her lip to keep from laughing. "That's true."

She snorted. "So. Ask away. Goddess forbid I spend time at the police station around actual criminals."

Laughter bubbled but she kept it in. The Flint spirit in Serenity ran strong. "I know you didn't have anything to do with Alaric's death"—she hoped and prayed, but she'd been mistaken before—"and I owed your mom a favor or two." Which was now paid in full. "I also care about you."

Sigh. "Whatchya want to know? I've already told you everything. I haven't seen Dru, either."

That sounded very defensive, but Charlene stayed on course. "I was reading up on 'real' vampires. It seems that there are communities all over the world of people who drink or consume human blood."

"Yeah. That grossed me out, but Alaric told me not to worry about it. His way was the old way, but together we would be strong enough to change whatever we wanted. I liked that modern idea."

"See? That's something you haven't told me before."

"I didn't think it pertained."

"It might not—but it's an interesting point, growing away from the ancient toward modern views." Change often scared others.

Was it a motive to kill?

"It's why Alaric was glad to find out that I was a true witch, tracing my ancestry back to Armand Sheffield."

"How did he find that out?"

"I don't know. I probably told him."

Charlene pushed aside the cabbage and ginger salad she'd been mixing and reached for her pen. "You are truly magically powerful, as he claimed to be . . . but he wasn't really, was he?" She jotted that thought down on the kitchen tablet next to the fridge.

"He was . . . but it's all so confusing. When I was with

him, everything made sense." Serenity blew out a breath, back to being annoyed.

Charlene set down the pen. "The article made me wonder if Alaric used his teeth to . . . drink blood."

"Yuck. I never saw him do that. He never tried to do that with me. Just tasted my blood, that one time."

"*How* was he going to turn you into a vampire, then?"

"The blood transfusion was going to happen that night at two in the morning. Between me and Alaric. He wanted Elisabeta and another guy too, but I said no way."

"Why two in the morning?"

"I read an astrological chart, and that was the most fortuitous time to raise the dead . . . which I double-checked with my spirit guides."

Accepting that this was true came easier now than it had a year ago. "Did you ask your guides if you should do the spell or transfusion?"

"No." Serenity spoke in a lower voice. "I knew the answer wouldn't be positive."

"I see." Charlene leaned her hip against the kitchen counter. Serenity'd had a very close call of her own making. "Did Alaric have enlarged eyeteeth? From what I read online, some 'real' vampires have custom prosthetic fan—teeth."

Serenity sucked in a breath. "I . . . I guess so. Not abnormal though."

"Did you notice them the night of the ball?"

"Uh . . . yes. I thought they were sexy—part of his vampire persona as an immortal being."

Alaric had been very sensual. Primal. "The spell cast . . ."

"A traveling through the cosmos spell. He was supposed to be waiting for me in his house. The stake wasn't part of the plan that I knew of." She sniffed. "I really do want to find out who killed Alaric—even if he was a fake."

"Have you had a change of heart?"

She paused, then admitted, "My mind is clearer this morning than it has been."

"That's so good to know."

"Yeah. I guess I was stupid to fall for him like that."

"Not stupid. Don't say that." The oven timer went off for the first batch of egg rolls. "Thanks again for calling me back. Shoot me a text if you think of anything else?"

"I will. Bye."

Charlene turned her phone off and got the egg rolls out of the oven.

Jack appeared at the kitchen table. "Those smell amazing. I don't often miss food, but I like a good spring roll with wasabi. Well, I used to."

"Ah, Jack. I don't have wasabi. Will ginger do?"

"It's fine." He rotated the bowl on the table. "That slaw looks good too."

"Serenity called. Alaric had fake teeth."

"He did? See, serious about his image. Did you tell her about his mom, and his real name?"

"Shoot! I forgot." And there was no way she was going to call for a fifth time.

"Forgot what?" Celeste asked, trailed by Tommy and Joey. Asher wasn't with them.

Charlene glared at Jack, who grinned.

"Nothing. Bad habit of talking to myself since my husband died. Apps are about ready if you want to wait in the other room. We're doing Asian tonight."

"Can we help?"

Celeste was a real sweet young lady—who was dipping her toe into the dark side, tasting blood with Asher. Asher had worn a vampire costume at the witch ball and maybe was into the scene more than he'd admitted. "No, thank you."

"I'll run up and get Asher." Celeste bolted back toward the main staircase.

"He doesn't need you to fetch him," Tommy grumbled as he and Joey shuffled off toward the living room.

"Trouble in paradise," Jack remarked. "Tommy probably thought he had Celeste for the taking until Asher showed up on the scene. Who would you choose, Charlene? The dark-haired bartender or the dreamy-eyed loner?"

"Neither." With that, Charlene brought the appetizers to the sideboard for her guests. She'd set out saki and plum wine, glasses, as well as bottles of water, and she perused her selection to see if there was anything else. Wontons, soy sauce, slaw . . . It was the last happy hour with this particular group and she wanted it to be special.

"What's this?" Chloe asked. "*Salem Confidential.* How intriguing."

Charlene had placed her new book on the coffee table to read later and now Chloe held it up. "Salem is all about the witches, but pirates are so cool too. Is this good, Charlene?"

"Don't know yet—you can borrow it after I finish." Charlene stepped away from the buffet. "Should be done tonight."

Tommy finished reading the long title over Chloe's shoulder. *"Secret Societies. Rum Smugglers. Hidden Tunnels."*

Celeste, who'd returned with Asher on her heels,

brought her clasped hands to her heart. "I love Salem. It's amazing."

Tommy, Joey, and Asher clustered around Celeste.

"Awesome!" Joey said. "What's it about? I know Seattle has an entire section of city preserved from where the new part of town was built over it."

"I've been there," Asher said. "Cool music scene in Seattle."

"Grunge is old news," Tommy scoffed. "LA is fresh again."

"Like you know!" Celeste laughed, clearly enjoying the tension between the young men over her. "Jersey City isn't a music mecca, that's for sure."

"Is there a city below us, Charlene?" Joey asked.

"I don't know. Just picked that book up today." At Celeste's questioning glance, she explained. "I'm interested in all things local to Salem, and I hadn't heard about the smuggling or tunnels before. It's sure to be informative."

"Where'd you hear about it?" Asher slung his arm over Celeste's shoulders.

"Hmm. I can't say." She shrugged. That was honest, anyway. For some reason the police were keeping the news of Orpheus's death out of the paper so she really couldn't admit to being there.

"My favorite kind of history is the haunted history like Salem has," Tommy said.

Charlene eyed the sepia cover with an outline of Salem on the front. A ship's mast. "I hope it's not too dark. I don't like being scared before bed."

"Me either!" Malena agreed. She and Judd walked full plates to their armchairs before the fireplace.

Emma loaded up a dish from the sideboard and handed

it to her hubby, in step behind her. "Us too, Tommy. We love the haunted tours in New Orleans. All of the tombs and voodoo magic. Zombies. Vampires. Ghosts."

"I've never been to New Orleans," Celeste said. "I'd love to go."

"The haunted tours are silly ways to scare people," Asher declared. "It's stuff not on the map that are the real deal. I can take you to the most haunted places in New Orleans. Ten times more thrilling than here."

"I'll go," Tommy said.

Joey elbowed him. "Don't think you and me are invited. I think it's a Celeste-only invitation."

Tommy's expression fell while Celeste peeked up at Asher.

Asher rubbed his jaw and hid a smirk.

Emma brought her plate to the sofa next to Gabriel. "I liked them in New Orleans just fine. We've done the haunted city tours in every major city that we've traveled to, Tommy. You get interesting tidbits. Key West, Savannah, New York."

Charlene handed Tommy and Joey plates and ushered them in the line for food. "I have a friend who claims to see ghosts around Old Burying Point cemetery. Even captured orbs on film."

"No way." Tommy added slaw next to his egg rolls.

"That I'd like to see!" Asher showed enthusiasm for the first time all night, knocked out of his studied ennui.

"Have you ever seen a ghost?" Chloe asked.

Jack appeared with a shivery laugh. "Go ahead and answer that one, Charlene."

She averted her eyes, not wanting to lie. "Well, I heard about the white lady at Old Burying Point and a crying child in the Hawthorne . . . but I honestly never saw a ghost in either place."

"I don't know what I'd do," Chloe sighed. "Probably faint."

"Not like you, Charlene," Jack said. "You were determined that I was a bad dream. Remember?"

She ignored Jack and reached for the bottle of plum wine to top off her guests' glasses. "Now, where is everyone going for dinner tonight?"

Jack's laugh echoed around the room and Silva sauntered in, tail high. She stalked toward Jack before the fireplace and swatted at his leg.

"Do you have a window open, Charlene?" Celeste asked. "I just felt a chill."

"Let me check." She glared at Jack, but he'd disappeared—which was very smart of him. He'd gotten her a couple of times already today.

She fussed with the windowsill and turned back to her guests. "There. Now, do you need any suggestions?"

"We've loved everything that you've recommended," Emma said. "I'm so glad that we stayed the full week to see everything."

"Us too," Olivia agreed. "Three days wouldn't be enough."

"This was the most exciting Halloween I've ever had," Celeste said.

"A dead guy at the same party as us," Emma said. "Sad. Gruesome. I sure hope they find out who did it. Will you let us know, Charlene?"

"Of course." Not that she wanted her B and B to be remembered for a dead vampire. She'd pour on the customer service so it wouldn't be what they recalled first.

Asher nodded at Charlene before he left. "Thanks for letting me crash here. I've patched things up with my roomie so I'll be back at the house."

Celeste lowered her eyes. Joey gave Tommy's arm a hopeful shove. Maybe this meant the hookup was over and Celeste would be back with her friends until they flew home to Jersey City in the morning.

"You're welcome."

After her guests all left and she'd loaded the dishwasher, Charlene sat down with a glass of wine before the fireplace, without Jack, and opened the book. The maps were in bold colors but vague, hinting at secrets in Salem.

Silva curled up next to her and purred her contentment. Charlene scratched the cat's chin.

The pages were easy to read in larger print with images every new chapter. Charlene loved the author's humorous style.

Lucas had been right that it made Salem seem scandalous. Brothels, gambling, smuggling not just molasses, but slaves. Jewels. The ship owners would unload certain items to be taxed and stored, and hide others to keep from paying a fortune on their cargo.

Charlene skimmed each of the ten chapters and was done in two hours, just about the time she expected her guests to return.

She had more questions than answers. Where exactly did the tunnels go?

On a hunch, she looked Patrick Steel up in the Salem directory.

To her surprise, his phone number was listed, so she called before she talked herself out of it, or imagined Sam telling her to mind her own business.

"Hello?" a gruff older voice answered.

"Hi . . . I'd like to speak with Patrick Steel."

"Who's asking?"

"Charlene Morris. I live here in Salem and I just finished your book. *Salem Confidential*."

"Yes?" His tone lifted from wary to jovial.

"I loved it."

"You did? Wonderful!" She remembered his booming voice as a pirate in costume. "Where'd you get a copy? Online?"

"Actually, Evergreen Bookstore. Brick-and-mortar." Charlene laughed. "Lucas recommended it."

"He's a good guy, that one."

"I agree." She waited for a few seconds to see if he'd speak, but he remained quiet. "I had some questions."

"Oooh?"

Charlene could tell that Patrick would need some more cajoling before talking to her about his hard work. She couldn't begin to imagine the time it took to organize an entire book, and the man had his doctorate. Intelligent. Creative. Funny. He was probably used to making hundreds, if not more, for his speaking engagements.

"Is it possible for us to meet tomorrow for lunch?" Wednesday her guests would all be checked out by eleven. Avery would come in after school if lunch with Patrick went late.

"Sure . . ."

"My treat, of course."

"I can do that, I suppose."

"Sea Level?"

"All right. Anything in particular you want to know?"

"There is so much fascinating information. Lucas said that you were hoping to do tours, but the city said no."

"It set me back some, don't mind saying. I hope they'll

come around and when they do, I'll be ready. I've got everything I need to lead an informative tour."

"I'd love to see the tunnels."

"You would?" He chuckled.

"What's funny about that?"

"It's just that after five years I've got interest in the tunnels again. Makes me want to dust off my tour guide license."

"Who else—"

"See you tomorrow at noon. Bye!"

Well, hell. Who else was interested in the tunnels? Orpheus came to mind. Maybe Orpheus had more to do with Alaric's death than she'd supposed. Brandy had said that she'd been wrong before too, meaning that Orpheus could be the killer.

She left the book on the stairs for Chloe to browse and went to bed.

CHAPTER 14

Charlene was sorry to see her guests go on Wednesday morning. Everyone said they'd had a wonderful time, which was all she could ask for.

"I'm glad I have this lunch date," she told Minnie, blinking her eyes clear. "Otherwise I might need a good cry."

Minnie laughed and patted Charlene's shoulder. "You care about all your guests, that's why. They'll be back, just wait and see."

Charlene and Jack talked strategy before she left. "Butter him up. Tell him he's brilliant. I hope he's not an author snob," Jack said. "You know the kind."

"Not personally." This was her first author that she'd ever met and maybe she was a bit nervous.

Charlene had worn her hair long, curling the ends. She smoothed her dark jeans down her thighs, then adjusted her thin wool turtleneck sweater. "He sounded like a gentleman over the phone, and he knows the waterways and tunnels better than anybody."

Jack crossed his arms. "What's your fascination with them?"

"I won't tell you until I get back. Just in case I'm totally wrong, and then I won't have to look like a fool in front of anybody but Dr. Steel." His book had hinted at secrets too volatile to be put in print and she hoped to learn a few.

"You could never look like a fool. How am I supposed to be patient with an exit like that?"

"See what more you can discover about Allan and Melissa Mayar. Still haven't heard from Sam and I don't want to bother him. He wants every communication to be through the proper channels."

"Until the murderer is caught. Do you have your pepper spray?" Jack dangled a wool string in front of Silva, who loved the game, but couldn't touch him no matter how hard she tried.

"Good idea. Just in case." Laughing at their antics, she darted into her bedroom, opened her closet, and dug out her pepper spray.

If she *happened* to drive by Elisabeta's and Alaric's house on her way home from Sea Level, well, that was the route she *might* take if she wanted to pass the Commons. A simple note in Elisabeta's door to request a call could be construed as neighborly. She didn't have Brandy's magick sachet so her pepper spray would have to do.

"Bye!" Charlene ventured into the cold. Instead of rain, a light snow was falling, fluffy flakes that melted as they touched ground. She drove to Sea Level, charging her cell phone on the way to ensure a full battery.

What did poor Nancy Drew do? No cell phones back then, only pay phones in Superman-sized red boxes. Yay, technology.

Ten minutes later, she circled around to find a parking spot. She hadn't heard from Sam today. What would he think about her lunch with the author of *Salem Confidential*?

"Well, if the man called to check in, he'd know." She pulled into a parking spot, feeling lucky.

Sea Level had two floors and she entered on the street. She passed the small reception area and noticed a man next to the window alone, a red wool cap on his head, a full gray beard, weathered hands clasping a cup of coffee. She hardly recognized him without his eye patch and parrot.

She strode to his table. "Dr. Steel?"

"Depends who's asking." His deep chuckle sounded like it came from rusty pipes. "Not the FBI or the tax collector, are you?"

She sat down across from him and put out her hand. "I'm Charlene. Thanks for meeting me today."

"Please, call me Patrick." He shook her hand. "Nice place here." His blue-gray eyes were hooded by thick brows that were mostly white.

Charlene gave him a friendly smile. "I run a bed-and-breakfast here in town, so I send a lot of customers this way. It's one of my favorites." She unzipped her jacket and shrugged it off. "The clam chowder is wonderful, but then everything is. The oysters are their specialties and can be cooked in various ways. You can't beat the lobster rolls, served either hot or cold. The seafood pie is filling, and they have fabulous mussels."

"You're sure you don't waitress here, or maybe own the place?" He slurped the last of his coffee and sat back. "My editor treated me to dinner after my book came out five years ago. How 'bout I have what you're having?"

Charlene placed both menus at the edge of the table and peered at him from behind her bangs. "Deal." She chuckled. "I worried you were going to be pretentious, but that was way off."

Patrick boomed a laugh. "Not a pretentious bone in my body."

"I have to confess that I saw you on Friday night."

He wrapped his hands around the coffee mug, clearly trying to reach back as to the circumstance.

"At the witch ball?" She unrolled her paper napkin. "Your pirate costume was so good. I wanted to vote for you to win but the alien beat you out by two feet of scales. I was a judge."

He roared with laughter, smacking his palm to the table. "That was some party. You know Lucas?"

She nodded.

"Alien and Aphrodite. Great choice for king and queen."

"I guess they're hanging out now." She shrugged. "Could be a romance brewing."

"Would you like to hear the specials today?" Their waitress popped over, harried, hand on her slim hip, fuzzy blond hair held back by a pink band. "I'm Maura."

Charlene didn't recognize her. She listened carefully as the young lady spouted off a couple of appetizers and entrées in a rushed pace.

Patrick shrugged. "Sounds fine to me, but Charlene is going to order for us both. Says she sends customers here from her B and B all the time."

Shelley, a brunette waitress wearing a Sea Level T-shirt, skirted past their table. "Hi, Charlene. This handsome guy one of your guests?"

"No, Patrick Steel is a local writer. I just finished his very scandalous book titled *Salem Confidential*." She lowered her tone. "Secret societies, rum smuggling, and secret tunnels."

"Hidden tunnels," Patrick corrected. "That last part always trips people up. Publisher's choice, though. What can you do?"

"That sounds exciting," Shelley said brightly.

"You can pick up a copy at Evergreen Bookstore—but there are only a few left in stock," Charlene informed her.

"I pass by the bookstore on my way home." Shelley grinned at them both. "Nice to meet you, Patrick. Charlene, you having the usual?" She winked at Maura. "Mind if I take this table?"

"Whatever," the young girl said, moving to where a family of four was being seated.

"Patrick, this is Shelley." Charlene gestured to the waitress. "She'll never steer you wrong on what's the best fish of the day."

He tipped his head. "Pleasure."

"Hidden tunnels. Is there one under here?" Shelley bopped her foot to the wooden floor. "We're so close to the water that I'd hate to have the restaurant collapse."

"The tunnels have mostly been filled in or reinforced to be used for sewer pipes or utility lines. No point in digging new holes when they're already there." Patrick lifted a shoulder. "See the wharves? Only four left and there used to be over fifty at the height of the international sea trade."

Charlene peered out the window. She'd been to Derby Wharf and the lighthouse many times.

"Imagine each of those man-made strips of land with warehouses on them, some two or more stories high," Patrick said. "Salem was very prosperous."

Now the strips were vacant, except for the lighthouse. "What happened?" Shelley asked, pen over her order pad.

"Times change. Travel changed. War, taxes . . ."

"I'll make sure to get your book tonight." Shelley rolled her eyes. "Otherwise you'll never get a chance to order. I grew up in Boston, but there is so much I don't know about Salem. Would you like to look at our menu, Patrick? Or has Charlene recommended something for you?"

Charlene laughed. "Now I'm more intrigued too—and I read the book already. One sitting. We'll start with the chowder, please."

After Shelley left, he raised his brows up and down. "You're the real thing, aren't you?"

Her cheeks warmed at his compliment. "I found your book fascinating and bought a copy for my den. Some days my guests enjoy sitting around the fire and reading, instead of touring. Rainy days especially."

He glanced around the restaurant as if looking for someone. "You mind calling that Shelley girl back? If it's okay with you, I'd enjoy a beer with lunch."

"Of course. I'll join you."

Shelley dropped off two iced waters and Charlene told her they'd both like a beer. "We have a big selection. Any in particular?" she asked.

"Heineken," Patrick said.

"Corona Light for me," Charlene added.

Shelley hurried off.

Patrick bent over and reached for something in the brown leather sling on the floor next to his chair. He pulled out a large roll of yellowed paper, tied with a blue ribbon.

"What's that?" She held her breath.

"The maps I used to research my book."

Charlene's pulse raced as she studied the old maps— he'd brought three and laid them across the table. A thrill of anticipation made her heart flutter.

"May I?" She changed her chair to sit next to him, and Patrick showed her the many tangled paths through the underground of Salem.

"Are the waterways connected to the tunnels? You hinted at a connection in your book but didn't say."

Patrick pursed his lower lip and glanced around the restaurant as if to make sure they weren't overheard. "There are things in Salem that one doesn't talk about in plain language." He held her gaze. "Most of the tunnels I've found and marked were created to simplify movement of cargo beneath the city. Not all. The founders wanted Salem to be a major city on the East Coast. Late eighteenth century, early nineteenth."

She listened, fascinated. He had the presence of a bard.

"To put that in perspective, the witch trials were in 1692, 1693. The height of the sea trade here was the mid– seventeen hundreds, especially after the Revolutionary War, through the War of 1812."

"Over two hundred years ago," Charlene said.

"America is a young country." Patrick lifted the maps

when Shelley brought their beers and set them on the table.

"I forget that, because of all the history around us all the time, it seems old."

They clinked their glasses and he took a long, thirsty sip.

"Bootleggers used the tunnels but so did the men in town. Okay, young lady. Stop hedging around the subject and tell me what you really want to know."

"The Hawthorne Hotel. Where would it be on this map?"

He brought the second map to the top of the stack. "Here. The hotel site started out as a small home on the Commons when it was used for the townsfolk to graze their livestock. Water them too. There was a river once."

"You hinted at a secret reason for filling in the river."

He raised his beer and drank. "The Salem Marine Society wanted to create a public area that all could use. Leveling the hills filled in the waterways and allowed for relatively even streets. Houses. And what is built aboveground provided a camouflage for what was being tunneled below."

"Why was it a secret?"

"Dynastic power. There were certain families in Salem that held the most wealth and power. They wanted to keep it amongst themselves."

Familiar story, unfortunately. "The waterways became roads?"

"Exactly."

"Not tunnels."

"Don't sound so disappointed." Patrick chuckled. "Underground tours might be forbidden, but I can take you on a walking tour and show you."

"I would love that! You mentioned in your book that mounds in the grass might be the brick from the ground settling around the tops of the arches of the tunnels."

He nodded sagely. "It's all there, right before us. If you see glass blocks in the street? Those are actually there to allow natural light into the tunnels."

"Is there one under the Hawthorne Hotel?"

He waved his hand dismissively. "Filled in a very long time ago, but it was used for deliveries when it was the Franklin building. It's only been the Hawthorne since 1925."

They laughed. "No time at all. You also hinted at something about chimneys in your book?"

"You paid attention!" Patrick rubbed his hands together. "Yes. The houses that were connected often had more chimney stacks than fireplaces as a marker."

Charlene burst out laughing. "You're kidding. Nobody caught on?"

Patrick grinned. "In the historic section of town, especially. The rich ladies of the day wouldn't want to get their clothes or shoes wet—they didn't have dry cleaners back then or automatic washing machines. You may have noticed that the weather in Salem on the harbor can be damp?"

"Yes. More drizzle here than in Chicago."

"Well, the neighbors that were family or friends had tunnels leading from their homes to their friends' homes. To their family business." His eyes glittered. "Imagine all of the cargo coming in from the ports on those ships. Jewels, silks, spices. I think the tunnels were used as commonly as the streets above in some places."

"It makes sense."

He used his index finger to point to the hotel on the

map. "There's Derby Street. In the old days it separated the houses from the wharves."

Charlene closed her eyes to imagine how it must have been—busy and built up.

She took a sip of her icy cold Corona. "Why are there so many secrets surrounding the tunnels?"

"Politics is my guess—our forefathers here in Salem thought to run the newly-born US—by hook or by crook."

"That's not as juicy as pirate treasure."

"There's *no* treasure." His bushy brow rose in caution. "Fools have been lost under the city searching for El Dorado. Idiots."

"No lost city of gold?" Charlene sat back when Shelley delivered a tray with two steaming clam chowders and a side dish filled with hunks of French bread and crackers.

"I get a little passionate." Patrick rolled up his maps and put them in the leather bag.

Charlene felt a sense of loss when he tucked them away and he laughed at her expression. "We can look at them again after. You might be a convert."

She'd always loved Salem's history. "Might be."

Patrick unfolded his napkin and stuffed the top into his plaid shirt, removing his wool hat at last.

Shelley offered him his bowl, then one to Charlene, putting the bread basket in the center. "Anything else?"

She turned to Shelley. "I'd like to order the lobster rolls for our main course."

"You got it! How's your beers?"

"I'll have another," Patrick said.

"I'm fine for now." Charlene breathed in the salty aroma of her chowder. "Let's eat!"

After a few moments, Charlene said, "I just can't get the idea out of my head that there are roads beneath Salem."

"The city is safe enough." Patrick chuckled. "I know of one entrance that isn't watched so much, by the Old Burying Point Cemetery. You know where that is?"

"Of course! I recommend it to my guests—they're always hoping to see a ghost." She could make a fortune off of Jack, but never would. He was hers alone.

"Well, here's a story for your guests." Patrick paused dramatically. "Diggers went too deep and one poor soul dropped into the tunnel below—rats and stinky water, and the corpse of a woman from hundreds of years ago." He wiped his mouth and snickered. "The construction guy fainted," he said. "His coworkers pulled him out and they realized they'd uncovered a secret tomb, probably from the Underground Railroad days when Salem hid slaves."

She spooned her chowder to her mouth and swallowed. "You should have put that in your book. Readers would love to know things like that."

"I suppose I could always write another one. Been thinkin' on it for a while."

"Definitely, you should."

"When *Salem Confidential* came out I had some acclaim, but not what I'd hoped for. And now twice this week?"

"That's right," Charlene said. She'd been so interested in the subject that fact had slipped her mind. "You mentioned last night that someone else had talked to you about your book."

"Guy offered me five hundred bucks just to go down

there." He gestured to the floor. "I said no. It's against the law."

Charlene studied her nearly empty crock of chowder to hide her reaction. Five hundred bucks? "How odd!" she managed.

"A book is like a child," Patrick said. "You want them to be popular and well-liked, and I admit I had delusions of grandeur. Hoped for a series on any of the major networks but it didn't pan out. It was for the best, really."

"I'm sorry to hear that." Charlene glanced toward the kitchen, but Shelley was with another table. "Do you know who it was that wanted to see the tunnels?"

"Didn't get a name. Tall guy. Dark hair."

Well, that described Alaric, Orpheus, and Dru. Not to mention Asher and Tommy. It even described Sam! Asher had cash, and lots of it.

Charlene watched Patrick drain half of his second beer, hoping it might loosen his tongue. Was a trip under the tunnels really against the law?

"Rolls are on their way," Shelley called as she passed to deliver lunch to a different table.

Patrick finished his clam chowder, scraping a crust of bread along the bottom of the dish. "You've got good taste, Charlene. This was the best chowder I've ever had."

She set her spoon alongside her empty bowl. "Were you serious about the tunnels being illegal? It seems that doing individual tours of this underground tunnel system might be a great source of income."

"I'm set for money," Patrick assured her. "Thirty years as a professor in history . . . I started writing after my wife died to ease the loneliness."

"I'm sorry." She could relate to that.

"Some of the tunnels are on or under private property so you can't just wander around willy-nilly. You need to have a license to operate tours and I've let mine lapse. Liability insurance is through the roof being below ground—if I could get it."

"But it's obvious that folks are interested. You'd be a perfect host. If your pirate costume is anything to judge by, you have the knack for entertaining. You could wear it while doing the tours!"

Patrick gave a hearty laugh. "No, no. It's cheaper and less hassle for folks to just read my book. Sometimes the past needs to stay buried."

"I'd like to take you up on your offer of a walking tour aboveground. I can pay you. You're so knowledgeable."

"I'd do it for free, friend to friend, so that we aren't tweaking the city council's nose." He raised his almost empty beer to her.

"Awesome." Her stomach jumped with excitement . . . Surely she could wear him down and get more information about the guy who'd requested a tour. She had a hunch that it tied in, but she couldn't get the pieces to gel yet.

She finished her Corona. "I'm still curious about this other man . . . I wonder if he was one of my guests interested in your book? Everybody wanted to read it." That could be Tommy or Asher, if there was a connection.

"Funny name." He tapped his temple. "My memory's not so good these days, but at the time I figured it was made-up so I didn't commit it to mind."

"Asher?"

"No. Crazier than that. Had flashy earrings; I remember thinking they had to be cubic zirconia."

She pleated her paper napkin, attempting for casual

even though her heart was racing. "Did he give you a hint of what he wanted?"

"Nope. Like you, he'd read my book and wanted to see the underground for himself." He pushed his empty bowl away, wiped his mouth, then drained his Heineken.

Shelley cleaned the table then returned with the two lobster rolls. "There you go. Hope you left some room."

"I'll be boxing half mine to take home, but let's see how Patrick makes out."

"Enjoy!" Shelley smiled at Patrick. "I bet you'll eat every bite."

"I might at that." He glanced at Charlene after Shelley had hustled away. "No need for a fork and knife right?"

"Right. Just go for it." She sliced hers in two and picked up the smaller one. The half-pound chunks of lobster slid from the sides of her bun, but she picked them up and popped them in her mouth.

He didn't need any more encouragement and dived right in.

The opportunity didn't arise again for her to question him about the mystery man, but it had to be Orpheus. Asher had flashy rings, but nothing in his ears.

They both devoured their meal, and Shelley had been right. Not a speck of lobster or bun was left on Patrick's plate. As she paid the bill, Shelley placed a plastic container for the remainder of her sandwich. It would make a nice lunch for the following day.

"I'd love to take that tour. Let me know when it's a good time. I have an hour or so free right now." She hated to press the author, but this was for Serenity.

"Can't do it this week. Can I get your card? I'll call you to set up something next Tuesday."

Hiding her disappointment, she reached into the side pocket of her purse and handed a card to him. "Thank you, so much. I had a great time. I hope you'll give some thought to doing a second book."

They shook hands on the street. Patrick hunched his shoulders and jammed his red hat over his white hair. "I just might. *Salem's Secrets*?" He mused over the possible title. "There's a guy out there who wrote *Salem's Secret Underground*. Now that's catchy! Good book too."

"I'm happy to help you brainstorm over another lobster roll," she offered.

"I'll be in touch." Patrick bundled up under his wool coat and wrapped a plaid scarf around his neck, then strode into the brisk Salem wind.

"Darn it." Charlene returned to her car. "I really wanted to take that tour."

CHAPTER 15

Charlene got behind the wheel of her Pilot and dialed Kevin's cell phone number.

"This is Kevin!"

Hearing music and laughter in the background, she checked the time on her radio. It was two in the afternoon and he must be working his bartender job at Brews and Broomsticks. "Hi, Kev, it's Charlene."

"My favorite B and B owner. What's up?"

"You do amazing tours around Salem."

"Is that a question?" He laughed.

"Nope. I'm thinking out loud. What do you know about the underground tunnels?"

"Folks always want to see those, but there is no official tour. In fact, it might be trespassing. I went in as a kid, and later snuck in. After nine-eleven happened, the powers that be really tightened security under Salem Town Hall and the other government buildings."

"That makes sense." She shifted on her seat, still in *park*. The heater kept the inside of the SUV nice and toasty. "What's with all the drama around the tunnels?"

"What do you mean?"

"Like, why are the tunnels referred to with such hush-hushiness?"

Snorting, Kevin said, "I think I understand what you mean. The thing is, Salem has a lot of history under the city streets. Our forefathers knew how to build to last, but after two hundred years they haven't been kept up. Some of the tunnels are dilapidated. Broken. Filled with sewage and completely disgusting."

"Ew."

"Why do you ask?"

"Well." She bit her lower lip. "I was hoping I could talk you into taking me inside them."

"Got your tetanus shot?"

"Funny."

"Not joking," Kevin countered. "But if you're up for it, I can ask around and see where we might still be able to get in that isn't locked or patrolled. I got a buddy that works at Oregon State Hospital and there were tunnels there. I don't know if they ever closed them off."

Where was that in conjunction to Derby Wharf? She and Jack could look it up later. "You'll check for me?"

"I will. Dare I ask why we'd be risking the plague?"

She shivered at the idea of disease-ridden rats. "Can I get back to you on that?"

"Deal. I hope it's not a rumor of buried treasure. That's

been debunked! Gotta run. Stop in sometime for a glass of wine, on me. Haven't seen you in months."

He had an amazing girlfriend who took up his free time, but Charlene didn't point that out. She happened to like Amy a lot. "You have your tour guide license?"

"Where we'd be going it wouldn't help. If we get caught, you pay the fine."

"All right." That was only fair.

She ended the call and put her phone on the dashboard holder. Her purse was on the opposite seat, and she unzipped it to reveal her pepper spray. And a pen. And her business cards.

There was just enough time to take the scenic route around the Commons and Alaric's rental house before she should be home. Avery no longer needed her guidance in cleaning the rooms, but Charlene liked to be there to hear about her day.

Her phone dinged a text. Brandy?

Serenity only spent half the morning in tears—an improvement. Cops just left with questions about the exact last time she saw Alaric. The meaning of the pentagram. No respect whatsoever for our religion. Nothing's changed in three hundred years.

Charlene stayed focused on her loose plan, not wanting to get sidetracked by Brandy, and drove away from the wharf toward the Hawthorne Hotel. She passed by the ornate building, trying to imagine it as a little house with a yard. The fenced-in Commons, surrounded by elm trees, once an open field with cows and chickens. A river. So different from now.

The bandstand had finally been refurbished. The lawn pristine. It was a place for the people of Salem like always. According to Patrick's book, the historical homes around the common lawn used to be connected.

Another ding. Then **I know you read my text.**

Charlene gripped the wheel and called via Bluetooth. "I was trying not to bother you since I was calling so much."

"That was Serenity. Me?" Brandy blew out a loud breath. "I want to know what you're up to."

"What does that mean?"

"I broke a bottle of your house wine," she exclaimed. "Fine, that could be slippery fingers. But then the letter C showed up on the counter when I dumped the change. My angels have been whispering your name. What are you doing?"

"Nothing!" She glared at the phone. "I just had lunch with the pirate from the witch ball—the author?"

"Patrick Steel."

"Yes. He's so smart. Very intelligent. I hope he gives me a tour from the street of the underground tunnels."

Brandy clicked her tongue. "The tunnels are closed."

"I know that. That's why Patrick said it would be from the street level."

"Closed for *security* reasons."

"Government?"

"Not just that. The tunnels were a maze of pathways, not all as safe and supported as the main tunnels. They lead to banks and the museum as well as the prison and the courthouse. Some are filled with water and sewage." Her tone rose.

"Why are you so worked up? Patrick and Kevin both already told me this too."

"I am not worked up."

"Maybe you should have some tea or something. Relax." Charlene breathed in, then out, as an example.

Brandy snorted. "Where are you right now?"

Charlene slowed to round Washington Street, toward Alaric's house. "Just driving home." This close to Alaric's and Elisabeta's, and her reason for driving by, made her ask, "Did you ever give a statement to Officer Jimenez?"

"I did. She's an odd duck—she asked not only about Orpheus, but our stop at Alaric's to visit Elisabeta. You might have warned me that you'd told them everything."

"Just what they needed to know. Nothing personal about you or Serenity."

"Oh. Thanks."

Charlene rolled past the rental house, slowly, then stopped in the street. No other cars were coming.

The curtains were closed. She could see the road kitty-corner behind the house that the man had jumped from the second-floor window to run away on.

She was sure Orpheus had asked Patrick for the tour.

The black cat dozed on the corner of the top porch step, eyes closed, body relaxed.

No car in the driveway, or sign of anybody home. Charlene could leave her card in the door with a message to call. She was 100 percent certain that Elisabeta had answers.

"Where are you?" Brandy asked again. "Why am I thinking of Alaric and Elisabeta?"

Charlene's eyes widened. "I'll call you later." She jammed her thumb to the *end call* button. That was too spooky. "Stop reading my mind, Brandy!"

Goose bumps slid up and down her spine and she reached into her purse for the card and pen. There was a basement entrance to the side of the house. Patrick's book had said those were put in later and not part of the original home design of the nineteenth century. The cat startled, then meowed, jumping to the dead grass.

Asher appeared from the basement to the lawn, bending down to pat the cat on the head.

Her stomach clenched and she gripped the pen tighter. Celeste was right behind Asher. The girl had shadows in her cheeks and bags under her eyes as if she hadn't slept in days. Red marks were on her throat.

Asher and Celeste walked up the front porch stairs and into the house, followed by the cat.

He had said that he'd made up with his roommate after a huge fight and moved back. Elisabeta had said three of them had come from New Orleans.

Asher was tall, like the man who'd jumped from the second story of this house to run down the road. Maybe Elisabeta knew he'd been there—maybe not, if they'd been arguing.

Had the fight been about Alaric, and Alaric's death?

What if Elisabeta was the killer?

Charlene blew out a slow breath and aborted the plan to leave a note. She had to talk this over with Jack. Celeste was supposed to be on a plane home to Jersey City.

Why had the young woman stayed? Yes, she'd been infatuated. Was Asher using some kind of vampire allure?

She shook off the chills dancing on her nape and put the car in gear, driving on before she got busted for snooping. Reaching the other side of the park, Charlene called Brandy.

"Hey—it's me. Listen, can you ask Serenity if the name Asher sounds familiar to her? I think I discovered the third person from New Orleans. If it's true, he's been in our sight the whole time. At the witch ball. In my house as a guest." Her stomach clenched. "He's at Elisabeta's." With Celeste.

"I'll ask her—but first, tell me what you were doing."

"I have questions for Elisabeta, but I realize now that just dropping her a note to call me probably won't work." She needed a better plan. "Do you know how Alaric earned his money?"

"Serenity said he just had it, but I'll press her for more when I ask about Asher. He was a guest at your B and B?"

"Sleeping with a guest, a sweet girl, rather than registered himself. Asher had plenty of money and was tossing it around. Being the big shot. Celeste is in love. Sound familiar?"

"What is with these bad-boy types?" Brandy exhaled. "Rhetorical question. Talk to you soon."

Charlene arrived home just as another dusting of snow was starting to fall. She'd give Avery a ride home tonight. A bike wasn't warm or safe transportation in the fall or winter.

Maybe it was time to think of getting a second car . . . something inexpensive but safe enough for Avery to borrow.

She parked in the driveway since she'd be going out again and climbed the stairs.

The Halloween decorations were now all Thanksgiving and fall. She opened the front door and breathed in the scents of spiced apple and caramel.

Avery sat on a stool in the kitchen chatting with Minnie. Her big eyes were emphasized by blue-and-silver eye shadow and her lips a pretty pink. Now a senior in high school, she enjoyed mixing things up. Her denim coveralls had black-and-white patches and she wore one black Converse and one white. Just because she could.

"Been here long?" Charlene asked.

"Just arrived and deciding on what kind of pie to have before getting to work." Avery sniffed and pointed to the bag. "What's that? It sure smells good. Buttery. Garlic?"

"Half a lobster roll. I had lunch with an author today at Sea Level." Charlene put it down on the counter and smiled at Minnie. "I see you made more progress on switching out the decorations. Looks very nice."

"I like the cornucopia next to the shell by the door but so does Silva, so I don't know if it should stay there. Too much temptation."

Charlene nodded, then turned to Avery. "Would you like the lobster roll instead of pie?"

Avery hopped off the stool and crossed to the bag. "You kidding me? I only had lobster once and it was the best thing ever!"

"Dig in. You can have pie later."

Minnie wiped her hands on her apron. "I remember being able to eat like that—enjoy it while you can, sweetie."

Charlene shrugged out of her jacket. "I saw Celeste down by the Commons today, with Asher. Didn't she leave with Tommy and Joey?"

"I thought she did," Minnie said. "Her room's empty."

"That's really strange. Oh well." She grinned at her crew. "What's the plan for the afternoon?"

Minnie gestured to Avery, who had washed up and was now biting into the lobster roll. "Avery's going to clean out the rooms and switch the linens. I did two of the suites before she got here. Sheets and towels already in the wash."

"Excellent. Our next wave comes in tomorrow. Three of the four suites and one single."

"But all full again by Friday." Minnie nodded proudly. "I made chicken pot pie for you to have for dinner, and lunch if you need something ready for guests tomorrow. I won't be here, don't forget. Doctor checkups all day."

"Thanks for the reminder." She needed to be here the whole day, which meant no running around the tunnels—aboveground, or below, for her.

"Everything okay, Minnie?" Avery asked in concern, lowering the lobster roll.

Aww. That girl has a big, tender heart.

Minnie put a hand on Avery's shoulder. "Prize for getting older—more doctor appointments to make sure everything is running smooth. I'm healthy as a horse, Avery, and plan on staying that way."

Avery offered the roll. "Wanna bite? I should've asked. Sorry!"

"Thanks, but no. You need more meat on your bones, while I could use less." Minnie patted her round hips.

"My bones are fine. It's my legs that are skinny."

Charlene shared an amused look with Minnie. "Let me change out of these boots and I'll be back to help with laundry."

"Take your time," Minnie said. "We've got this under control."

Charlene knew they did, so she went to her room. She kicked off her boots and hung her coat in the small closet, then returned to her sitting room.

Using the remote, she turned on the television, sat on the love seat, and called for Jack. "Jack? Are you there?"

She needed to talk to him about Orpheus and Asher. The hospital and the wharf. The tunnels. Everything. Nobody was better than Jack for her to bounce ideas off of. She whispered again, "Jack?"

Hugging her pillow, she sat back with disappointment. He was a no-show.

Sparkles of light lit the room for a brief moment, and then there he was. Magnificent as always.

She grinned. "You had me worried."

"I come to you whenever I can—and after your remark earlier, I hadn't gone far. How was lunch?" He sat in the armchair across from her to see her better. "Did you solve the crime?" He'd changed from his chinos and button-up shirt earlier to a blue wool sweater and a pair of gray slacks, moccasins on his feet.

"Lunch was terrific. Patrick showed me his maps he used for the book. I thought that perhaps the waterways and tunnels might be connected, but I was wrong. The roads are built over the tunnels and most of them are filled in or blocked off."

"Whoa. Wait a minute." Jack raised his hand. "Why did you want to know that?"

"Alaric's body was found near Derby Wharf. He'd done a disappearing trick. Did Serenity actually use a spell that helped him travel? How did he get from the Hawthorne Hotel, to sea?"

"Excellent questions. Did Patrick help?"

"He nixed one of my ideas—which is helpful, in a way."

"Which one?"

"That maybe there was a tunnel or secret passage from the Hawthorne Hotel to the wharf."

He flashed his white teeth and chuckled. "Oh. That's very interesting. Did you get to see the map?"

"Yes. There *was* a tunnel for delivering cargo at one

time, but it was filled in a while ago. I guess when the Hawthorne was built? It used to be the Franklin Building, and before that, some guy's house."

He crossed one leg over the other. "That's right. I remember that from history class."

"Patrick offered to give me a tour of the tunnels, but from the street, since having one underground isn't allowed."

"What would you learn?"

"Where the tunnels are. Where the entrances and exits are—people in the old days used them as much as they did the roads. But even Brandy told me that it was a bad idea to go underground. Kevin said I needed a tetanus shot, but he'd take me. I think he was kidding."

Jack stood up in alarm. "I don't want you going down under the city. It's dangerous. What is Kevin thinking?"

"He's game if I am. The property owners and businesses that still use them have strengthened the tunnels so that they're safe. Kevin's been down there and knows the ones that aren't. Sit down, Jack. You know he'd never put me in harm's way."

He sat but wasn't happy about it. "When are you supposed to do this?"

"*If* I do it, it can't be until Friday or Saturday with Kevin—Patrick can't fit me in until next week."

"What's the hurry?" Jack demanded.

"Two men are dead, Jack. We want to help Serenity, right?"

He glowered. "Where is Sam in all of this? Shouldn't he be the leader of the pack? Or is it too *dangerous* for our pretty boy?"

"Sam and I are no longer texting each other during a case. He's not going to stop by for coffee. He wants to meet at the station to go over information, when he has it to share—or I do." Charlene set her pillow aside. "Says it's more professional."

"Didn't think he knew the meaning of the word." Jack gave her a pointed look. "He's always made it personal, dropping in all the time."

Jack exuded agitation with frenetic energy that made his image quiver until he calmed himself down.

She spoke in a soothing voice. "Well, no more."

"Why the sudden change of heart?" Jack tossed a plastic mouse to Silva on the windowsill.

"It will keep the boundaries clear for both of us." She would miss seeing Sam, though she wouldn't admit it.

Charlene clasped her hands and brought the subject away from the detective. "Patrick said that Salem used to be extremely wealthy. Where did all of the treasure from the ships go? Were leaders of the community lining their own pockets?"

Jack snorted. "Maybe there was some of that, but Salem's forefathers set up the Peabody Essex Museum to house local artifacts as well as priceless objects from overseas. To keep them protected, not for personal gain."

"I have a strong desire to check out the museum myself." She grinned at Jack. "Admire some of that amazing treasure."

"The priceless items would be heavily protected." Jack rubbed his hands. "Not out in the open, up for grabs."

"I know . . . but Dru works there. Maybe he could pull some strings." Dru, who she'd love to chat with. "Brandy mentioned the tunnels used to lead there. And to the banks. That doesn't seem very secure to me."

"A bank vault is extremely secure. It would take a team of professionals to get away with a break-in."

"Not if you have a secret passageway that leads inside the vault." Charlene got to her feet with a smirk.

"You have a point," Jack conceded, "but I'm sure they've been closed off for a great many years."

"You're probably right. Kevin mentioned heightened security after nine-eleven—that was a wake-up call. Hey, you ever heard a rumor about treasure buried inside the tunnels?"

"No." Jack placed his hands on his hips. "Not surprised, though."

"Kevin said there wasn't any; so did Patrick."

"Was the author a snob, like we feared?"

"No way." Charlene laughed. "I told him that I'd been a little nervous and he was nothing but sweet about it."

"I'm glad you had a nice lunch." He bent down and grabbed the mouse from Silva, who lifted two paws to get it back.

"I asked Patrick who had contacted him last week about an underground tour and the tunnels."

His eyes narrowed. "Don't keep me hanging. Who was it? One of our vampires?"

Charlene perched on the armrest of her love seat. "He couldn't remember the name, said it was weird. I asked if it was Asher, because of all the money he's been flashing around, and he said the name was stranger than that."

"Like *Alaric*?"

"Maybe. But listen, I have reason to believe that Asher is on friendly terms with Elisabeta and, surprise, surprise, he might be the third person who moved from New Orleans with them to form a new coven."

"Where did this information come from?"

"I saw him with Celeste on the way home from lunch. Strange, right?"

"Where did you see them?" Jack was agitated once again. Arms folded, he paced the small room.

"After lunch I took a quick drive around the Commons."

"That's an odd way to come from the wharf."

She shrugged, face hot. Busted. "Just had a feeling something wasn't right, so I did a quick check. You always tell me to trust my instincts. At Elisabeta's place I spotted Asher climbing up from the basement and into the house by the front door. Cat liked him, which means he lives there. Probably. The cat was hostile to Brandy and me."

"Charlene," Jack growled.

"Sorry. Remember the tall man running down the street? Well, that could've been Asher as well as Orpheus. And maybe it was Alaric who contacted Patrick, but I think it was Orpheus."

His brow arched. "Brandy questioned him, you said, and he told her under her spell that he did not kill Alaric."

Charlene nodded. "Orpheus was ticked off that day at Alaric for betraying the coven—but not furious. Still, something is giving me that tingle that there's more to it."

"We've talked about this before. A murderer isn't going to blink over telling a lie that will save him from jail. Tingles or no tingles. Doesn't happen."

With an eye roll, Charlene continued, "Patrick described Orpheus's diamond earrings to a T, which is why even though Orpheus may not have killed Alaric, I'd bet money he was the one who contacted him about the tour."

"So we're back to Orpheus." Jack scratched his head.

"What if he was able to get past Brandy's spell? He is the most logical candidate for being the murderer." She studied the area rug on her floor as if the answer was in the floral pattern. "Then again, I strongly feel that Elisabeta, Asher, and Alaric were all working together, and then something went wrong."

"Very. Two supposed vampires are dead and two more are still in town. I know you don't want to think about this, but Dru can't be crossed off your list. Or what if it was someone who just doesn't like vampires?" Jack tossed the mouse in the air and let it spin. "Did you ask Patrick if it was Orpheus?"

"I didn't. The chowder came and the conversation had moved on." She hadn't pressed, just in case it got back to Sam that she was discussing Orpheus after he'd asked her to keep quiet.

He caught the mouse and twirled it by the tail just out of Silva's reach. She knew he was piecing together all she'd told him. Charlene had been through this with Jack a time or two.

"I think I'm right, Jack. The diamond studs were huge. If he was planning to kill Alaric, wouldn't he stay under the radar? He was at the witch ball, partying with Brandy."

"I don't believe we're dealing with great minds here."

She chuckled. "The only men I've seen wearing diamonds that big are rock stars or famous athletes, not your average Joe."

Jack rubbed his chin and stood before her. "Orpheus had his reasons for wanting Alaric dead. Jealousy. A punishment for sharing details of the vampire coven. He had a secret about Alaric that he didn't tell you. If he didn't do the actual deed, maybe he was working with someone, like you think. Who?"

"Elisabeta." Charlene answered right away. "She might've wanted Alaric dead for replacing her with a younger, prettier, more gullible woman who turned out to be a powerful witch! Serenity is the real thing."

"Which Alaric was not."

Charlene got up and crossed her arms. "Serenity and her immediate family, and all their ancestors, are very powerful. He needed that power since clearly he didn't possess it himself. When did he discover that she was a witch? Before or after Salem?"

"Why does it matter?" Jack asked. "Once he discovered it, it wouldn't be difficult for him to introduce himself." His expression turned stern. "I can imagine that louse enjoying the game."

"*When* matters." She tapped her finger to her chin. "I need to get Elisabeta to talk to me. She can answer that question among others. She might know Alaric's secret."

"She has a lot of answers. Yet she's hiding away without talking to anybody."

"Hiding is right. I need a good plan. That's why I was going to drop off a note—"

Her phone rang and she put her hand to her thumping heart.

"Brandy!" She answered and put it on speaker so Jack could hear. "Hello?"

"Nothing more on where Alaric got his money, and Serenity never met an Asher through Alaric. It was a popular name in the nineties and still rising."

Charlene sagged down into the armchair. "Oh. I guess that would have been too easy."

"This is really starting to poison the sacred energy in our home. I don't like the negativity. Should we smoke Elisabeta out of her hole and make her confess?"

"How? By holding a knife to her throat? I thought we were hoping that Orpheus did it."

Brandy sighed. "I wish I could believe that. It has to be *that* woman."

Charlene felt for her friend and asked in a soft tone, "How is Serenity today?"

"More tears. I think she regrets breaking up with Dru. She's feeling a lot of guilt, but I can't pinpoint from where."

"That's not good!" Jack said. "Guilt because she had something to do with killing Alaric?"

Charlene raised her brow at him.

"Tell me about this Asher," Brandy said.

"He's fascinated by the vampire world, to an unhealthy degree, from what I saw—although he was very polite. He convinced Celeste to taste blood the other night at a beach bonfire. And now Celeste is with him and Elisabeta at Alaric's house."

"No!" Brandy said loudly. "One predator dead and another to fill his cape. We can't let that happen."

"We can't," Jack agreed. "What are we going to do, Charlene?"

"Okay. Let me think. I'll call you back, Brandy."

She hit *end* and tossed her phone to the coffee table, overwhelmed for a moment by all the sadness and darkness in the world, though she did her best to be the light. "All we ever get around here is death! Sometimes I wonder why I moved here at all."

"Don't say that!" Jack's voice was sharp, his eyes angry—worse, scared.

She stood up to face him, apologetic. "I didn't mean it, Jack. You know I don't. I love it in Salem. Being with you makes it all worthwhile."

He lifted a hand as if to touch her cheek, then dropped it. "I was miserable before you came along. Now with Silva and you, I have a family."

CHAPTER 16

Charlene wished she could give Jack a hug at his confession. She too felt like they were family.

He cooled the warmth in her heart with, "I think you should call Sam."

"What?" She was sure she hadn't heard correctly and jiggled her earlobe.

"I do." He folded his hands behind his back and stared out the window at the oak tree, the leaves an orange-red.

"Why?" Did he believe her to be in danger?

"Ask him about the tunnels. I bet he could take you and he'd make sure you were safe. No offense to Kevin, but Sam can carry a gun with him. I have a lot more faith in a weapon against a killer than the ability to make a martini."

Dark tunnels. Possibly dangerous. Sam would be good

to have around. "I don't know. He won't break the rules if the tours are no longer sanctioned by the city."

"Sam's a detective. He is the law. Who's going to give him a ticket?"

"Officer Jimenez might."

Jack waved his hand. "Sam makes his own rules! I think you should follow your hunch, Charlene. You've been right before."

She'd also been wrong. "If there is a physical path that hasn't been blocked or filled in, it might explain how Alaric reached the shore . . . but so could a lot of other things. Maybe he was fast enough to walk out when the lights went off in the ballroom."

"How long would you say you were in the dark?" Jack's brow rose. "Five minutes?"

"Less than that."

The clock had struck midnight when the lights had been shut off. Charlene paced behind her small love seat, trying to think of any small detail she may have forgotten. The band, the punch bowl, the photo booth, the excited people wondering if it was all part of the show.

Jack waited for her answer, his toe tapping with silent impatience.

"Maybe three minutes."

"What happened next?"

"Stephanos pounded on the door, in the dark. There were lights from costumes and party favors, but not bright. Lucas was on the stage with the band, calling for calm, then the gorilla opened the door from the outside. It all happened so fast."

"Then?"

"Elisabeta gasped. Serenity shouted and pointed at the cape, flush to the floor. It was obvious that Alaric wasn't there." She frowned. "I lifted the cape and found the stake—smaller than a baseball bat—with the red goo on the tip."

"And called Sam." His eyes pierced hers. Not in anger, but searching for answers.

Yet she still felt a twinge of guilt. "Well . . . yes. Just because . . ."

"You had a hunch," Jack said definitively.

"Yeah." She nodded and held Jack's gaze. Even though the blood on the tip could've been fake, as it was Halloween, she'd had a sense that there was more to it. "But I had no idea that Alaric was dead. He might not have been at that point."

"Did you see anything out of place?"

Charlene dredged up her memory of the ballroom just before midnight. The band had quieted; folks had stopped dancing. Celeste and Asher were there, chanting. There'd been an air of anticipation to hear the winners.

Alaric had hijacked the spotlight to make his point. "It was a crowd of people in costume. Oh!" Charlene straightened, her hand to her heart. "What if Alaric never left at all, but put on a mask and melded in with the party?"

Jack swore. "Devious. Genius."

"Both." Charlene stepped toward her back door that led to the porch, swiveled, and returned to her door connecting to the kitchen, her mind on fire. "He needed to prove to Serenity and Orpheus that he was the real deal when it came to being a vampire. He wanted immortality but he was human."

Jack nodded. "Why leave the bloody stake?"

She continued pacing in frustration. "I don't know. It was O blood type, the most common."

Jack swirled away from the window to face her. "If he

was in a different costume, he could have just walked out at any time."

Charlene wondered if Sam had thought of this already. Probably—he was the professional while she was the amateur. She sighed.

"What?"

"I need to talk to Elisabeta and get the truth."

Jack scowled. "You can't do any more drive-bys of the rental house, especially now that we know Asher is there. It's possible that he and Elisabeta were in on the murder together."

She considered the possibility. "Let's set aside Orpheus as the murderer. Why would Elisabeta and Asher kill Alaric?"

"Anger at Alaric for choosing Serenity over them."

"All right." She narrowed her eyes, trying to envision it. "They killed Alaric. And then had to kill Orpheus to protect whatever secret Alaric had?"

She and Jack looked at one another—she saw in his expression that he agreed it could be a possibility.

"I need proof." She shrugged.

"Elisabeta isn't just going to confess. And it's much too dangerous for you to confront her at her home. What if Asher and Celeste are there too? Three against one is not a fair fight, even with your pepper spray."

"I'll need to tempt her into a meeting with something she wants desperately." Charlene tucked her hands in her pockets to warm her fingers. "Elisabeta believes that Serenity has true witch supernatural powers. Maybe I can find out if she still wants to be immortal. I know Asher does, if he's drinking blood."

Jack crossed his arms. "Assuming she wants immortality, what then?"

Charlene felt the hum of adrenaline course through her. "If she knew I could contact someone with great power on her behalf, it might earn me a conversation, and that's a start."

"I don't like this," Jack said. "If she is a killer, your reaching out to her is like a flag before a bull. Promise me you won't meet her alone?"

"Promise. Brandy would come with me—but that would be more of a hindrance than help. Might start a full-out war!" She chuckled. "For the best results, it would have to be Serenity."

She called the Flint house and Brandy answered. "I've been praying to the Goddess that you've got a brilliant plan to stop Asher and Elisabeta."

"Well . . . I don't know about brilliant, but I'm fairly sure it might work. I need to get Elisabeta to open up to me. I know she'd never do it willingly unless I had something special to offer in return."

"Like what?" she asked warily.

Charlene swallowed. "Please think about this before saying *no*. This is hard for me to ask . . ."

"Then don't," she interrupted.

"Brandy, just hear me out. You can't help me with Elisabeta, but Serenity can." She crossed her fingers and looked at Jack. "What if we set a trap with Serenity's necromancy powers as bait?"

"No. Just, no way. Sorry. I wanted your help to keep my daughter out of trouble—not toss her right into a boiling pot of pitch."

Charlene bit the inside of her cheek at the dramatic response. "Just ask her if she can help."

"No." Brandy hung up.

Charlene gripped her phone and winced. "Not the outcome I'd hoped for. But you know what? I can suggest it to Elisabeta and see if she bites—and then I can conjure my own witch later."

"Who?"

"I can hire Amy, Kevin's girlfriend, for a onetime performance."

Jack nodded but then repeated, "Even then, you can't meet the woman alone."

She relented at his serious expression. "Fine. I'll see who I can drum up—but you agree that the bait to lure Elisabeta from her house is good?"

"If I wanted to be an immortal vampire and a witch offered her necromancer services, then yes. I'd jump on it."

"That's one hurdle over." She blew out a breath. "How can I contact her? I don't have her number, and I never delivered my note. I have to reach her now, or it has to wait until Friday."

"A lot can happen in two days."

"Like someone else dying? Or Dru going to jail? I don't have Elisabeta's number, but I do have Celeste's." She stood. "I'll call her and see if she can get them all to meet for a drink or something."

"In a public place."

"Of course!"

He tugged his chin, then nodded once.

Charlene sat before her laptop and pulled up the information on her guests.

"Hello?" Celeste answered a few moments later.

"Hi! It's Charlene—from the B and B?"

"Oh. Hello. Uh, did I forget something in my room?"

"No." She cleared her throat. "I was driving home today and saw you with Asher. Did you miss your flight back to

Jersey City?" She had visions of Celeste being held against her will, though it hadn't looked that way.

"Oh!" Celeste laughed. "No. I decided to move to Salem for a while. I just love it here and Asher . . . he's great. I'm crashing with him and Beta until I find something."

Beta. Short for Elisabeta. Already chummy. "I'm so glad!" Charlene tapped her nail to the keyboard. Now what? "How about I treat all of you for drinks? I'm always on the lookout for new places to show my guests, but I hate to drink alone. I'd love to get to know you better."

"Can't speak for Beta, but Asher's right here. Hey, hon, Charlene wants to buy us a round of drinks. Doesn't want to drink alone."

She heard masculine mumbling.

"No! We are not meeting her at the Bunghole," Celeste said, her hand partially over the phone. Then, "Oh. Okay. Charlene, next to the Bunghole, which I guess is a real liquor place that used to be around during Prohibition, is a bar called the Pirate's Cove that Asher likes."

"Got it. Your roommate is welcome too." Charlene couldn't be more suggestive than that. "Tie Elisabeta up and toss her over your shoulder" probably wouldn't go over well.

"See you in an hour?"

"Perfect." Charlene would have just enough time to grab a drink, then be back to take Avery home at seven.

She ended the call and faced Jack. "While I'm gone, do you mind seeing if there is even a hint of a rumor of a tunnel near the Derby Wharf?"

"You got it." They changed places, he taking her seat

before the computer. "Bring your pepper spray and tell Minnie where you're going. If you aren't back by eight, I'll make a scene."

"It's still in my bag . . . I'll be back before you know it!" She added the address of the bar to her GPS. Two blocks from the Commons, which put it in easy walking distance for them.

She entered the kitchen. It was odd not to prepare for happy hour as they'd done for the past week, but the chicken pot pie Minnie had made smelled savory and delicious.

"Off again?" Minnie asked.

"I'm meeting Celeste and Asher for a drink at a place called the Pirate's Cove—just in case I don't come back," she said jokingly. She hoped.

"Have a good time. Text me if you need me to drive Avery, if you decide to do dinner too."

"Thanks." She crossed her fingers in her jacket. "See you later!"

CHAPTER 17

Charlene scored a choice parking spot in front of a ten-foot-tall one-eyed pirate, which reminded her of Patrick and his pirate costume. She didn't think the name very original but she was pleasantly surprised when she stepped into the bar.

The interior was gold and dark wood, pinks, purples, blues—it resembled Aladdin's cave. Not shabby at all, but very unique ambience. Another great place to suggest to her guests.

She sat at the bar, which had six wooden barrels instead of stools, and ordered a Corona Light. A neon sign over the bar blinked red-and-black: ORDER A BACARDI SHOT FOR A CHANCE TO WIN YOUR NUGGET OF GOLD.

Fun. When the thirtysomething bartender dropped off her beer, she introduced herself. "I'm Charlene. I own a nearby bed-and-breakfast and my guests always ask for recommendations. This place is amazing!"

"Thanks. Nice tae meet ye. I'm Callum, from Plockton in the Scottish Highlands. Great place tae be from, but never tae go back. I'll get ye a menu and the first beer is on me." He had reddish-blond hair to his chin, two days' worth of beard, blue eyes, and a great smile.

"No, please, let me pay. I'm meeting friends here. We might snag a table and get some appetizers."

"Sure." Callum grabbed half-a-dozen menus from under the counter and slid them onto the smooth wooden bar. He saw a speck on one and snatched it back, spraying disinfectant on the plastic before wiping it down with a towel.

"Did you do the décor?"

She admired the heavy drapes that floated overhead and covered the walls. A four-by-four sunken table in the center was surrounded by dozens of colorful cushions on the floor. It smelled nice and clean. Booths lined the front window.

"Aye, that was me. Bought a dive and turned it intae a magical place where ye can dream and leave the world behind for an hour or two."

"You sure did. What made you create Aladdin's theme?"

"Loved that tale growin' up. I wanted tae see the world, have experiences that no Scottish laddie ever could. Me parents raised sheep." He crinkled his nose. "I wanted tae create me own destiny."

A dreamer, she thought. But a doer too. "I certainly wish you well. Was Salem the first stop in your journey, or have you seen the world, made your fortune?"

"I'm in the middle of me story. Plan tae stay here a few

years, hopefully make some dough, and then off I'll go again wherever the wind sends me."

She smiled at his enthusiasm. "Sounds nice."

"Och, are those yer friends?"

Turning on her stool, she almost gasped. There stood Elisabeta with Celeste and Asher. All three were dressed head to toe in black. Pale makeup, black liner. Velvet cloaks. Very gothic and theatric, like they'd just walked off a stage.

"Halloween's over, mates," Callum joked.

Asher studiously ignored him and ushered Celeste into a booth, then Elisabeta.

She slid off her barrel and grabbed the menus, dropping a five on the bar counter. "Thanks," she said, turning to greet the wannabe vampires. Was this the beginning of a new coven—Asher, Elisabeta, and Celeste?

Charlene scooted in next to Celeste, who was glaring at her as if Charlene had pulled a fast one.

"Hi," Elisabeta said coldly from across the table, where she and Asher sat shoulder to shoulder. "What in the hell are you up to, lady?"

"Drinks. This is on me."

"I can afford my own drinks," Elisabeta declared. She whirled a large diamond around her pointer finger.

"It would be my pleasure . . . that was all I meant." Charlene glanced at Celeste, next to her. "What would you like?"

"A rum and Coke." Celeste flicked a gaze to Asher as if to make sure it was all right. Asher nodded.

"Me too. A double. For Elisabeta as well."

Callum came over and Charlene placed the drink order. He said, "It'll be right up."

"He's kind of cute," Elisabeta whispered. "I'd like to bite his neck." She purred and caressed Asher's forearm.

Celeste squirmed uncomfortably. If Charlene had to guess, they'd already had the conversation about sharing. Were Asher and Elisabeta a modern-day Bonnie and Clyde?

"Thanks for coming." Charlene passed out the menus. "Elisabeta, I'm really glad you joined us. I've been wondering how you are."

"Since you broke into my house?" Her thin lips were pinched. The lines in her face were more pronounced—even in the dim lighting.

"I did not!" Charlene lifted her head high. "You opened the door."

"And your witch friend pushed it in. Where is she?" The woman scanned the bar. "I'd love to see her again. Especially in a dark alley. Alone."

Charlene swallowed hard. "Home. Anyway, I wanted to discuss our mutual friend, Serenity. I have an idea that might be beneficial for you."

Silence weighted the table as the three wannabes looked at each other.

"So why did you invite these two," Elisabeta huffed, "if it was really me you wanted to see?"

"You said you wanted to welcome me to Salem!" Celeste pouted.

"I told you that was a lie," Asher said. "This was a setup."

Charlene refused to rise to the bait. This was about saving Serenity and keeping an open door for Celeste. "I do, Celeste, and Asher. Elisabeta, I would have come to see you tomorrow, but this is better."

"About Serenity?" Elisabeta laughed and caressed the

red marks on her neck. "The baby witch misses us. Truth is, Alaric got to her before he was killed." She leaned into Asher and chuckled low as she stared at Charlene in amusement. "She wants the blood."

Charlene hid her reaction and countered, "I don't think so. She's stronger than all of you."

Elisabeta crooned, "You send her to me, the baby witch, and we can discuss a new plan for eternal life."

How about confessing the old plan?

Callum dropped off their drinks and left. Charlene raised her bottle of beer to the others at the table. "Cheers."

"So what is it that you want, Charlene?" Elisabeta sipped her rum and Coke. "I don't trust you or that she-witch, and asking us here tonight . . . well, it got me thinking. You must want to turn your fancy B and B into a luxury coven for us."

Asher laughed. Celeste blushed and lowered her eyes.

"That's not it." Over her dead body.

"Then what is it? I hardly think you'd offer Serenity on a platter. Let me guess—you really believe that *I* killed Alaric."

Charlene's cheeks heated but she didn't look away. "Did you?"

"Ballsy of you to come straight to the point." Elisabeta *tsked*. "No. I didn't kill him, although I wanted to at times. I wonder what you'd do if I said *yes*?" She started to laugh as she studied Charlene's sweater and jacket. "Are you wearing a wire?" More loud laughter erupted from Morticia.

"No wire. Detective Holden would be horrified if he knew I was here." Charlene had to bluff her way out of this uncomfortable situation, but how?

"We should go," Asher said, his eyes narrowed at Charlene.

"Let's finish our drinks," Celeste said. "I'm a bartender and this is an excellent brand of rum. Can I get my nugget of gold?"

"You're a fool, Charlene Morris, thinking to ride in on a white horse and save Serenity from jail when it's obvious she killed *my* mate." Elisabeta's eyes hardened. "I know she had something to do with his death, and I will find out. When I do, she is a dead witch."

"Serenity did not kill Alaric. She loved him." Charlene's stomach churned and she couldn't even pretend to drink her Corona. "Do you believe in her power?"

"I saw it for myself," Elisabeta admitted. "I'm not big on telepathy or anything, but I have the occasional premonition. I can see auras sometimes." Her tone was defensive and dared Charlene to argue.

Charlene ran her fingers up and down the chilled bottle, praying for inspiration. "Did Alaric choose you for your powers? Serenity's are far greater and she's descended from centuries of witches. That could make a woman jealous."

Elisabeta raised her hand. "Alaric chose me because he loved me. Unlike all the other cows in the herd, he loved *me*. You tell the witch that—she had nothing on me. If she only knew . . ."

"So what?" Asher demanded, cutting off Elisabeta from spilling her guts. "You're just going to go around and ask everyone until someone confesses?"

The three of them laughed, even Celeste, and Charlene knew she was losing the crowd.

Better to concede than get crushed. Especially if it got her closer to the truth. "I guess so." She stayed seated rather than run and hide her head. "Asher, I know you were involved with Alaric and Orpheus. Was that why Orpheus was in town? He believed you were going to be immortal, but not himself? He hinted at a secret Alaric held that could ruin him."

"When was this?" Elisabeta asked. "I haven't heard from Orpheus since he went back to New Orleans."

Charlene lowered her eyes so she didn't give the man's death away. Elisabeta didn't know he was dead, which meant she didn't kill him. She peered at Asher from beneath her bangs.

"I spoke with him the night of the ball, when he was dancing with Brandy." Implying that was the only time, without saying so.

"The mama witch." Elisabeta touched her cheek with a hard gaze. "I owe her for that."

Tension so thick it could be sliced with a knife eddied around them. "What do you know of the underground tunnels?"

Asher and Elisabeta both eyed her in feigned surprise. "Tunnels?"

"Legend, myth. Hearsay. Can't get into them." Asher didn't crack a smile. He drained his drink and thumped the empty glass to the table.

Charlene knew they were lying and that they wanted her to know they were lying. She played along, hoping for a clue.

"I just read a fascinating book on the subject by a local author. Evergreen Bookstore still has some copies."

Celeste wriggled on the booth seat beside her. "I saw the book. You had it at your bed-and-breakfast. It's true, guys. Tommy was really interested in it."

"Forget Tommy. Forget the book." Asher scooted to

the end of the bench in the booth, stood, and reached for Elisabeta. "It's time to leave."

Elisabeta stayed seated and twisted a skeleton ring on her middle finger that had a large emerald in the center. They all had gemstones. Gold. Platinum. Money wasn't a worry. How did they earn it? "Just leave us alone, Charlene. We won't bother you; you don't bother us. Everybody will be fine."

"What about Serenity?" Charlene touched Elisabeta's hand—warm and full of life despite its pale color.

She yanked it away. "That I can't promise."

"Neither can I, then." Charlene had two seconds before they bolted. "Were you happy with Alaric? Orpheus implied that all was not rosy between you."

Elisabeta's pale face went chalk-white. "Damn him—he gets drunk and can't shut his mouth. He promised not to make a big freaking deal out of it."

"What?" Asher slouched against the table.

"Alaric discovered I'd slept with Orpheus one night when he was out prowling." She glanced at Asher. "Just the two of us. After the—er . . . disagreement."

"You didn't!" Judgement stamped Asher's face.

Charlene's beer soured at the back of her throat.

"Yeah." Elisabeta jammed the short straw into her drink and sucked it dry. "Things went south real fast—that was the final blow. We moved here—to find Asher's witch."

Woman scorned. Even a vampire in love could feel jealousy, and payback was only one step away. "Alaric's, you mean?"

Elisabeta blinked into the present. "Alaric was a weak man. Mortal. He wanted to be immortal so badly that he pushed us aside. Not the makings of a good leader. Or a mate."

An admission from the heart that Alaric was blood and bone. And had his faults.

"Charlene's right to question you," Asher said harshly. "You were jealous of Serenity—I felt bad for you. You failed to mention you cheated first."

"Asher!" Celeste leaned across Charlene with red cheeks. "Don't yell at her. You and Alaric also argued about Serenity."

"Shut it!" Asher straightened from his slouch.

"The night of the ball?" Elisabeta asked. "You didn't tell me you argued. Over what?"

Asher clasped his mouth tight, shooting visual daggers at Celeste.

"He shoved Alaric, mad that he chose Serenity over both of you. Alaric told him to be patient and stick with the plan." Celeste's eyes glittered and she touched a red mark on her neck. "You'd all be together soon. In re-birth."

Charlene gave Celeste a sideways glance. Pieces of the night dropped into place. Celeste and Asher talking heatedly by the door before Asher teased her into dancing, when there was no music. He'd stuck to Celeste like glue after that. To make sure she kept quiet?

"Before you go," Callum said, ushering Asher back into the booth. The tension rocketed but Asher sat, scooting Elisabeta close to the wall. "Would ye like tae share an appetizer?" He tapped the menus. "We have some interesting dishes that ye willnae find anywhere else. Scrumptious." He put two fingers to his mouth, smacking his lips. "I highly recommend the haggis."

"No haggis for me," Celeste said, nose crinkled.

The door slammed open.

"An ill wind," Elisabeta murmured.

Two officers in Salem blue burst in and to her horror they handcuffed Callum. "You have the right to remain silent." Charlene remembered being given her Miranda rights. Wasn't funny then. Wasn't funny now.

"Callum?" Charlene searched his handsome face—but it wasn't so handsome anymore. He had a wild look in his eyes.

"Lemme go!" He tossed his head back and spit on the police.

"What did he do?" Charlene asked. Elisabeta, Asher, and Celeste all remained quiet as they watched Callum get arrested.

"We're bringing him to the station to answer some questions on the missing owner of the bar. Have any of you seen Kendrick George?"

"Don't know who that is." Charlene rested her elbow on the table.

The police bundled the cursing man out of the bar.

"What just happened?" Celeste murmured.

"Dunno. But we're splitting." Asher stood and held out his hand for Elisabeta and Celeste. Charlene got up to let the girl join them.

They didn't tell her good night as they dashed out the door.

Charlene followed. Some of the other patrons looted the alcohol behind the bar. A harried policeman jostled her at the threshold as he went inside and flickered the interior lights.

"Everyone out!" he shouted.

Eager to get away from this place and the people, Charlene ran to her car.

She knew she wasn't supposed to call Sam anymore, but this was ridiculous. Starting the engine and locking the doors, she dialed his cell.

"Charlene?" Sam asked in concern.

"Hi! I know we agreed to do things by the book, but I was just having a drink by the harbor . . ." She didn't say with who so as not to completely compromise their deal. "And the cops arrested the owner!"

"It wasn't Pirate's Cove by chance?"

"Yes, it was. How did you know?"

"We've had a team on surveillance for the last few days. People reported that the owner wasn't around; some new guy claiming to be his cousin was running the place. An offensive smell came from the oven each night."

Her stomach churned. "Oh no, Sam."

"What?"

"He told us about some amazing appetizers he had that no other restaurant did. Said the haggis was delicious. That was when the police arrived."

"Glad you didn't order the appetizers." She heard a faint chuckle. "I have a pretty good idea what ingredients were used to make it so special."

"Me too. I think I might puke."

"Poor thing. Go home and let Minnie feed you amazing food that will have the proper ingredients. Who were you with?"

"Well . . . Celeste, Asher, and Elisabeta." Charlene rushed ahead to give him information before he shouted at her. "She said the reason that they all moved from New Orleans was that she had an affair with Orpheus, and Alaric found out. Can you believe it?"

"What I can't believe is that Elisabeta and you were in this bar at the same time. Please tell me how that happened."

"I invited Celeste and Asher. They're all living in the rental house together. Sam, why don't they know about Orpheus being dead yet? I didn't say anything but I'm very curious."

"You're curious? Imagine that. Charlene, you have one chance to tell me the truth."

"That is the truth! Elisabeta thinks Serenity had something to do with Alaric's death and threatened her life if she were to find proof of it. I mean, Elisabeta might not have committed the murder—but maybe her and Asher did it together? She's more involved than we think."

"*We*?"

"Uh, I meant you, of course."

"You and I will have a lot to discuss when I see you in the morning. At the station. Nine sharp."

She clenched her teeth. "Sam, I can't leave the bed-and-breakfast tomorrow. Minnie is off and Avery wasn't on the schedule. I mean, I can ask her, but that would be three at the earliest."

"Make it happen or I will send a squad car." Then there was silence and she only had her thoughts for company during the drive home.

CHAPTER 18

Charlene hurried home, her mind reeling with new information. Elisabeta had appeared interested when Charlene mentioned Serenity—but then she'd concluded wrongly that Serenity had been "turned" by Alaric.

It had to be a lie that Alaric had seduced Serenity into drinking blood. Telling tales was only one way of many that he'd used to create his vampire persona. It was laughable compared to Serenity's actual bloodline, which ran true without fear of death, or what came after.

Charlene parked in the drive next to Minnie's Volvo. The snow had stopped but it was still chilly. She burst through the door.

"Hi, Minnie! Hi, Avery." She drew a quick breath. "It's been quite a day. You ready to stick your bike in the back?"

"Yeah," Avery said. She tossed on her jacket—black,

which matched her black-and-white coveralls. "How was Celeste? I liked her."

"I hope she's all right with Asher. Not sure about that man." Minnie tied her squirrel hat beneath her chin. Avery straightened the tail, managing to keep a straight face.

"She seems infatuated. We'll keep an eye on her in case she decides to go back to Jersey City and Tommy or if she needs our help. Asher is quite a few years older." And wants to be a vampire.

Jack appeared in the foyer. "Hurry back, Charlene. I want to hear what happened. Glad you made it home before eight or the lights would have flickered like a short!"

She lifted her hand to her impatient ghost.

"I'm ready," Avery said, zipping her coat. "I didn't like Asher. I thought he was creepy. Trying too hard, while acting like he wasn't."

"Good observation." The three of them stepped outside and Minnie drove off with a beep as Charlene helped Avery with the bike.

They each got in the front and Charlene started the short drive to Avery's. "How was class today?"

"Good. Aced my English test."

"Congratulations! You're doing so well. I'm proud of you."

"Thanks." The teen adjusted the heater.

"Do you mind filling in tomorrow after school? I need to go to the police station."

"Sure. Everything okay?"

"It is." Not okay exactly, but there was nothing she wished to share.

Avery chattered nonstop the whole way—when there was a pause in the monologue, Charlene asked. "Avery, you've lived here all your life. Have you heard about the underground tunnels?"

"Sure. Pirate treasure is buried in the floor but there are booby traps, like in *The Goonies*."

Charlene laughed. "You're kidding?"

Avery cracked up. "In freshman year we went in one as a dare. By the old cemetery? It was so spooky and disgusting. It's supposed to be haunted and there's all these *keep out* signs."

"That only served to entice teenagers?" Charlene teased.

"I was fourteen, in my defense." She giggled. "Just a kid. And I had a crush on Josh, who liked my friend Trish."

"The things we do for love." Which brought Jared to mind. What she'd do to have him back for a minute, or a day.

Charlene parked in front of the teen house. Avery hopped out and got her bike on the sidewalk, waving goodbye.

"See you tomorrow!" Charlene shouted with the window half down. Once the girl was inside, she drove home, chuckling over her comment of being just a kid.

After the car was parked in the stand-alone garage, she hurried inside. Only a few dim lights lit the place, no sounds from a TV or music or laughter greeted her, and as always when her guests left, it seemed too empty.

Jack drifted near her and whispered, "Welcome home. Stop fretting. You'll have a full house tomorrow. Let's enjoy tonight—we don't have to hide in your suite or the wine cellar to converse."

At that, she locked the front door behind her with a lighter heart. "You're right. That is a perk."

"I have a fire lit in the living room."

"Thoughtful as always. Just let me heat up some dinner."

He followed her into the kitchen and as she warmed Minnie's chicken pot pie, he poured a glass of wine for her. "Thank you," she said with a smile. "You won't believe what happened tonight."

"Pirate's Cove. Was the place a dive?"

"I thought it might be, but it was actually really cute. Like the inside of Aladdin's lamp. Until . . ."

"Until what?"

She shivered and shook her head. That whole stinking mess at the Pirate's Cove would probably scar her for life. Nice guy like that, chopping up poor Kendrick George and making appetizers out of him. Freakin' crazy!

"Let's save it until after I eat."

The kitchen table was set and Jack took his usual seat opposite hers.

Charlene removed the pie from the microwave and jumped as whiskers brushed her leg, followed by a hearty purr. Silva had emerged from wherever she'd been napping, tempted by the smell of the savory chicken. "Hey, baby."

Jack said, "Celeste and Asher showed up?"

"Bringing Elisabeta—she was onto me from the start." Her cheeks heated as she recalled the mortification of being discovered and called out for it.

"Oh no!"

Charlene cut a little piece of chicken for Silva and put it in her dish. It was attacked and gobbled up before she could place her own dinner on the table.

"Elisabeta wanted to make her point, believe me."

Charlene sat down with her wine, sipped, then bit into her pot pie. "But as strange as that all was . . . well, the guy who served us was certifiably crazy! Made our vampires look like saints."

He laughed.

She spilled what had happened and how, ending with the cops dragging Callum away. The shock of it still made her queasy. She pushed aside her plate.

Compassion showed on Jack's handsome face. "I'm so sorry, Charlene. What a horrifying experience."

"It was—but worth it." She straightened and focused on the positive. "I learned a lot."

"Like?"

"We'd considered that Elisabeta and Asher might be working in tandem. The more I think about it, the more I believe that Asher is our killer."

"He was at the Hawthorne Hotel for the witch ball," Jack said, raising a finger.

"Where Celeste overheard him arguing with Alaric about Alaric choosing Serenity over him and Elisabeta."

Jack raised a second finger.

"Alaric, in that same argument, told Asher to continue the plan, which I think alluded to them all being immortal, eventually. Maybe Asher didn't agree?"

Jack didn't add a third finger. "Not strong enough."

"What about the money he flashes around? Where does he get it? Security jobs online? Joey is right; that could mean anything . . . Maybe he cracks online security?"

"Too nebulous. The fact is, Asher drinks blood." Jack added a third and fourth finger. "The guy seems guilty just from that. And his hold over Celeste?" He lifted his thumb as well. "I can see it."

Charlene sipped her wine. "And to top it off, Elisabeta didn't know Orpheus was dead."

"It's really too bad that you can't text Sam about this."

She agreed, but she hoped to return to their friendship once this case was over. "I'll see him tomorrow at three." Hopefully nothing terrible would happen between now and then. "Did you read Patrick's book?"

"Not yet."

"I'm interested in your take on it since you've lived here your whole life. What did you do this evening?"

"I was researching that skin disease. I would love to help find a cure. Charlene, it's miserable for people who have it, and so they live afraid of the daylight. In medieval times, they probably only went out at night, which would have made them true monsters. At least in this time in our history, they can cover up. Stores are open at night, restaurants. But still . . ."

"His mother, Melissa, probably gave Allan a story to make his suffering bearable. And somehow that turned him into believing he was a vampire."

"Another monster." Jack rubbed his jaw. "Reading the case studies has made me melancholy. Did I waste my life? Not do enough for humanity—I went to Harvard. Returned home to Salem to buy a big house. Married a beautiful but vain woman."

"Jack. Don't ever say you wasted your time here. It's not true! You lived a full life while you could. You gave to charities. You were a caring doctor."

"I'd like to go back and do things differently." He propped his elbow on the table.

"We can't change the past." They both knew that very well.

"Or . . . there's no reason why I can't continue to expand my knowledge and do more." He lifted his gaze. "These days doctors are online. I don't have a current license, but maybe there is some way I can help people over the internet. They don't need to see me."

"Let's look into it, Jack." She wished she could hug him. He'd had a temper when they'd first met, but it had waned once she'd discovered his killer. "You need a purpose, besides just hanging out with me and Silva."

"Do you think I could do it?" His image wavered.

"I know so. And how lucky for us to have a doctor in the house."

Thursday went by in a blur of greeting guests. Avery and Minnie had prepped the rooms with fresh flowers and the folder of what to do and where to eat, the happenings surrounding Salem. Clean linen, fluffed pillows, wine, chocolates . . . each space was an oasis.

"Nice group so far," Jack said as she got ready to leave for the police station. Avery was at the kitchen table with a slice of pie. Today she was dressed in jeans and sweater— nothing crazy, though she'd dyed her hair a silvery purple.

"You'll be okay? I feel terrible that I have to leave with another couple still to arrive." She'd never left Avery in charge and didn't like putting that much responsibility on the girl. Sam had left her no choice.

"I can handle it," Avery said, her shoulders back, her head held high. Pride shone from her eyes.

"She can handle it," Jack agreed. "I'm here too."

Charlene nodded, confident in the two of them. "Call me if you get stuck or need something. I'll text on my way home."

She left the house with great reluctance but knew if she tried to back out of the three o'clock appointment, Sam would probably send Officer Jimenez after her. That woman wanted nothing more than to lock Charlene up and toss the key.

Arriving at five till at the station, Charlene entered, not bothering to hide the chip on her shoulder.

"Hello," she told the receptionist—a different young woman than the last time. "I'm Charlene Morris. I have an appointment with Detective Holden."

"Have a seat." The woman, so preoccupied with entering information into the computer, didn't even glance her way.

For that, Charlene didn't bother politely saying "thank you" as she took the farthest chair along the wall. The waiting area was crowded with bedraggled people—a mix of men and women, all annoyed at having to sit and cool their heels.

She shifted on the hard plastic. There was no paper to be read or magazines—most folks scrolled their phones. Taking hers out, she played solitaire to pass the time.

Twenty minutes later, the receptionist called, "Charlene Morris."

She hopped up and made her way through the sea of extended legs. "Pardon me. Excuse me." It wasn't their fault she was in a bad mood. Besides, manners had been ingrained in her from childhood.

Her chip had grown to be the size of Texas by the time she reached the desk. Charlene couldn't wait to let Sam have it.

She recognized Officer Bernard, a polite man from Haiti who'd always treated her kindly, and gave him a pleasant smile.

He tipped his head. "This way."

She followed him down the hall to the right, where Sam sat behind his desk. She noticed the piles of papers stacked up to his elbows, and behind him a hodgepodge of file folders.

"Ms. Morris," the officer announced as Charlene strolled forward, stopping an inch from his desk.

Sam looked up without his customary smile. "Be seated."

She did. Her anger at him dissolved a little, seeing the amount of work scattered all over his office. Guilt sunk in. The wait had nothing to do with teaching her a lesson, only being overworked.

"You've been busy." She swallowed back an apology, still ticked that he'd forced her hand.

He didn't answer but continued reading a piece of paper.

Her unease grew and she knew she wouldn't be giving him a piece of her mind after all. She schooled her features and waited for him to speak, treating him with the professionalism he deserved.

Minutes later he swapped what he'd been reading for a report from the stack at his elbow. "I finally had a chance to go through this. Thank you for bringing it in. You mention a book in Orpheus's room. There was no book."

"There was—on the bed. Orpheus knocked it over"—when Brandy was interrogating him—"and I picked it up. I set it on the table before we left."

Sam smoothed his mustache and lasered her with his brown-eyed gaze. "Not there. I checked in evidence and his possessions in the morgue."

"I have no idea what happened to it, but it intrigued me so much that I bought my own copy from Lucas Evergreen. I have the receipt." Charlene folded her hands on her lap to hide her trembling fingers. It hadn't been a crime scene at the time, so she didn't understand his anger or his questioning.

"What else did you see in the room?"

"I told you. It wasn't much." She nodded at the report, which had been very thorough.

"Tell me again."

Charlene went through everything, including the dirt on the boots and the cloak visible below the mirrored sliding door. "I thought that maybe Orpheus had been in Elisabeta's home earlier that afternoon. That he'd been the man we saw running away from the upstairs window."

"Why were you upstairs again?" His mustache quivered, but no smile was hidden underneath.

"Because we heard a noise and knew someone else was in the house, even though Elisabeta had said she was alone."

"A smart person would have left through the front door and alerted the police if they believed something nefarious was going on."

"Never said I was smart. Just curious by nature."

He ignored her attempt at humor. "Did you see his face?"

"No. Which is why I'm not positive. Just a tall man in a vampire cloak. Possibly with dark hair. But now . . ." Now her money was on Asher.

Sam knocked his knuckle to the report. "I finally had the chance to interview Elisabeta Sala."

"When was that?"

"This morning. She showed up with an alibi on her arm. Asher Torrance. Said they were together all night."

"Well, that's not true. Asher was with my guest, Celeste. They were together after the ball." Charlene leaned forward. "Asher and Elisabeta were in a vampire coven with Alaric in New Orleans. Asher stayed with Celeste the last few nights at my B and B."

Sam's jaw clenched. "He signed a statement saying otherwise."

"Celeste heard Asher argue with Alaric about Serenity. Elisabeta was jealous of her. That's why I wondered if they were working together against Alaric."

"What else?" Sam tapped the desktop.

"They all expected to eventually be together as immortals. Oh, I forget what Celeste said exactly, but something about the plan would go on."

"Celeste's last name and number?"

"Celeste Devries. Just wait a sec while I get her number." She pretended not to hear him tapping his pen on the desk and muttering under his breath. His impatience had her jumpy, but she found the number as quickly as she could.

"I'm worried about her. These crazy vampires are able to control the women that fall for them. How do you think they manage that, especially with someone as strong as Serenity?"

"Drugs?"

"She said that they didn't do drugs, and I believed her."

"Hmm." Sam's focus was beyond her at the wall of files that tipped to the right.

"I wonder how they get their money. No one seems to work, but they can afford to rent expensive housing. Granted, they probably spend little money on food, since they prefer blood, but they flash around jewels and cash."

"What sort of jewels?" Sam alerted like a coyote to a rabbit. "Elisabeta had plain rings on this morning. I checked. Gold, silver, platinum. Titanium."

"Orpheus's earrings were at least five karats each. Elisabeta also had diamonds and emeralds when I saw her last night. Alaric had given a star sapphire to Serenity on the night of the ball. He claimed it was a family heirloom, and she was to use it for the spell later."

Sam jotted that down on the back of a folder. "Does she still have it?"

"I don't know. Probably." Charlene shrugged. "I can ask her if you want."

"I don't understand this whole vampire thing. What's wrong with meeting a nice girl and drinking a good bottle of wine together? Am I just old-fashioned?"

She shook her head. "Nope, I kind of like that."

"My sworn duty as an officer of the law is to discover who killed Allan Mayar, not to pass judgment on his lifestyle. Between you and me, this is a tough case."

"Sam, I wonder if you've checked his medical history? There's an actual skin disease that blisters in the sun—it's an allergy of some kind. It's possible that he really had a physical reaction to sunlight."

"How do you know about that?"

"I was curious as to why Serenity would believe Alaric's vampire story. Both she and Elisabeta agreed that he had a severe reaction to the sun. It added to his vampire persona."

"Your curiosity is going to be the death of you, Charlene."

She bit back a smart remark and said, "I'm careful."

"Like last night at the Pirate's Cove?"

"I had my pepper spray and I was in a public place surrounded by other people."

His stare couldn't be colder. "It sounds like you at least gave it some thought."

Oh! She pursed her mouth.

Sam dug through the papers on his desk and dragged out a black-and-white photo taken from a security video camera.

"Do you recognize this man?"

Charlene accepted the photo. "It's Orpheus."

"Real name is Carl Stephenson. He's from Alabama originally, before moving to New Orleans. The earrings he was wearing the day he died were part of a jewelry heist done by a theft ring called Night Shadows, three years ago."

Charlene studied the grainy photo. Orpheus wore black-on-black. If he hadn't glanced at the hidden camera, it would have been difficult to identify him. His hair was covered by a sleek black knit cap.

A smaller figure followed behind him. Not Alaric. More feminine.

Elisabeta?

"This is why we haven't announced his death—we're working with the police in Louisiana. You told me last night that Elisabeta thought that Orpheus had returned to New Orleans. I couldn't ask her directly this morning without causing suspicion or playing my hand."

"I see."

"I'd appreciate it if you continued to keep quiet about it."

"Of course!" Why was he telling her this?

"The book was missing from Carl Stephenson's hotel. The clerk swears she didn't take anything out. I'm going to tell you something else that needs to stay between you and me."

Tingles raced across shoulders. "All right."

"Carl didn't jump to his death. He was already dead before he was pushed off that balcony. We got the report back from the coroner yesterday. He'd been choked."

Charlene, chilled, stared at Sam in dawning horror. "Somebody was in the room with us? In the closet?" Fear rocketed through her.

"A strong someone." His eyes narrowed. "It's very important for you to tell me exactly what you saw. Go through everything one more time. You have to realize the danger you and Brandy might be in. I saw a decanter and glasses out in the room."

"He offered us wine. I didn't want any, but Brandy said yes . . . then she didn't drink hers."

"That's a good thing. It had GHB in it."

"What?" Brandy's witch senses must have cautioned her from drinking the wine, though she hadn't said as much to Charlene.

"That's the reason I asked about the drugs with Serenity. GHB can lower your inhibitions. It's why it's called the date rape drug. You go along with anything—even trying to kill a pretend vampire." He pounded his desk with his fist. "You realize that Serenity would have killed him to make him immortal?"

"We don't know that for sure."

He gave her an icy glare that made her shrink back in the chair. "Are you trying to scare me, Sam? I already am. You don't have to be heavy-handed."

"I'm worried that you are going to ask one question too many to the wrong person. The reason I told you about Carl is that Officer Jimenez mentioned she'd slipped up by referring to him as a victim—and you noticed. Of course you did. You're like a bloodhound."

She wanted to apologize and give him comfort. But she could do neither. "I don't mean to be. I might have inherited that trait from my mother."

He groaned. "That's about the best excuse I've heard yet. Your mother can be a real pain . . ."

"I know. Only too well."

"Look, I shouldn't be saying this, but we're closing down on our killer. This is important, Charlene. I need your cooperation, and for you to not ask any questions that will disturb the investigation. Understood?"

A harried officer arrived with a file in his hands. "Sir? When you have a minute?"

Charlene took that as her cue and stood on quivering legs.

"Charlene?"

"I understand, Detective. You can count on me."

CHAPTER 19

Charlene had three missed calls from the Flint household by the time she left the station. They were the last people she wanted to speak to right now. Sam had made it brilliantly clear that she needed to step back and do nothing. She clicked her phone off so she wouldn't be tempted to answer it.

She had one agenda right now. To get home quickly and talk things over with Jack.

The moment she stepped inside her warm and brightly-lit home, her mood took an uphill swing. "Hey, Avery! How did it go?" The clock on the stove read four-thirty. "Any problems?"

"Easy peasy." Avery slicked a short silver-purple lock of hair over her ear but it sprang right back. "The Jenningses, Toni and Robert, are so cool. They come from

Missouri and do a lot of traveling. Their kids are out of college and Toni said that it's their time to have fun."

"Good. Did they like their room?"

"Loved it! After they unpacked, they came down to thank you for the wine and flowers. Said it was the nicest welcoming package they've ever had. I mentioned the happy hour and that you'd be back soon to greet them. They decided to go out for a walk."

"I can't wait to meet them. Way to go, hon. You handled it like a real pro. You've also practically got everything set up!" Charlene pulled the chilled platter of shrimp she'd prepped earlier from the fridge and placed it on the counter next to a couple bottles of her house wine. "Give me ten minutes to freshen up."

"You've got thirty. No rush." Avery gathered silverware and plates for happy hour.

She entered her suite and smiled at Jack. "I wasn't sure if you were going to be arrested or not," he teased.

"Jack," she whispered in a tone just below the sound of the television, yanking off her boots and tossing her jacket over her love seat. "Orpheus *was* murdered. And he's part of a theft ring. Those diamonds in his ears led back to the heist."

Jack raised the volume of the TV with a lift of his palm. "Huh?"

"Yeah. Sam told me so that I'd stop asking questions and interfering with the investigation. They're working with the police in Louisiana."

"What else did you learn at the station?"

"Orpheus tried to serve Brandy drugged wine at his hotel. Jack, somebody was in the closet while we were there. She didn't drink it. Good thing."

"Did she know it was drugged?"

"I think her sixth sense alerted her—she didn't say anything, but set it aside." Brandy'd proved yet again she was a powerful witch!

"Another woman with good instincts."

"Yes. I also found out why Sam won't write off Serenity from his suspect list. And, unfortunately, he has a point."

"What's the reason?"

"He believes that Serenity intended to murder Alaric to bring him back to life. Just as Alaric planned to kill her." Charlene rubbed her chilled arms. "I refuse to believe that, but it could be a biased opinion. I wish I could be a fairy godmother and whisk Celeste away from Asher and Elisabeta."

Jack laughed. "Please, not another mythical creature. We have enough as it is."

Charlene grinned. "We sure do! I told Sam my theory about the women around the vampires being under some sort of vampire allure, or brainwashed."

Jack folded his arms. "I wish there was a way to snap them out of it."

"Reminds me of those young girls who were burned at the stake." Charlene tilted her head. "Why did they all point the finger at each other and act crazy?"

"Group hysteria." He stopped pacing and studied her. "You must be exhausted. It's been a difficult day."

"Nothing compared to poor Sam—you should see his office. He's on overload." She never kept secrets from Jack, so she found herself blurting, "Sam says they're closing in on the suspect."

"He's doing his best, but I must admit this is not an

easy one to solve, not even for a clever guy like me." He struck a pose like *The Thinker* and made her laugh.

She turned on her phone. "What do you think Brandy and Serenity want?" She showed Jack the now four missed calls. "I can't tell them anything. I promised Sam. If I don't respond, they'll know something is up."

"Your decision, but if it were me, I'd delay as long as possible."

"Right. Oh, I asked Sam to check into Alaric's medical history and mentioned that skin disease—I think you're right about how it could have affected him mentally."

Jack nodded. "Imagine that poor kid going to school? I found his elementary school transcripts. Grades only. They moved around a lot and he missed years completely, resulting in low scores."

"What a nightmare for him." If that was her child, she would want to keep him from the hurts of the playground. Give him a way to feel special rather than like a freak. "Maybe pretending to be a vampire was his way of coping." Charlene shrugged. "Makes me almost feel sorry for him."

"Watch your heart. Alaric, as an adult, manipulated people to make his way." Jack winced. "I have to keep telling myself the same thing."

"He wanted Serenity's power to help him achieve something he could never do alone." She was so grateful that the spell hadn't happened—it would have ruined Serenity's life as well as taken Alaric's.

The sound of a dish crashing to the floor made her jump back. "I have to go—but we'll talk later. Search the Night Shadows theft ring in Louisiana."

She slipped on her sneakers and entered the kitchen.

Avery looked up, guilt on her face. "I'm so sorry!"

Charlene reached for the broom. "Accidents happen—it's okay. Glad it was the bread dish and not the shrimp."

"Really?"

"Really!"

They had the mess cleaned in minutes and a new ceramic tray loaded with garlic rolls and chicken wings instead of the loaves of banana and pumpkin bread Minnie had made.

Silva, sensing that they were in a hurry, meowed by her dish.

"It's not time for dinner, fat cat. How about a treat?" Charlene opened the jar and gave her two that she chewed, kneading the kitchen floor as if she'd been starved. "I think you're feeling better."

Avery brought the food to the sideboard while Charlene greeted the newbies in the living room. "Sorry I wasn't here earlier, but I promise to make amends. I'm Charlene, and you've met Avery. We're so happy to have you here."

She smiled at all their expectant faces, putting them at ease. "Please introduce yourselves and don't be shy. Pour a drink and enjoy the appetizers. I'll make my way around and get to know you one at a time."

A few people turned to speak with those closest to them, so Charlene stepped forward and grabbed a bottle of red and one of white. "Who's going to be first?" She waved it at them. "And if you're a shrimp lover, come and get 'em!"

That broke the ice. Everyone came forward to accept a glass of wine, grab some food, and mingle.

Charlene poured herself a generous glass of cabernet and placed a few shrimp and chicken wings on her plate,

with a garlic roll to top it off. She greeted the couple behind her. "Hello! You must be the folks from Florida?"

"Good guess! Was it the tan that gave us away?" The
woman was of medium height, tanned and toned with
highlighted hair to her shoulders. Her husband, standing
behind her drinking a merlot, raised his glass to her.

"No, your exuberant faces! Cheers," she said and
clicked her glass with theirs.

"Well, I'm Jennifer, and my husband is Chase. This is
such an awesome place—outshines the photos online."

"Why thank you. You're staying—what? Three days?"

"We're not committed right now. We might hang here
longer or go visit Boston or Martha's Vineyard."

"It all sounds good." Charlene turned her attention to
the tall, solidly built husband. "Okay, I'm curious what
you do for a living? My guess is you're both fitness train-
ers or salsa dancers," Charlene added for a touch of
humor.

They both laughed and nudged each other. "Hardly, no!"

"I'm a police officer in Sarasota," Chase said. "Doesn't
get much tamer than that." He glanced at his wife with a
grin. "Had to break up a fight once with two senior citizens over a parking spot for their fancy golf carts. Jay-
walking is a big infraction too."

"He's kidding." Jennifer used her knuckles to chuck
his firm jaw. "My guy's tough. He's caught looters, broken up the occasional drug ring. I'm proud of him, but
don't want him in a big city where he could be killed."

Chase did a few salsa steps. "Is that why we don't
move to Miami?"

The pair drifted away on a chuckle as another couple
came forward. Charlene felt as though she was in a re-

ceiving line all by herself—but she knew Jack wasn't far away.

"Hello, I'm Fredrick and my beautiful wife is Marjorie." The handsome older couple shook her hand. "This is a very pleasant spot you have here. Big lawn."

"One of the nicest things about having all this space is we never see any neighbors." She lifted her glass. "Complete privacy, a beautiful garden, a wonderful landscaper, and a mile walk into town." She turned to Marjorie, knowing she was about to share a woman-to-woman thing. "I moved here after losing my husband. We both worked in advertising at a firm in Chicago. I knew I had to get away and here I am—with my own little piece of heaven."

Marjorie took her hand. "This is remarkable! And to think you achieved this yourself."

"I can't take all the credit. Couldn't have done it without my wonderful cook, Minnie, her husband Will, who's the gardener, and my youngest member of the staff who most of you've already met, indispensable Avery. Together we make a dynamo team." She lowered her gaze. "At least we think so."

Fredrick sipped his wine and glanced around at the other guests. "It's a nice group you have here. All very friendly. Marj and I love to sit back and watch people for entertainment. We like to guess what they do, where they're from; it's our own unique entertainment."

Marjorie shook her head. "That's what happens when you're our age and have nothing else to say at dinner."

Charlene laughed. "I won't keep you, but what do *you* both do?"

"I'm an adjunct professor at Columbia, and I'm called upon to lecture at other well-known institutes a few times a year."

"And you?" she asked his wife.

"I run several salons in Manhattan. Keeps me busy." She laughed softly and they moved on.

Charlene refilled drinks and listened to the various conversations as people got to know one another, completely in her element.

"Charlene, what's your favorite thing to do in Salem?" Felicity Summers, the only guest she hadn't met yet, was seated in Jack's favorite chair in front of the fireplace. The positioning of the wingback had hidden her from sight, but obviously needing a refill, she'd lifted her wineglass and spoke for the first time.

"I didn't see you sitting here until now. You must be Felicity?"

"The one and only." She giggled. "Is it possible to have some more wine? And shrimp? These are delicious."

"Of course." Charlene half-stepped toward the sidebar but then stopped. "My favorite thing is welcoming new guests. Wait one sec while I get your wine. Anything else?"

Felicity nibbled her last shrimp. "Uh—maybe some of those chicken wings? I'm so hungry and it's an hour till dinner."

Jack whispered in Charlene's ear, "You are going to spill it on her, I hope?"

She bit back her grin and poured the wine. A couple she hadn't met yet said, "We'll take this over for you. You've done so much."

Charlene gave them a warm smile. "You must be Toni and Robert Jennings. Avery was singing your praises earlier. This is so sweet of you."

"No problem, dear." Toni took the wine. "We have

children of our own, and they never quite grow up, do they?"

Charlene had no answer for that. "Thank you." She made a plate for Felicity and joined the others who'd now settled in the living room.

Holding court was the overdressed—and much impressed with herself—Felicity. "I'm kind of by myself here." She lifted her perfectly straight shoulders, revealed in a form-fitting wool dress. "As you can clearly see. First time on my own and I've booked like a zillion tours. What do you all think about the witches? Any believers?"

Fredrick leaned back on the sofa. "Are you referring to those poor young girls that were unfairly hanged without proof of any kind—with no legal representation, just a bunch of wealthy landowners who had more to gain than lose?"

"Well, I don't know about that, but I'm thinking more modern-day witches. Like some of the tours I've booked claim they not only exist, but are a big part of the society here. Educated, highly respectable people, living amongst others in a normal way. Doesn't that scare the crap out of you?"

Charlene rose from her chair. "Not at all. When I first moved here, not much more than a year ago from Chicago, I didn't believe in the paranormal either." She felt Jack behind her and smiled. "One of my best friends is a self-professed witch. You're drinking her wine."

Marjorie put down her wine with a stricken expression.

"Not to worry," Charlene assured her. "The Flint family can trace their line back centuries and they're immensely proud of their heritage. Brandy runs the most successful winery on the East Coast."

"It tastes wonderful." Marjorie picked up her glass again.

"That's not spooky at all," Felicity said dismissively.

"There are rumors of ghosts, of course, but the scariest thing I've heard is that a vampire coven wanted to set up roots around here."

Just then the fire leaped and crackled as Jack blew on the flames. Felicity gasped. Everyone else laughed.

Charlene raised her glass with a smile. "Welcome to Salem. I have books on the shelves about various local religions. Feel free to borrow anything that captures your interest. I recently bought one called *Salem Confidential* that makes a fascinating read."

"You're a firm believer in the occult?" Jennifer asked. "You kinda have to be, living here and all."

Charlene sipped her wine. Things were not black-and-white as she'd once believed. "There is more to the world than meets the eye."

"What's the book about?" Chase asked.

"Rum smuggling. Secret societies. Hidden tunnels." Charlene picked it up and showed it around. "If you want more information about the paranormal element here in Salem, go see Kevin at Brews and Broomsticks. He runs some of the tours and has great stories. I've been on several and they're a lot of fun."

Felicity grinned. "Single, I hope?"

"Yes, but spoken for."

"Not taken. The evening is looking up."

"She's something else," Jack remarked. "Not in a good way."

It wasn't long before her guests drifted out—all in high spirits. Charlene cleaned up the food from the sideboard and put it away. By seven, she'd dropped off Avery and her bike and decided to stop by Brews and Broomsticks to chat with Kevin.

The bar was a favorite of hers. Only a mile from her bed-and-breakfast, it had a decent-sized parking lot, good music, fun atmosphere, and the best drinks supplied by one of the nicest men she knew.

"Hey, Kevin!" The place was hopping on a Thursday night, with a small country band on the stage. She sat at the counter, her purse strap over her knee.

"Charlene—what can I get for you?"

"Merlot, please."

"I was about to call you, but I didn't want to be the bearer of bad news."

Oh no. "What happened?"

"My contact at the Oregon State Hospital no longer works there, and all of my pals in the tour guide system are very reluctant to go below."

"Why?"

"Increased patrolling by the armed guard. Hefty fines of a thousand bucks if you're caught."

"Wow. That's a lot of money."

"I think it's smart for the city to protect its assets, but why not just block them all off and snip the mystery, right?" He scanned the patrons at the bar counter, but no one needed his attention.

"Well, I read this book about it, and the author hints at Masonic beginnings and sordid secrets. Oh—that would be a great name for his second book." Charlene dug a pen from her purse and wrote *sordid secrets* on the back of a cocktail napkin.

Kevin delivered her wine. "I can still take you aboveground, but isn't the author going to do that next week?"

"Yes. But you know that I'm as patient as a kid promised an ice cream and I want to see for myself." She smiled at him over the rim of her wineglass.

"Tomorrow? I don't have to be here until two, so let's do the tour around noon. I'll let you treat me to lunch at Longboards when we're done."

"Sure. Sounds great—and I do appreciate it. You think Amy would want to come along?"

"I'll ask her, but she's been busy at the theater. She's got the role of the Ghost of Christmas Past. Something about Scrooge?" He rubbed his head. "Can't remember the darn name of it."

"*A Christmas Carol.* That's amazing." She sipped her wine. "Kevin, I've sent some new guests this way. One is a tigress named Felicity. Be warned."

He chuckled. "I can hold my own."

"Have you heard anything *interesting* lately?"

His brow arched. "I got to meet the king and queen of the witch ball—giant couple. They were so happy they'd won that I bought them a round."

She laughed. "When did they come in?"

He thought back. "Let's see. Last Saturday night? Can't believe Halloween was a week ago tomorrow."

"You've heard nothing about a dead vampire?"

"The dude that washed up on Derby Wharf?" He shrugged. "Someone told me that Alaric disappeared right from the room at midnight. Crazy."

She took another drink of her wine. "How do you suppose he got from the Hawthorne Hotel to the wharf, Kevin?"

Kevin slapped his palm down. "Ah-ha! That's what you're after. You want to see if there is a way for somebody to have staked him—yeah, I heard about that—and then dumped him from the hotel, through a tunnel leading to sea?"

"Is it so far-fetched?"

"Yeah. It is. I called my buddy and left a message. Listen, we'll check it out tomorrow during the day, by foot, to see if it's possible even by road."

"You're a great friend, Kevin. But we need to keep it quiet."

"The detective . . ."

"Doesn't want me poking my nose where it doesn't belong. But this is for Serenity. She can't go to jail."

"Jail, no way. Hard to believe that her and Alaric actually hooked up. Here's a well-respected witch and she has to explain that she put a spell on someone who then vanishes and winds up dead."

She leaned over the counter and smacked his arm. "Dead on."

"Bartenders hear a lot of stuff not meant for their ears."

"What do you think of Dru?"

"Dru and Serenity used to be attached at the hip. He's a good guy. I like him."

"He works at the Peabody Essex Museum. Another of the major places the tunnels went to."

"Oh—those are closed, for sure." He frowned. "They have to be. Why don't you ask Dru?"

"I don't know where to reach him other than work." She hadn't wanted to call the guy there. What if he got in trouble? But she would, she decided. First thing in the morning.

Just then a crowd of people came in, hooting around a pretty woman with a fake wedding veil and a tiara.

"I'll see you tomorrow. Noon. Where should we meet?"

"The Hawthorne." She wanted to check out the ball-room again. She placed a ten on the counter and left him to serve the bridesmaids and the bride-to-be.

She returned by nine to the bed-and-breakfast, pleased that her guests were still out. Opening the door to her suite, she saw Jack teasing the cat. He floated around the room as Silva tried to catch him.

"Playing games," she said with a smile. "That poor girl doesn't know what to make of you."

"Her instincts are sharp and clear."

"Silva wants to catch you and can't. An endless source of frustration." She plopped down on the love seat and put the blanket over her legs.

"Even though I can't snuggle with her, I'm still her playmate."

"You are so sweet, Jack. She adores you." Charlene pointed to the laptop, open to a text that looked very official. "What's that?"

"More stuff on Allan. If possible, could you try to find out about his earlier years? How deep the vampire fantasy went. When did it start?" The air around Jack whirled like a mini-tornado in her suite. "Maybe someone from his past surfaced to kill him."

Charlene shook her head. "I can get away with asking questions to the locals because I live here in Salem, but tracking down family in Ohio? Almost impossible. We don't know who they are or where they live."

The wind in the room died down. "You're right."

"Kevin doesn't think we'll be able to get inside the tunnels to poke around, but he agreed to take me on the walking tour. Did you read Patrick's book yet?"

Jack lowered his eyes. "I got into it, but put it down to do a little more research on Allan."

"I understand, but it's really important for you to finish it so we can be on the same page when I get back from the tour tomorrow."

"I won't let you down."

Jack was stuck in the confines of his home and property and she knew how frustrating that must be. He wanted to solve this mystery as much as she did.

She heard a beep and looked down at her phone. "Five missed calls. Now what?"

Jack crossed his arms with a rueful chuckle. "You can't keep ignoring the Flints. What if they turn you into a toad?"

CHAPTER 20

Brandy answered the Flint home phone on the second ring. "Hello, Charlene. You don't need to wonder how I knew it was you—I just did. Now, why have you been giving us the cold shoulder? Because I refused to let you use Serenity as bait for a possible killer?"

"I'm sorry I suggested it, all right?" Charlene said. "It was in poor taste."

"To put it mildly."

"Did you have something urgent to tell me? I've been extremely busy with new guests arriving."

"Serenity wants to talk to you—she's being very secretive." With a huff, Brandy covered the receiver and yelled, "Serenity! It's for you."

Serenity answered. "Hello? No, Mom, I don't want you to listen in. Sheesh. I'm going in the other room—don't eavesdrop."

There was a muffled noise, a door slam, and then Serenity said, "I swear I'm going to get my own place. There is zero privacy here."

Mind-reading crossed all kinds of lines, she imagined. "You called?"

"Pick me up tomorrow at ten," Serenity instructed. "We'll get a coffee at the shop where I first met Alaric— we can talk freely."

Ten might work, if she rushed breakfast. "I'll try to make it, but I have new guests to take care of first."

"Whatever!"

Charlene, on the verge of asking for Dru's phone number, realized the young witch had hung up.

"I tried, Jack," Charlene said, placing the phone on the coffee table.

"You did." Jack rattled the TV remote in agitation. "All we seem to get are dead ends." He ran a hand through his thick hair, his face concerned. "This has gone on long enough. Where is Sam when we need him?"

"You must be desperate if you want Sam to help solve the case," she teased, hoping for a brief smile.

"My empathy is with the poor kid with the skin disease who turned into a modern-day monster. Why was he killed?"

"We will find out, Jack. Now, did you locate a tunnel access close to Derby Wharf?"

"Took me all of five minutes," he boasted. "I kept the map in *favorites*."

She shoved aside the blanket to stand at Jack's shoulder. "What am I looking at?"

"This is the Derby Wharf and the lighthouse." He tapped the screen. "This is the Derby Tunnel."

"Just a few blocks separate everything. Kevin and I are

going to try and use Patrick's book to see which houses might be connected. We want to estimate how far Alaric's house is from the Hawthorne, and then the wharf."

"Good. Is Elisabeta still a suspect after speaking with the police?"

"Her alibi with Asher was a joke, and Sam knows it. I still think she has more motive than anyone—well, other than Asher. Another thing that keeps running through my head is their financial situation. If they don't work, how can they afford an expensive rental? And it easily could have been Asher hiding in the closet. He'd have ducked in while we were knocking on the door, or perhaps before Orpheus came home. He had the motive to kill Orpheus, but he had to wait until we left. He fits the description perfectly. It all adds up."

"You've already solved it in your mind," Jack said. "Let's hope you're right."

"Me too!" Her head pounded with the weight of it all. "I'm ready for a romantic comedy and a hot cup of tea."

"Your wish is my command."

Jack flicked his hand and Netflix appeared. Silva was already curled up on the love seat. They spent the remainder of the evening laughing at misguided lovers that found their way to each other again, not a single vampire or magic spell in sight.

Friday morning, Minnie arrived like a breath of fresh air. Her gray curls were held back with an orange headband and her round brown eyes were bright.

"How was the doctor?"

"All good. Wants me to lose a few pounds, but he tells me that every year." Minnie tied on her apron and popped a corner of banana loaf in her mouth. "It's not going to happen. How'd it go yesterday?"

"Great. We have a couple checking in later, and the two singles. I have a coffee date with Serenity Flint at ten, and an appointment with Kevin at noon."

As she was getting dressed, she received a text from Serenity. She no longer needed a ride. Family issues, she'd said, confirming she'd meet her at Aroma at ten.

"Another busy day in paradise."

Charlene greeted her guests for their first breakfast as Minnie brought out ham slices and scrambled eggs. Charlene limited herself to a single cup of coffee so that she wouldn't be over-caffeinated when she joined Serenity at the coffee shop.

She arrived at the coffee shop five minutes early and lucked out with a parking spot only a few stores away. The front exterior had a long window facing the street. Sheer blue curtains draped on both sides. If open, Alaric would have seen Serenity clearly. Closed, he'd see a form but not enough to make an identity. And wasn't the meeting at night? It had to have been to protect Alaric's skin.

Charlene walked inside the dim shop. Fresh-ground coffee warred with autumn spices to get her attention. She craved a pumpkin spice latte with nutmeg.

"Over here!" Serenity called.

Turning in the direction of a shadowed table, Charlene lifted a hand as she approached. "Thanks for the text."

Serenity gestured to the steaming mugs before her at the wooden table. "Have a seat. I've already got the drinks."

Charlene frowned. She'd planned on treating.

"Don't worry. I think you'll like what I ordered for you." Serenity grinned as Charlene inspected the drink before removing her coat and taking a seat.

"What is it?" She lifted the mug and sniffed the whipped topping. Nutmeg.

Serenity giggled mischievously.

"How did you know that I wanted a pumpkin spice latte?"

"Can't spoil the magic." Serenity shrugged her slim shoulders.

Charlene took a long sip, enjoying the flavors. "I guess you're feeling better?" Good enough for jokes, the minx.

"Yeah." Her smile faded as she picked up her drink and waved it under Charlene's nose. "Soy and cinnamon. It's what I was drinking when I met Alaric. It doesn't taste as good as it did back then." Serenity placed it away from her, eyeing it with regret.

Bad connotation due to the fact Alaric had died? Or the realization that he would have taken her life too? That wasn't love.

"Let me get you something else," Charlene offered.

Serenity scrunched her nose. "No, thanks." She ducked her head and lowered her voice. "I'm going to meet a *friend* later."

"Dru, I hope?"

Charlene hated the maze she sometimes had to navigate with secrets and omissions. Who knew what and who she could talk to. Much like Kevin, being a bartender and gathering people's secrets.

Serenity sucked in her bottom lip as she fidgeted with a white square napkin.

Charlene didn't expect an answer. She picked up her mug and sipped the pumpkin spice latte, giving Serenity as much time as she needed. "Yum, so good. Thank you."

"You're welcome." Serenity tapped the table with long, slender fingers and fingernails painted black. "Funny you mentioned his name, because I invited you here to discuss the Dru situation."

Charlene glanced around the interior to see if the tall, dark-haired young man was joining them, but no. Only mothers and a few children filled the few tables. "Have you been in touch?"

Watching her, Charlene remembered Elisabeta's threat to kill Serenity if she discovered it was her that had harmed Alaric.

"Yeah. I hate not being honest." Serenity held Charlene's gaze. "I've talked to Dru at length. He didn't kill Alaric. You have to help him—he's terrified."

She was already helping Brandy with Serenity, at risk to her friendship with Sam. "Did he call Detective Holden, like I suggested?"

Serenity wound an auburn strand of hair around her finger and shook her head. "He's supposed to go down to the station, but he's afraid he'll get tossed in jail. He doesn't want to involve me either in case they decide to detain me for more questions."

Charlene liked this Dru guy.

"It will be okay, Serenity. If he didn't do it, then he won't go to jail."

"That is not the way the world works. Mom said you were naïve, but even I know that."

Her cheeks warmed at the rebuke and she focused on finding answers. "Serenity, this may sound strange, but after all that went down, do you . . . still feel an attraction toward Alaric?" Elisabeta had hinted that she might, if Alaric had turned her.

Serenity wrapped her hands around the mug, still not drinking it, but holding it. She flushed scarlet to her roots.

"Why do you want to know that? We had a very sexual relationship. The chemistry between us was off the charts." Her cadence was defensive.

"You said that Alaric saw you from outside and so he came in?" There was a window, with curtains. "Did you meet in the daytime?"

Serenity toyed with the loose strand of hair like a nervous tic. Winding. Releasing. "I work at the vineyard during the day so it had to be after four—it gets dark by five. Mom was riding my ass about how to unpack the new gift bags for Christmas, as if I haven't been working there my whole life, right? Anyway, I needed to blow off steam so I came here. It's usually me and Dru's hangout. I was in a funky mood."

"So what happened? Can you tell me what you remember?"

"It was like a movie." Her blush lessened only slightly. "Alaric sat down opposite me and he was just so charismatic. His eyes gazed into mine as if he could see my soul."

Charlene cleared her throat to keep the young woman in the present rather than the past. "When was this?"

"Oh." She blinked and thought back. "Three weeks ago, now. Dru and I had gotten into a big fight about where we were going to live, and I'd moved back to Mom's house with Grandma."

She'd been very vulnerable. Charlene sipped her latte, taking comfort from the warmth of the mug.

"It sounds stressful." Charlene leaned forward. "Can you remember what Alaric was wearing when he burst in and swept you away?"

Serenity half-smiled. "Definitely. He had on this Victorian shirt and jacket. Soft black leather gloves. A broad-brimmed hat. Jeans and boots. Goddess, but he was sexy."

"Did he order coffee or a latte?"

"No." Her gaze brightened. "He sipped from mine. Just picked it up and drank."

"What did you do?"

"I was as shocked as you look, at first, but then he started speaking with his deep Southern accent. Told me that I was beautiful and he could see the power in me. Told me that my aura was gold, which meant I was special. I do have gold in my aura. It's the witch in me."

Charlene nodded. Elisabeta had said she'd seen auras too and had probably fed this information to Alaric to trick Serenity into further lowering her guard.

She swallowed her anger down, her empathy for Alaric gone in the face of his actions toward Serenity. Sipping from her drink—had he somehow found a way to put something in it?

"How are you feeling now?"

Serenity glanced out the window, curtains open to let in the morning sun. "Better."

"Like, how?"

"Clearer minded." Serenity traced circles in her foam.

"Do you still think that you loved Alaric?"

She clenched her jaw, tears on her lashes. "No. I don't. Which makes me really upset."

Charlene patted her hand. "Can you tell me what the plan was for you the night of the ball?"

"There are lots of things that I don't remember, and I haven't told Mom or Grandma because I know they'd freak out." She lifted emerald eyes. "What if I did have something to do with his death? The police keep insinuating that I wanted him dead—which is sorta true, but only to revive him!"

This was what Sam had warned her about. Was Serenity guilty? "What do you mean, hon?"

She dabbed the corners of her eyes. "We had planned an elaborate ceremony to welcome the Day of the Dead, as you know. It's a very powerful day and a good omen."

"To perform your necromancy ritual. Two in the morning." She encouraged Serenity to tell her again and listened for anything that might free her. Dru. Celeste. God, she wanted everyone to just be okay. Was that too much to ask?

She knew firsthand the grief from when life didn't play fair.

"I was going to raise the dead." Serenity gulped and rubbed the hollow of her throat. "I told him I couldn't kill him. I was very shocked when I woke from my faint and saw the stake there, with blood. Is that what killed him? I don't even know, and I can't ask the police because to admit that things are fuzzy might land me in jail."

Charlene was speechless, so she sipped her latte. Serenity didn't remember? The young woman was right to be afraid.

"I'm a very powerful witch, and I have access to centuries of magick. Alaric wanted me to share my spells with him. On some level, I had to know that he wasn't a true vampire, but it didn't matter." She glanced at the napkin rack on the table, then back at Charlene. "Why didn't it? It sure does now, when it might be too late."

"I don't know, Serenity." Her temples pounded. It didn't look good.

"I feel like such a fool, Charlene. Mom and Grandma, they wouldn't have been taken advantage of like that."

If what she suspected was true, Brandy had almost been a victim of GHB too. She drank her latte. "You might be surprised. They both love you very much."

"I know that. It's why I don't want to see their disappointment."

Charlene patted Serenity's hand. "Serenity, this is changing the subject, but I'm curious . . . what do you know about the underground tunnels?"

She straightened, alert. "Why?"

"I read a book that came out five years ago. It got me thinking."

"About what? The tunnels are closed for good reason. It's very dark down there, like, spiritually. Bad things happened."

Was she talking recently? Was this a confession? *No.* Just . . . no way did Charlene believe that Serenity, a professed good witch in a line of good witches, would resort to murder. She had no reason.

"Have you been down there?"

"Yeah, of course. Supposedly haunted, but I never saw anything. Me and Dru used to sneak down there in high school. Everybody does it. Or they used to until the cops got more strict about it."

Her stomach clenched. "Dru knows about the tunnels?"

Serenity got quiet. "We *all* know about the tunnels, Charlene. Most of them have been filled in, or the businesses have cleaned them up and use them for storage. No gold, no ghosts, no secret passageways."

End of that subject. "Can I get Dru's phone number from you? I have some questions about them and maybe he can help."

Serenity scribbled his number down on a piece of

paper and handed it over. "There, I've given you his number and now you need to do something for me. Help him. He's missed work all week. Personal time. He's afraid to go in, in case the police are after him. He can't lose his job at the museum."

Charlene finished her latte, eager to get home to Jack with her theories, but she had to be sure of something. "What do you mean, that you can't remember pieces of the night?"

"No matter how hard I try, I can't recall things . . . like, I was supposed to meet Alaric at twelve-ten at his house. That was the plan." She lifted her gaze and Charlene glimpsed terror. "He wasn't there when Elisabeta and I got there. What happened to him? I don't know. Did I—"

"Serenity, listen to what you've just told me. You were with Elisabeta the whole time, or at the ball in full view. You didn't do anything wrong."

"I ran ahead of Elisabeta to the rental house, terrified by the stake. How did it get there? Alaric wasn't there. I vaguely remember Elisabeta telling me to calm down. She gave me some water, but then I ran."

"You didn't stake him. I promise. There wasn't time for you to stab him when the lights were out. The stake was a prop from the photo booth. Somebody set that up."

"I was very vague with the police." Her eyes darted. "I honestly don't know where I was until three that morning."

Her stomach churned. "Were drugs used for the rituals?"

"Not that I took or saw. Craziest thing Alaric wanted me to do was drink blood, and I passed on that . . . I said I wanted to wait until after the ceremony." Serenity shivered, her nose curled. "Still can't believe what an idiot I was to go along with that. I hate the blank spaces in my mind."

She hadn't had Alaric's blood like Elisabeta thought.

"I suggest talking with your mom and grandma—maybe there's a spell or something they can use to bring back your memory."

"I can't talk to them. Or the police." Serenity curled another strand of hair around her finger, eyes wide. "I can't go to jail."

CHAPTER 21

Charlene put a hand over Serenity's and realized they were cold and shaking. "I'll help you anyway I can. Serenity, what if Alaric put something in your tea, or your mouth, that first instant he met you? You wouldn't notice, if it was just a little bit."

"You think he drugged me." Her eyes widened and she shook her head, but then stopped.

"I think he knew you from New Orleans. I think he targeted you."

Shock emanated from Serenity. "How? I've been over that with Mom and Grandma. I don't let people know that I'm a witch, duh. You'd have to know me personally."

"I'll go with you to speak with Detective Holden," Charlene said. "He's got your best interests at heart."

Serenity stood up, pale and distressed. "I don't think so, Charlene. He wants to pop someone in jail—and I'd be handing myself over on a platter." She grabbed her jacket and bag. "I've gotta go." She turned and rushed out of the coffee shop like a ghost was chasing her.

Charlene brought the mugs to the counter, her thoughts spinning. Her appointment with Kevin wasn't until noon, so she went home, knowing Jack would be anxious to hear about their conversation.

Out on the street she patted her jacket pocket where she had Dru's number. She was in no condition to talk to him, but it was like a scratch-off lottery ticket—she wanted to see if the number would be a winner. She called and it went to voice mail—she left a message. Hopefully Serenity would convince him to talk to her.

The minute she opened her door, Silva pounced on her. This was a new trick of hers—she'd hear the sound of Charlene's car, then hide behind a plant near the doorway and make a sneak attack.

Minnie stepped out of the kitchen. "Good thing you're home," she said in greeting. "We've had a few calls this morning about renting rooms next week. I wrote their information down." She wiped her hands on her apron. "Our new crowd loved the pumpkin muffins."

"Thanks, Minnie. You're a champ as always."

She curled her arm to show her muscle and grinned. "You just missed Detective Hottie on the house phone. Told him you were out and he didn't seem too pleased. You better call him back."

True to his rules, he hadn't used her cell number. Nothing personal. Business.

"Not sure if I want to face a snarling Sam right now, but I'll take care of it after I speak with our prospective guests." She picked up the notepad with the list and smiled at Minnie. "You have any leftover breakfast?"

"Sure. There's plenty of muffins and some fruit."

"I'll just grab a small plate and take it to my room to record our guests on the computer. We should send Christmas cards this year to each of them."

"And who is 'we'?" Minnie shook her head and muttered to herself, fixing a plate for Charlene. "Here you go. Would you like coffee with that?"

"No, thanks. Just water."

"Of course."

With a full plate and a bottle of water, Charlene made her way to her suite. She entered expecting to see Jack, but he wasn't there. She went into her bedroom, removed her boots, washed her hands, and headed for the sitting room, hoping her full-time guest would make an appearance.

She took a seat at the computer and ate her "now brunch" as she ran through her scheduled guests, noting the free days and rooms. Pushing the plate away, she returned each call. In less than an hour she had the B and B half full for the next two weeks. She'd expected a lull until the first two weeks before Christmas, but this extra money would keep the bankers happy.

"What are you grinning at?" a voice she was accustomed to asked from behind. She felt that familiar chill and spun around on her chair.

"New bookings," she told Jack.

Jack sat on the love seat since she'd claimed the computer's leather chair. "How did the coffee date with Serenity go?"

"I'm scared for her, Jack." She leaned toward him. "Serenity told me that she has gaps remembering what happened that night. All it would take is Alaric slipping a drug into her latte or tea unnoticed, and she could be rendered helpless. You should have seen her expression when she realized he might have drugged her without her consent. She didn't need or want drugs and was adamant."

"It's very widespread, unfortunately, and often the male counterpart is never charged." Jack clenched his jaw. "She had no knowledge of the drugs as her memory was wiped clean."

"It wasn't his charisma or extreme arrogance that gave him power over women," she spoke slowly, understanding for the first time. "That vampire act was a show. It wasn't magic or great power, but a roofie."

"Gamma hydroxybutyrate acid, or GHB. I'm ashamed of myself for not questioning this before." Jack covered his face with his hand.

"Don't blame yourself, Jack. We all believed what she told us—no drugs." Charlene gnawed at her bottom lip. "At their first meeting he took a drink of her soy latte and kissed her. Could have done it right then. It would explain their 'chemistry that was off the charts,' right?"

"Agreed. Small doses that she wouldn't notice, working his image as the sexy vampire to heighten her libido—in conjunction with the drugs." His upper lip lifted. "This conflicts with the empathy I feel for him as a child."

"Alaric would keep away from her family as much as possible. If they caught on to him, they'd destroy him. He was smart enough to know that."

"Exactly. You're getting good at this." Jack had a hint of pride in his eyes.

"Why, thank you, sir." She jumped out of her chair. "Can't Serenity be tested so we'd all know for sure?"

"Too late for that. That type of drug is normally out of the system within twenty-four hours." Jack put a finger to his lip. "Elisabeta is still living in the house they rented. Would she admit to drugging Serenity against her will?"

"No way. She's still loyal to Alaric; don't ask me why. She does the drugs, remember? For her orgies." Charlene and Jack exchanged a look. "That doesn't sound so good. What if they are doing that to Celeste now? We, or I, have to get her out of there."

"Agreed, but you can't do this alone." Jack appeared to her right, at her desk. "It's too dangerous."

"I can ask Kevin if he'll help when we do the tour. Which means I should leave soon. I also need to call Sam. I want to protect Celeste as well as Serenity. I don't think Sam knows about the gaps she had the night Alaric was killed. If it was done against her will, she can't be guilty, right?"

Jack gave her a compassionate half-smile. "Can you put Sam off until later?"

"No." She went to the door and opened it.

"You want privacy?" he asked.

She nodded.

"Tell Inspector Clouseau to hurry up and solve this before we embarrass him again."

"Not so funny," she whispered and closed the door behind her. Jack put Sam down because he was jealous.

Minnie looked at her strangely. "Thought I heard you talking to somebody. You all right, dear?"

"Yeah. Just have something on my mind."

"Can I bring you a tea and a sandwich? You don't eat often enough."

"Tea sounds nice. I still have to call Sam, and I don't want to."

"Why on earth is that?" Minnie put a hand to her ample chest. "He's a darling man and very fond of you.

Come on, admit it. You might be developing feelings for him too. That can get confusing at times. You may think you're not ready—"

"Minnie, thanks for your concern, but I just need tea and some of your lemon cookies that I spotted earlier. Please?"

"Fine!" Minnie huffed and marched back to the kitchen.

Charlene leaned back in the heavily upholstered chair near the fire and closed her eyes for a second. What could Sam want? Was he going to tell her something about the case, or ask where she'd been?

She hated his questions because most of the time he didn't like her answers, and then she'd get in trouble again. How she constantly put herself in danger, how it was his business and hers was running the bed-and-breakfast. Yada, yada.

After Minnie dropped off the tea and cookies—nose high—Charlene took a long sip of the herbal tea, hoping it might soothe her nerves.

She pressed Sam's number and waited to hear his grumpy voice.

"Hey, Charlene! Thanks for calling me back. My sister Sydney, you remember her and Jim?"

"Yes, of course. How are they?"

"Doing great. They wondered if they could book a room over Christmas and asked me to check with you. Otherwise they'll look for another hotel in town."

"Oh no, they won't!" She laughed, feeling better already. "Tell them I'll reserve a room right away. Do you know how many nights they plan to stay?"

"Three, then they're headed to Boston."

"Great." She bit into her lemon cookie.

There was a pause that turned awkward as it length-ened.

"Did you want to ask me something else?" Charlene asked. "Or should I come to the station?"

His tone shifted from friendly to official. "I have an-other question about Carl, aka Orpheus. You were the last one to see him, and Brandy of course, but I don't think she's a reliable witness."

"Why? Because she's a witch?"

"No," he drawled extra-patiently. "Because her daugh-ter is involved and her views might be tainted."

Serenity had expressly told her not to discuss her situ-ation with Sam. She cleared her throat. "I have to meet Kevin in a few minutes. He's taking me on a tour of the tunnels. Aboveground." So far.

"Why?"

"I met with Dr. Steel, the author of *Salem Confiden-tial*, and he told me about the underground tunnels and some of Salem's more notorious history. Rum smuggling, pirate treasure."

Sam blew out a breath. "The tunnels are closed, Char-lene, for a reason. They are dangerous—"

"I know!" She cut him off before he could lecture her. "How about I stop by after I do the tour with Kevin?" That way if there was anything good to help the case, she could tell him right away.

"Don't go getting into trouble, Charlene. And remem-ber to keep our conversations confidential while you're with Kevin."

"I know. Can your question wait?"

"Yes."

"Talk to you later!" When she clicked off, her mood had lightened and she couldn't deny that surge of anticipation. Maybe that's exactly what the doctor ordered. A few laughs with Sam once this was over.

Charlene took note of the gray, dreary sky and grabbed a foldable umbrella. She dropped it into her bag, next to the pepper spray—the two looked similar in shape and size, black, cylindrical, with a red button. Her book by Dr. Steel was already there for her and Kevin to use.

She parked in the lot near the Hawthorne Hotel and went inside. Had the ball only been a week ago? Peeking in the cute windows as she rounded the corner, Charlene entered the hotel off of Hawthorne Boulevard.

Kevin wasn't in the lobby so she wandered into the bar. Made of wood and with a large fireplace, it was a cozy watering hole frequented by locals as well as guests of the hotel. The food was tasty and artistic.

She stepped back into the lobby, eyeing the Victorian love seat where Serenity and Alaric had snuggled so close. And now, Alaric was dead and Serenity a person of interest in the tragedy.

Shaking off the sadness that accompanied death, Charlene went into the ballroom directly behind the bar, which seemed massive without the people inside dancing and partying, celebrating Samhain and Halloween.

The far right corner was where the band had been; the far left, the photo booth and the long table for the punch bowl of sangria.

Small tables had been along the back wall for folks who needed a break from the dancing. The mezzanine on the second floor overlooked the ballroom.

Charlene crossed the long wooden floor to where the tall vampire, probably Asher, she realized now, had drawn the pentagram. Nothing remained of it now. It must have been part of the spell by Serenity and washed away the next day by the cleaning crew. She got down on her knees to inspect the floorboards—they weren't even loose.

"Now why am I not surprised to find you in here?" a masculine voice asked as he entered the ballroom.

She sat back on her heels and sucked in a startled breath. "Kevin!"

"I'm assuming you aren't searching for a lost contact? I missed one heck of a party." Since Kevin also worked as a paranormal tour guide, Halloween was the busiest night of the year for him.

Charlene laughed self-consciously and rose from her kneeling position. "This is where Alaric disappeared. Nothing to be seen after his theatrical performance, except the cape, the stake—which was a prop from the photo booth—and this empty space on the floor." She pointed to the far corner.

She crossed the wood floor to where the photo booth had been to search around, not sure what she was looking for. There hadn't been blood, other than the tip of the stake. Six inches of carpet surrounded the very edge of the dance floor like a low-pile picture frame.

"What do you hope to find?" Kevin asked as he joined her in studying the floor.

"A secret exit," she rattled off. "A trapdoor. A way for Alaric to escape."

"The library is directly below us." Kevin raised his brow. "Walk me through what happened that night and where."

She liked that he didn't automatically discount her idea. "Alaric stood where I was kneeling, speaking in a commanding voice to the people, saying his name over and over again, until they started chanting it too. Orpheus was by the band. The dance floor was crowded but Alaric had everyone enthralled." She glanced up, feeling the color fade from her cheeks, her stomach woozy. "We have learned since that Asher had drawn the pentagram, and he was the one who got people chanting. He was counting down to the stroke of midnight. The lights went out. Brandy, Stephanos, and I were by the door, which was locked."

She and Kevin walked around the room. Large windows gave a view of the street and the Commons beyond.

"The lights were out for about three minutes. It wasn't completely dark because there were candles on most of the tables, and the bright costumes showed where everyone stood. We had the one exit blocked with tables to stop the flow of people coming in and out of the ballroom."

Kevin rubbed his smooth-shaven chin. "Alaric was there, and then *poof*, he was gone. Where did he go?"

"It was just a long enough period of time that he could have walked out on his own," Charlene surmised. "Maybe a quick change of costume? No magic needed at all, just a distraction to make people think he'd disappeared."

"But he never reappeared." Kevin crossed his arms.

"Exactly." She strode around the room, her instincts drawing her toward where the photo booth had been. She brought Dr. Patrick Steel's book from her purse. "The author of this book mentions secret passageways all over town from the 1800s."

"The Hawthorne wasn't built until 1925. Long after the original tunnels were made."

"It was the Franklin Building before that."

"Which burned down numerous times." Kevin lifted a brow at her. "My bartender friend said people have complained about the fire smell coming from the basement, but when they check? No fires."

She shivered. "Phantom flames?"

"Cute. I might use that in one of my tours."

"Kevin! Help me focus, please—where could Alaric have gone?"

They walked along the windows. "Do they open?"

The windows they tried didn't budge. The last one Charlene attempted, near the photo booth, did—not fully. If a man was very skinny and could contort his body into a U-shape, he might be able to slip through.

Kevin narrowed his eyes. "It would have been crowded, chaotic, people focused on where Alaric was standing. It might have been easy for him to slip away, but probably not through that window."

"He had help." Charlene studied the floorboards. A scrape of wood showed. Beneath the carpet runner was a square edge. Charlene pried it up; the exposed carpet revealed a wood square.

"A trapdoor," Kevin said with a grin.

Chapter 22

Charlene just knew this had to be the escape route! "What's directly below here?"

"The library, like I told you," Kevin said. "Nothing mysterious about that."

"Let's go see."

"Okay." They walked down the stairs and Kevin smacked his palm to his forehead. "Oh. There's also the men's room."

"The Franklin Building, all versions, would have had a basement too." Charlene looked around the space, getting a chill.

"This place feels older than just a hundred years."

"The Salem Marine Society is still housed on the top floor of the Hawthorne. This space was meant to be a retirement home for sailors—and that was in the late 1700s, early eighteens."

Kevin knocked on the men's room door but nobody answered. He gestured for her to join him and they both entered.

She pointed to the ceiling and a square cut out above the farthest stall.

"Alaric could have come down through here, changed into different clothes, and walked out."

"What was he wearing when he washed ashore?"

"He was naked."

Kevin's eyes narrowed. "Less DNA to transfer if the clothes are gone. Has Sam told you the time of death?"

"No. You know how that goes. The stick was a prop, with type O blood on it. I don't think it made the hole in Alaric's chest—it was the width of a baseball. There would have been blood around the floor then."

"You're right. Alaric wasn't killed upstairs. It's likely the hole in his chest was done later."

"To prove that Alaric, a supposed vampire, was actually human and dead?" That sounded like a point Orpheus might have made. Unless Asher decided to also make sure that Alaric was dead in the vampire sense and then been sorely disappointed.

Kevin jumped up onto the toilet seat and opened the door. A rope ladder descended and Kevin climbed it as agile as a monkey.

"What is it?"

"Just a crawl space for ventilation." Kevin wiggled halfway in, legs dangling. "He might not have come out here at all. This leads under the whole floor, but I can see a muted light. Natural. Probably the street."

"Let's go see." Charlene helped Kevin get down, gently tugging on his calves until his boots could reach the toilet seat.

"These are sort of like tunnels." He brushed off the dirt from his shirt and jeans.

"Thanks for doing that," she said with a shrug. "I never would have thought to look inside there. Alaric had to have been very fit."

He led the way upstairs to the lobby and they exited from the front door, going around the building to the side where they had the best view of the Commons.

Charlene pulled out Patrick's book again.

"What's that?"

"Dr. Steel's book. This has the underground history for Salem—smuggling, rum, secrets."

Kevin studied the area around the back of the hotel and pointed to a grate. "That's where the light is coming from."

He dropped down to inspect the metal.

Excitement had Charlene's stomach jumping. "Did he get out that way?"

"Nope. This is welded on—and hasn't been tampered with in fifty years probably." He stood and brushed his hands together. "Sorry, Charlene. It was a good idea."

"Is this the only one?"

Kevin blew out a breath. "Let's check it out."

After going around the whole block, they came across a basement access door. "Could this be it?" Charlene asked.

Kevin stopped and studied the entrance. "I don't know."

"Where did he go? How was he killed and where? His body somehow got from here"—she pointed to the brick hotel—"to the Derby Wharf." She put her hand in her jacket pocket. "Nobody saw him leave."

Kevin disappeared down the steep stairs and Charlene

peered over the edge. He twisted the metal knob on the door.

It opened. "Bingo."

Charlene followed him as he held the door open. "What is this?"

There were crates and old hotel furniture. "Storage, looks like," Kevin said.

Charlene used her cell phone for light until they found a switch. Two sets of boot prints were near the door. She carefully avoided them and walked across the cement basement to the main interior door. She opened that and it led to a back room like a forgotten office and more storage—this time of books.

"The library."

"Yeah," Kevin said. "Seems he came out this way—did he have help, or are the boot marks his from multiple visits?"

"Wish I had the answer. I did see Asher in the ballroom the whole night so I can't imagine it was him. Elisabeta is petite; she could easily slip down here. Orpheus had been wearing boots, but he's a large man. Brandy and I saw a pair of his boots in his hotel room. They had dirt on them."

"Dare I ask why the two of you were in his room?"

"Another story for another day." She would keep Sam's confidence.

Kevin shone his phone flashlight into the shadows. "We should get out of here and talk in the sunshine."

She looked around the dim space. "I'll tell Sam about this entrance when I see him after we finish our tour."

"We don't know for sure if this is anything—it's a possible route for Alaric to escape. Not how he ended up by the wharf with a hole in his chest."

"I know. I'd thought that maybe there would be tunnels from here to the water. Like in the old days, but Patrick said that they'd been filled in."

"There was one here, though?"

"Yes. He's going to show me a place in the street that's been cemented over where they used to bring in supplies for the Franklin Building."

"Is it in your book?"

Charlene handed the paperback over. "I wouldn't know what to look for."

"Let's skedaddle. It's giving me the creeps." They ascended the stairs together.

On the sidewalk she shook a few cobwebs from her hair. "I don't like spiders."

Kevin thumbed through the pages with interest as she dusted herself off. "Can't believe I haven't read this before. It's pretty thorough."

"After reading this, I'd like to get back to the Peabody Essex Museum. I had no idea that so many treasures were stored there from Salem's glory days." She sneezed at the remaining dust clinging to her clothes.

"Bless you. I've been there a million times and they're always changing things up."

"You should meet Patrick; you'd like him. He was a professor for thirty years and is very pro-Salem. I can see him as a militiaman or something back in the day, patrolling the Commons against the Redcoats."

They exchanged smiles. "I'd like that."

"You're welcome to come on the tour with me next Tuesday."

"What time?"

"Don't know yet—he's going to call me."

Kevin nodded. Standing on the corner, they faced the

Commons, the hotel at their back. "Let's imagine that Alaric left the ball on his own two feet."

"It seems likely," Charlene said. "He would go to his house nearby where Serenity would do the spell, with Elisabeta there to assist in the transfusion. Elisabeta was asked to wait to be immortal until after Alaric and Serenity proved it possible. Asher was also sidelined. Orpheus was not invited to the party, period."

"Where is his house?"

"He rented one of the historic homes across the park from here. Two chimneys—only one fireplace that I saw."

Kevin shaded his eyes as the sun broke from behind a cloud. "What's that mean?"

"It's supposed to indicate that the house or business had a tunnel access, connected to another house or business."

"You're kidding."

"No. Well, I don't know if it's true, but that's what the book says. Sounds silly, but it was important for the men and women not to ruin their clothes and protect their health during inclement weather. Tunnels were created as roads to connect homes of family or friends, and businesses."

"I feel like I need to pay *you* for the tour."

Charlene laughed at the role reversal. "My theory about Alaric going from the Hawthorne to his home to the wharf has holes in it. Which is why I need you. What would be the most direct route for someone to move a dead body?"

"You're assuming he would have been killed here, which might not be true."

She crossed her arms and scanned the area around

them. Gorgeous elm trees, bluish-gray sky, lovely historic buildings, and so much scandal.

"He wasn't at home when Serenity and Elisabeta were there fifteen minutes later. It seems logical to me that he just plain never made it."

Charlene reached for the book and put it in her purse as the weather started to spit and drizzle. "Traveling underground made sense in a way. Folks spent a fortune on their clothes and fabrics. Only the rich merchants would have the money, not the majority."

Kevin hunched his shoulders, scooting back under the protective awning of the hotel. "A warren of paths beneath the city. Most are filled in or blocked off due to the torrential rains that can cause flooding. It puts a lot of pressure on the old bricks and stones."

"It would be a nightmare if one collapsed and trapped someone."

"For sure, that's why they are more patrolled now. It's trespassing if you're caught on private property and that thousand-dollar fine is no joke."

"Patrick said it's okay to follow the paths above-ground. Where is the pedestrian mall from here?" Charlene knew the area but not the direct route. It was an upscale part of the city that included the Peabody Museum and blocks of quaint shops where no vehicles were allowed.

Kevin pointed to his left. "Down there about a mile."

"And the wharf?"

He gestured to his right. "Same distance—well, maybe just over a mile."

"Not so far to walk, but not so easy to carry a body and have no one notice. Not even on Halloween night." Charlene turned toward Alaric's rental house. "I'm hoping to see what's in the basement. Asher and Celeste were guests of mine until Celeste checked out. I saw them down there."

"Uh, will they be friendly?"

"Probably not." She shivered as she recalled their last meeting at the Pirate's Cove. "Alaric's house has two chimneys. A basement. It could be connected to the tunnels."

"That would be very cool—but then what?" He hunched into his jacket.

She swallowed and touched her throat. "Well, the tunnels, or just one, might lead to the wharf."

"I see what you're getting at."

"Either way, it would be easier to transport a dead body underground than carrying it through the streets."

"Agreed. If the connection can be made. What else do you know about this underground?"

"Just what I read." She patted her purse. "The tunnels were made from the wharves to the homes and businesses across Derby. Tons of cargo was taken off the ships and brought to the city—for sale or storage or personal use."

"Most of the wharves were taken apart," Kevin said.

"Except for four—one of them being Derby Wharf— where Alaric's body was found." Excitement coursed through her as they pieced things together.

Kevin pulled out his cell phone from his back jeans pocket. "Let me call my buddy and ask him about it. I wish that Patrick guy was here to explain this in better detail."

"Tuesday seems like forever." Charlene chuckled at her own impatience. "I think Asher and Elisabeta are dangerous, between the drugs, blood, and vampire scene. I'm afraid Celeste is being drawn into their crazy world." She gave Kevin a nod. "You call your friend, and I'll phone Patrick to see if he can answer that question specifically. Do any of the houses around the Commons connect to the wharves?"

Charlene's phone rang before she could dial out. She didn't recognize the number. "Hello?"

"It's Dru Ormand." The young man spoke fast. "Meet me at the Lobster Shack, and I can tell you what I saw inside that monster's house. Now or forget it."

"All right! Can I bring Kevin Hughes?"

"Come alone or no deal." Dru hung up.

Charlene whirled to Kevin in surprise, knowing she had to speak with Dru. "I have to go—will you take a rain check for lunch?"

"Sure." Kevin didn't question her further, having heard her part of the conversation. "You safe?"

"Yes. Meeting Dru, but he's being secretive." She shrugged. "Call me after you speak to your friend? I'll let you know what Patrick says when I get ahold of him. He might not be around this weekend though."

"You got it. Want me to make an anonymous phone call to the station about the Hawthorne Hotel open basement door?"

She grinned. "I would owe you a full steak and lobster dinner at Turner's. You *and* Amy."

"Deal!" Kevin waved and walked toward the bandstand in the park, phone in hand.

Charlene hurried to the Lobster Shack three blocks away. Would Serenity be there too?

When Charlene arrived at the quaint restaurant with big booth seating, she searched for Dru's dark hair, but didn't see him.

"Hey," a redhead whispered to her right.

She turned toward a wide-eyed young man in a suit jacket and slacks. His dark hair had been dyed auburn and didn't match the scruff at his jaw. His hand quivered as he gestured her to the booth and the seat across from him.

Why the disguise? Was he that scared of being arrested? "You might not remember me. I'm Charlene."

He didn't chitchat but launched his complaint. "I need your help so I can get back to work. The cops want to see me, but I almost got arrested when I volunteered some information at the department. Figured they'd want to know what I saw in Alaric's house."

She shrugged out of her jacket. "I know I sure do. You were at the station Saturday night?"

"Yep. When it seemed like the cops wanted to put me in a cell for murder, I asked to use the restroom and dipped out the side door." Dru pulled at his chin. "I interned at the Peabody for three months before I got hired in the security department. High level. My record needs to stay squeaky-clean."

"You broke into Alaric's house, though."

"Basement door was unlocked and he had drugs everywhere. Creepier than that, he had a refrigerator stocked with blood, labeled, like for a hospital."

He'd told Stephanos about the blood the night of the ball. Drugs probably weren't that big of a shock these days. Dru drummed his fingers on the table in a nervous rat-a-tat-tat.

"Where have you been? I tried to call you." She imagined him in a dark apartment with the lights on low. "Your place?"

"God, no. I must've slept through the cops knocking on my door Saturday morning but they left a card. I had no idea Alaric was dead. Serenity left a message for me to hide out so I've been laying low at my grandma's house." He kept on in a rush. "She passed away six months ago. Serenity's been bringing me food and stuff. I can't believe that freak was going to kill her."

"And Serenity was supposed to kill Alaric." Charlene studied Dru's earnest face.

"She wouldn't have done it. Not even if he drugged her, like you said he might have. I believe it. I saw pipes and powder, syringes." His voice broke. "She's a good person. I know she wouldn't have gone through with it. Serenity doesn't do recreational high."

"Serenity's shared everything?"

"Yeah. We've been doing a lot of talking, just the two of us. I would go to jail for her, if it helped. She says it won't."

"Did you kill Alaric?"

"No." Dru held her gaze with no sign of nerves.

"I'm trying to keep you both out of jail. Serenity doesn't know where she went until she remembers coming to around three in the morning. At her house."

"I was at the pier, drunk and stupid. Pissed." His knee jounced, shaking the table. "She showed up, out of it. Slurring. Off-balance. She kept on about the spell and Alaric missing." He paused. "I made sure she got home."

"Does she know that?"

"I told her but she thinks I'm trying to protect her and lying for her." He tugged at his reddish hair curling past his ears. "That's really how it happened. As an employee for the museum, I have the code to unlock the gate for the House of the Seven Gables and we waited under the trees there until the police came by. I knew I had to get her to the vineyard so I flagged down a ride and paid cash."

Charlene sank back against the cushion with a groan. "No trace that you were together or have an alibi."

"Which is now biting me in the butt, but when you're panicked and drunk you don't think so clear. I had no idea Alaric was dead." Dru scrubbed his stubbly cheek with his palm.

"Can I get you lunch?" Charlene waved to a passing waitress. "What are your specials?"

"Lobster club."

She looked at Dru, who nodded.

"We'll take two of those with fries and a beer, okay?"

Dru nodded again. "Sam Adams."

"Good for me too."

The waitress hurried off.

Charlene kept her attention on Dru. "Now. How do I know that you and Serenity didn't kill Alaric?" Serenity had been covering for Dru the whole investigation.

He straightened in shock. "S'cuse me?"

"What was Serenity wearing when she arrived at the pier?"

"Oh. Uh, her costume from earlier. The velvet cape kept us both warm."

"Did she still have a star sapphire?" She watched him for signs of evasion, but he seemed aboveboard.

"I don't know what that is."

"It was an expensive necklace on a gold chain. Dark blue, white striations in the center."

"No. Not that I remember."

"Alaric gave it to her. I can't imagine her taking it off." Serenity still in her costume confirmed that she'd been at Alaric's but bolted.

The waitress brought their food and drinks and left again, running her tail off on a Friday lunch hour.

"Hey, you said that you used a code to get into the private grounds . . . Will there be a record of that?"

Dru raised his bottle. "I can check with our security people once I'm back to work. I've been out on personal leave the last week. I'm due in tomorrow, but I'm terrified the cops will be waiting for me." He exchanged his Sam Adams for his club sandwich, taking a large, hungry bite. "I thought for sure the killer would be caught by now and I'd be off the hot seat."

Charlene broke a fry in half. "See if you can track down the driver you hired to bring Serenity home. It will at least give you a time marker to share with the police."

"Good idea. When did he die?"

"Alaric's body was found Saturday morning. We don't know the time of death."

"Serenity's been filling me in, but we have to be careful 'cause the police are watching her. There's no phone or internet at Grandma's place."

He was alone with nobody to vouch for him, besides Serenity, also under suspicion. She could understand why he was nervous. Charlene raised her head and set her sandwich down. "When you were at Alaric's that night, did you go through the whole house?"

"Yeah." He followed a bite of sandwich with a swallow of beer.

"What was in the basement?" She and Brandy hadn't made it down below.

"I think someone was living there."

Asher, probably. "What did you see?"

"Besides a bunch of drugs and clothes tossed everywhere? There was a coffin—open, and a stack of crates filled with stuff. Packing crates. No pictures or anything personal." He sneered. "It was a flophouse."

"Was there a fireplace?"

"Yeah. Not lit. Old-fashioned." He dabbed mayo from his mouth.

"Did you see a door or entrance into a tunnel?"

Dru dropped a fry to his plate in disbelief. "What?"

"You know," Charlene said, sipping her beer. This was not a bad club sandwich and she'd add it to her list of recommendations for her guests. "The smuggling tunnels."

"I wish they'd just shore them all up." Dru's eyes narrowed. "Nope. No strange entrance leading into the abyss that I noticed." His smile was derisive. "There's a lot of myth around the smuggling tunnels. Just be careful not to buy into it. There's no hidden treasure buried by pirates."

Charlene's cheeks heated. "I'll keep that in mind." She blew on a hot fry. "You should speak with Detective Holden. Do you want me to go with you to the station?"

"No. That place gives me the creeps. I wanted to tell them about the drugs and the blood, but they just wanted me to confess." Dru polished off his beer and his lunch like he wanted to get out of there. Fast. "I didn't kill Alaric. When Serenity was at the pier, she had clean hands—I mean, no blood or bruises. She doesn't even know for sure how Alaric died. There were no defensive marks on her."

"He had a stake through the chest."

"That was in the news." He shuddered. "Killed as if he were a vampire. Proved to be human in the end."

Charlene didn't elaborate on Alaric's troubled childhood. "What are you going to do now?"

"See if I can find the driver, like you suggested. I have to prove myself innocent—I don't trust the police."

"Dru." Charlene patted his hand. "The Salem PD is very good at their jobs. Not once have I had cause to doubt them and there have been a few . . . challenges since I've moved here from Chicago." She sat back. "Just so you know, I'll have to tell the detective that I spoke with you today."

Dru tensed with alarm. "Serenity said I could trust you."

"You can. I know you can trust Detective Holden too."

"Let me think about it. Thanks for lunch." With that, Dru left the Lobster Shack and blended into the crowd.

CHAPTER 23

"D r—" Charlene bit her lip before calling out Dru's name. The kid was surprisingly good at disappearing into the waiting patrons around the restaurant. Speaking aloud to herself, she said, "Sam isn't going to be happy. Between the Hawthorne Hotel and now not somehow convincing Dru to turn himself in?"

She wasn't making any points.

Charlene waved to the waitress for the bill and while she waited, she dialed Patrick, not at all surprised that she had to leave a message asking about the tunnels. Some days were like that—walking uphill both ways in a snowstorm. The old saying from her dad made her miss her parents.

When this was over, she'd call them for a good chat.

Charlene walked to the Salem police department, leaving her Pilot in the lot by the Hawthorne Hotel.

She checked in at the front desk. "I'd like to see Detective Holden. Is he around?"

He greeted her in the sitting area ten minutes later. "Charlene—great timing. I was about to take my lunch."

"Oh? Too bad. I just finished eating at the Lobster Shack."

"Ah. With Kevin? How'd that go?"

"I've got some news for you concerning the Alaric case."

His smile fled. "Okay. Come on back to my desk then."

They were not friends in this instance. She wished they could find a way past this awkwardness.

He ushered her toward the seat across from his desk.

"What is it?" His brow lifted. "Does this have anything to do with the anonymous tip about the Hawthorne Hotel's basement entrance?"

"It does not," she assured him, keeping a poker face. "I just had lunch with Dru Ormand and wanted to let you know. He called while I was with Kevin."

Sam's eyes narrowed.

"I asked him to speak to you and assured him that if he wasn't guilty, which he claims he isn't, then he has nothing to worry about, as you are a fair man who only wants justice done." She shifted. "For some reason he feels like you all wanted to toss him in jail when he was here to tell you about the drugs and blood at Alaric's house."

"When we went to inspect the house there were no drugs. Elisabeta let one of my officers in that morning. The blood in their refrigerator is not illegal." Sam shrugged. "What else?"

"Dru says that he and Serenity were together between twelve-thirty and three. What time did Alaric die? What actually killed him—the stake?"

Sam watched her carefully.

"Fine, don't tell me, but it might influence Dru's decision to come in."

He interlaced his fingers on his desk. "There's no reason not to tell you. The coroner's report said that Alaric died between midnight and three AM."

That didn't help Dru or Serenity. They were each other's alibi, but Serenity had told her about the gaps in her memory, so that was a concern for everybody. The PD would look at the facts. Dru had threatened to kill Alaric. Serenity had a spell prepared to kill Alaric and bring him back to life.

Her shoulders slumped. "Did you speak with Elisabeta and Asher about their alibis?"

"Neither are home." His eyes were steady on hers. She couldn't read his mind like Brandy might, but she wasn't sure that she wanted to.

"Celeste? I would think she'd be the easiest to break."

"Thanks for telling me that. We weren't sure who to call first."

"I'm trying to help, Detective. No need for sarcasm." She leaned forward, hands folded in her lap. "Did you speak with her?"

"I left a message."

"Sam! Is that it? No arrests?"

"That's how police work goes, Charlene. One step at a time."

She blew out a breath. "You had a question about Orpheus?"

"Carl Stephenson? Oh, that's right. Did you see any other jewelry in his hotel room?"

"He had some rings on. The night of the ball he was wearing platinum hoops, not the diamonds."

He fished a folder from the stack and opened it, then nodded. "Those were in his luggage. Thanks."

She wanted to help so badly. To end this case so that she and Sam could go back to being friends again. "I wish I could do more."

He ran his fingers through his mustache, a familiar gesture that always got her heart humming. "Serenity Flint is very tight-lipped." He stared at her coaxingly. "I'm sure she'd tell you things she wouldn't the police. Have you spoken with her?"

Confession time. A chance to repair the bridge separating them.

"I have, as you might know." Dare she tell Sam about Serenity's memory lapse? She would lose Serenity's trust as well as Brandy's, and yet with Sam looking at her like this, what was she supposed to do?

"What?"

"Well . . ." Charlene hugged her purse to her lap. "I need to ask you some pointed questions before I decide if I can betray a confidence."

Her stomach churned, but if it helped Serenity and found Alaric's killer and Orpheus's, she'd have to live with it.

His gaze narrowed. "Don't you know me by now?"

"Of course I do, but this is a delicate matter. Promise me that you won't be judgmental? That you'll listen to her with an open mind? Even if she talks about spells or necromancy?"

"I will." Under his mustache she noticed a hint of a smile.

Go time. "Serenity might have been drugged without her knowledge or consent . . . that's how Alaric had control over her."

Sam's jaw relaxed. "Well, that's a start. Now I can share the fact that Serenity has agreed to come in this afternoon to give another statement. She's also given bloodwork, but I doubt we'll find anything."

A weight lifted. "I'm so glad."

"She also said that you convinced her to come forward with some important information. Want to give me a hint?"

"I'd prefer you hear it from her." Charlene released a breath. "If it goes as well as I expect it to, I'm sure she'll convince Dru to follow suit."

"Thank you, Charlene. I know you don't like the sluggish pace we set there, but we must be thorough." His expression thawed slightly.

"I should go." She stood and gripped her purse tightly to her chest.

"I appreciate you coming by the station for this. I think it helps create a clear boundary. I'm the law."

She nodded and left, a part of her hurting over the loss of their previous camaraderie.

Charlene went home to talk things over with Jack, but her ghost was nowhere in sight. She hoped Serenity would tell the truth and clear herself, and convince Dru to do the same. Now, she had to figure out a plan to trap Asher into making a big mistake—he wouldn't break; she was sure of that. All signs, to her mind, pointed to the tall, lanky vampire wannabe.

Asher could have been hiding in the closet and run down the road behind Alaric's. So what if Patrick hadn't recognized the name as the man who'd read his book and inquired about an underground tour? At his age, he might get confused at times. She was much younger but was constantly losing her keys, forgetting things, checking in the fridge for what she didn't know. Stress worked in mysterious ways.

Now that she and Sam were on good footing, she texted Patrick if the name Orpheus rang a bell. She'd practically convinced herself that Orpheus had killed Alaric, and so Asher had killed Orpheus out of revenge. She just had to prove it.

Kevin texted with a message that he was still waiting to hear back from his friend—she replied that she was also waiting.

If she didn't find something to do for the next hour she'd go crazy! She pulled her note cards from her desk drawer. The front had a picture of her bed-and-breakfast on it, and inside was blank to accommodate whatever occasion arose.

She went through the list of previous guests and began thanking them for their visit, offering a 15 percent discount on future visits. By the twentieth her hand was tired. No wonder everything was done online—handwriting was time-consuming. No Jack, no Kevin, no Patrick.

By four, Charlene decided not to take being ignored personally and went to help Minnie with happy hour. "What can I do to assist?"

Minnie handed her a knife. "Slice the lemons for our sangria. We're doing Mexican tonight."

"Yum! What is that mouthwatering dish you're cooking?"

Minnie bent over to take a tray out of the oven. "Mini–cheese quesadillas and beef tacos. I made the sauce earlier and I'm just keeping it warm."

"Sounds good, smells great." Her lobster club had worn

off and she could hear her tummy rumbling. She snatched one of the steaming quesadillas and blew on it. After a sec she bit into the melty cheese and murmured her appreciation. Pointing at it as she munched over the sink, she said, "This is so good. Avery's missing out."

Fridays were the teen's day off so she could hang out with her friends after school.

"It's a new recipe I tried using jalapeño cheese. We can make them again."

At ten to five, Charlene helped Minnie bring the trays in and put them on the side table. Both women carried the large punch bowl of sangria, without spilling a drop.

The guests began arriving in twos. Fredrick and Marjorie were dressed for fine dining. They shared they were going to a top-notch steak house.

"I've never been there," Charlene told them. "I want to hear all about it when you get home."

"Of course. We read the reviews and it's a five-star!"

"I'm sure it is. So how are you enjoying your visit so far?"

"We're loving it. Nothing to complain about, not even the weather. Don't worry, Charlene, we'll recommend this beautiful B and B to everyone."

"I appreciate that, Marjorie. Fredrick. You should bring friends with you the next time you visit."

Charlene moved on to Jennifer and Chase. "Okay, tell me about your day. You look like you've been having a great time."

"We have. Went to Plymouth Rock, which in itself is overrated, but we had so much fun in the town around it. Great little boutiques and art shops. Funky bars and vendors on the street. So cool, right, Chase?"

"Must admit, I'm not the kind of guy that likes to walk

around all day, seeing a line of vendors trying to entice you in. But it wasn't like that. Laid-back. No hassle. Great winery and brewery too."

"Sounds awesome. It's still on my list of things to do." Maybe when her parents came to visit next she'd take the time to show them the sights, and experience it herself.

Glancing around to see if she'd ignored anyone, Charlene spotted Jack in a corner next to the fireplace, watching each guest. What was he thinking? He studied them as if trying to read their minds, but that was something he couldn't do—unlike Brandy Flint.

Playing the perfect hostess, she did the circuit, making sure she spoke to each of her guests and asked about their day. They were all important to her, and yet all she wanted right now was to shoo them out so she could retire to her suite and talk to Jack.

One sangria later she made her excuses and escaped to her rooms. Her cell phone blinked from where she'd left it on the coffee table.

With a flick of Jack's hand, he floated it toward her.

"Patrick and Kevin and Serenity?" Charlene glanced at Jack and blew out an exasperated breath. "I've been waiting for these calls for hours. And now all I want to do is sit with you and tell you everything that happened today."

"I'm sorry, but you left it here and I didn't want to interrupt you when you were busy with guests."

"This isn't your fault, but I'm bone-weary and just want to relax with you."

"Return the calls, and then we can."

She looked at the phone, then back at him. He gestured for her to go ahead.

She dialed Serenity first to make sure the girl didn't

need to get bailed out of jail, although she trusted Sam and knew he'd never do such a thing unless he had a really good reason. Still, it made Charlene glad when Serenity answered on the first ring.

"Charlene!"

"Hi—everything all right?"

"Yes. Dru said you gave him the idea to track down the driver for that night, and guess what? He did! Guess Dru tipped the guy really great and told him to make sure I was on the porch. I remember that part, a little. Dru is talking to the detective, who is being so cool. Can't believe it. We owe you, Charlene."

"I'm so happy things are working out. Do you happen to remember any more about a vampire named Asher?"

"No. I know like four Ashers, three girls, one guy. He was a pipsqueak in middle school."

Pipsqueaks grew. Sometimes into really tall men who would know that the Flint family was very powerful in a real way. And maybe even tell Alaric. As she thought this, she heard Serenity curse and say, "Asher Torrance."

"Go tell Sam, Serenity. Whatever you do, don't confront Asher yourself. He's very dangerous."

"I will. I'm still at the station."

That was the safest place for her until Asher was behind bars.

"Do you have the star sapphire necklace?"

"Nope. I must have lost it. I feel really bad about that."

"I don't think you lost it, hon. I suspect it was taken from you."

"Who would take it, and how?"

"My hunch is that Elisabeta put something in your water when you both were at the house. You were totally coherent when you left the ball that night, and yet Dru said when you were at the pier with him, you were out of it. You don't remember. Elisabeta said she gave you water—supposedly to calm you down. I bet she took the necklace back then."

"That bitch!"

Charlene nodded. "Elisabeta and Asher are not nice people. The necklace is very valuable, so make sure you tell Sam to search her house."

"Why wasn't Asher there that night?"

"Don't know, hon. Asher had been dancing with one of my guests, Celeste, and she overheard Asher and Alaric argue over you and the ritual. Alaric told Asher to stick with the plan."

"What plan?"

She shrugged, not that Serenity could see the action. "I think for everyone to be immortal."

"Jerk."

"Yes. Anyway, Asher decided to make sure Celeste didn't say anything about the plan, so he told her that he'd argued with his other roommate, Elisabeta, and needed a place to stay. She invited him to the bed-and-breakfast."

"I feel bad for her, another innocent girl, getting dragged into this mess. Do you think Asher killed Alaric?"

"I can't say for sure." She did, she did, she did.

She wouldn't be surprised at all if the star sapphire was also part of a jewel heist, but she had to let that thought go because Kevin was beeping in. "Got another call. I have to go. Stay alert, and tell Sam everything we just talked about."

"Bye, Charlene!"

She clicked over but missed Kevin. Patrick was on the line when she said hello.

"Charlene! How are you? I received your messages

and I admit you have me tantalized." He chuckled. "Orpheus was the name—you got it. Is it important?"

Charlene knew it! "Not important . . . it just was bugging me, trying to figure out who had contacted you. When was that again?"

"That Friday night."

"Oh. Hard to believe Halloween was a week ago. I hope you notice some sales—I've been bragging about how wonderful your book is. People love the idea of smugglers and hidden tunnels."

"Appreciate that. Thanks. I'll check in with Lucas when I get back on Tuesday."

She felt her spirits sink with disappointment—she'd hoped he would be able to show her the tour earlier.

"Well, let me know when you're ready. My friend Kevin Hughes is also interested in the tour."

"Wonderful! Ideas for a second book are coming at me faster than a snow flurry."

"What do you think of *Sordid Secrets* as a title? I hope you're able to concentrate more on the treasures still in Salem. I had no idea that there was so much wealth here all related to that time period."

"I knew you were into it," he said with a chuckle. "We'll talk later—no matter how curious you get, please stay out of the tunnels. I've been doing some structural work on parts of them and hope to get the city's approval to start the tours again."

"Let me know how I can help. I'm a pretty good fundraiser." She ended the call and immediately dialed Kevin. "You won't believe what's been going on. Serenity and Dru are at the station with Sam and all is well—she knew Asher in middle school!"

Kevin sniffed. "Middle school? Wow. If he was raised

in Salem too, he would know about the Flints and their magickal powers."

"That's it exactly. How are you?"

"Well, I'm ready to take you up on that steak dinner. Maybe tomorrow night—after we get back from the tunnels. *Underground*."

"What are you saying?"

"I explained the situation to my friend, and he told me exactly where to get into the tunnels below the Hawthorne Hotel."

"But they were filled up!"

"Maybe not. Who told you that?"

"Dr. Steel. He said he's been under them himself—back in the day, before they decided to keep everybody out."

"He sounds like a cautious old man afraid of a lawsuit. Where is my adventurous friend? I say we go check it out. But you can't tell Sam. Got it?"

She exchanged a look with Jack, who hesitated before saying, "You should go."

Tomorrow Asher should be behind bars and possibly Elisabeta too—the only danger she'd be in was getting stuck in the dark. Kevin had been in the tunnels before. "All right. What time should I meet you, and where?"

"In front of the Witch Tea shop. Dress warm. Boots or sneakers. Let's go see if it would be possible to get a body from the hotel to the wharf."

Not just a body. Alaric's body.

CHAPTER 24

Saturday-morning frost glistened on the ground. It was chilly outside, so Charlene wore her favorite black jeans, a light-blue cashmere sweater, and a warm wool jacket. She put on a pair of dangly silver hoops, reminded of the platinum earrings Orpheus had worn. She'd had dreams of vampire pirates as her brain tried to justify going in the tunnels.

She opened the door to the sitting room. Jack waited for her with a scowl on his handsome face. "I want you to be very careful with this," he said. "Why isn't Kevin picking you up like a gentleman should?"

"Whoever called him a gentleman?" she countered. "Besides, we both have things to do once we're done there."

"I know this is important," Jack conceded, "but I

worry about you beneath the city, even with Kevin and your pepper spray."

"I'm not at all worried. I have a flashlight with extra batteries." She blew him a kiss and let herself out.

Kevin, in hiking boots and a thick jacket, waited for her outside the Witch Tea, which used to be the old First Federal building.

"How do you feel about breaking the law?" she asked him.

"Not breaking it really, just . . . a mild bending of the rules. I do have my tour guide license."

"And you're putting it at risk."

"This isn't the first time I've been below Salem's streets, Charlene." Kevin shrugged, his eyes bright. "Unless you don't want to go?" He pulled a copy of *Salem Confidential* from his inner jacket pocket. "Got the last copy from Lucas yesterday. This Patrick Steel is brilliant. I know exactly where the Hawthorne Hotel is on this map."

"Lead on!" Charlene stifled the rising guilt at not letting Sam know where she was or what she was doing. "It had to be Orpheus who wanted to get an underground tour from Patrick—offered him five hundred bucks. Patrick is not bribable, however, and turned Orpheus down."

"Didn't I just say he was smart?"

She couldn't tell Kevin about Orpheus being choked before supposedly leaping from his balcony window at the Longmire Hotel. The historical Longmire . . . was it possible that it too was connected somehow to the tunnels?

Orpheus had been reading a book on Salem's sordid history. The dirt on the boots by the door. Asher had to have been down in the tunnels. But when? He'd been visible at the ball. Hadn't she seen him after Alaric disappeared?

Did Asher have to keep Orpheus quiet about . . . what? What secret?

"Earth to Charlene!" She raised her head at Kevin's voice. Though nine in the morning, it was gray and dreary—the fall air crisp. "Ready?"

"I'm ready!"

"Be careful, follow me precisely. I'd hate for you to trip over a piece of rock or brick."

"I'll pay attention."

"Most of the tunnels are shored up." He looked at her sneakers and his own boots. "Watch your step. Remember, there might be rats. We'll clomp and scare them away."

"How far to the Hawthorne Hotel?"

"In a straight line, can't be more than a mile. Nothing is far in the center of town. The city filled a few in when the sewer lines were added. Broke the chain of tunnels in a few spots when they did the work." Kevin stepped in the narrow space between the shops.

Charlene followed him and didn't dare look back at daylight.

Kevin stopped abruptly. "Hang on. I brought these." He put a headlamp attached with a band around his forehead and turned it on, then handed one to Charlene.

"I have a flashlight." She patted her purse.

"Hands-free is best." Kevin grinned. "You sure you can do this?"

"I'm sure." She nodded quickly, eager to get answers and satisfy her curiosity.

"Salem's tunnel system was arranged so that the merchants could bring the goods in from the ships without bothering the townsfolk." Kevin stomped on a metal slab. "According to Patrick's book, this used to be an elevator shaft. The boats would unload, and the shop owners would have their goods delivered and whisked below-ground. Usually guarded to stop thieves."

"You're pretty knowledgeable," Charlene teased. "I can tell you studied last night."

"I talked to another one of my tour guide friends. Be-cause the underground tour was nixed, the main guy doing it now changed the name from Underground Tun-nels to the Pirate Tour. They can walk the streets above the tunnels, pointing them out. City's happy. Stories still get told. No fines." Kevin unlocked a door to the Witch Tea building. "No adventure."

She laughed, a thrill of anticipation making her tone higher than normal.

"There's an entrance through here. I called Teresa and she agreed to let me use her access below."

Though morning, the back space of the tea shop was very dark.

"This way. Teresa told me that she uses this for storage so it's pretty clean and well-lit, but once we leave this space, we need to be careful."

Charlene entered the storage area, the scents of herbs and spices reminding her of her friend Kass Fortune's tea shop. She'd have to see if Kass had a basement. They crossed the cement floor to the door connecting to the main tunnel.

"Bolted from within, that's good." Kevin slid it back and walked out, the headlamp creating shadows along the brick and stone walls. When they were both in the corridor, he shut the door to the shop and Charlene's heart thudded.

"You know how to get back?"

"I do." Charlene made out Kevin's Adam's apple as he swallowed hard. "This way."

Dirt and stone crunched beneath her sneakers. Kevin's boots created an echo as he strode forward. She hurried after Kevin into the dark, the rubble and dust in the tunnel musty and dank.

"It smells old." She reached out to touch the rough brick, which scraped her fingertips.

"Couple hundred years," Kevin said, stopping to admire the pieces. "See this brickwork? Made local."

"It's in such good shape."

"Protected from the elements down here," Kevin said. He pulled the book free from his jacket pocket and read it, the headlamp flickering ominously. "This way to the Hawthorne."

They walked for about ten minutes, then Kevin stopped to check the map again. The path was about four feet wide with arches on either side. Occasionally there would be a door, or a filled-in place where a door had been. Wood trusses lined the ceiling.

Eerie shadows that could be rats or mice darted around the corners. Charlene was glad for her extra flashlight, just in case. She'd tossed nuts and a bottle of water into her purse as well. Not that anything would go wrong.

"You know where we are?" Charlene asked. Her voice was much more confident than her racing pulse.

"Yeah." Kevin's headlamp bobbed in affirmation. "We continue on, then hang a right at the crossways."

Rocks sounded behind them. Rats?

Kevin shone his light in the dark, but there was nothing there.

Charlene's temple pounded. "What about the pier?" She risked a glance behind her, certain a giant rat would be sneaking up on her. "Does this particular tunnel lead to the water?"

He patted his map he'd copied from the book. "It's a mess of corridors so it's hard to say."

"I thought it would be more of a direct route."

Kevin chuckled. "That was the original point of the tunnels. Smugglers had to bring in legal and not-so legal goods. Legal aboveground, illegal below. They'd have had their own passageway from the wharves."

What washed in, could go out. Like Alaric. Dead or alive?

Charlene shivered and wrapped her jacket tighter around her body. She followed Kevin past a series of brick archways over alcoves with a knee-high wooden shelf in each. "I think these were beds. According to Patrick, Salem used to be part of the runaway slave Underground Railroad."

Charlene imagined the scared people running for their lives finding shelter here beneath Salem's streets. "Poor folks."

They went on a bit more. To the right were new wood braces on a tunnel. "That must be some of the construction Patrick was talking about."

"What?" They stopped to admire the clean lines.

"Yesterday he warned me to be careful of the new construction."

"Huh. He must own some of the property above us. My buddy said the permits to do anything down here are a bitch."

They kept walking and passed a warren of cubbyholes. "What's this?"

"On the flip side of the antislavery coin, the Chinese were forced to live down here. Couldn't be seen by the 'good' citizens of the city." Kevin snorted. "The men, however, managed to make their way down to gamble. Or"—Kevin waggled his brows at Charlene—"visit the brothel."

Charlene scoffed. Brothels were old news—she'd read the book too. "And opium."

"You got it. People and their vices." Kevin slowed to compare the doorways in the stretch of tunnel they were passing now. They had to go around fallen timbers and bricks, but so far the path had been passable. "Can you imagine having these doorways connect, house to house? You'd better hope to have good neighbors."

Charlene followed Kevin carefully over a broken truss. "No. I miss the fresh air and we haven't been under-ground long." She checked her phone for the time—forty minutes had passed. As expected, there was no cell service down here. "I wouldn't like it at all."

"I know what you mean. Even though this is drier, I prefer the cold, brisk wind in my face. This is claustro-phobic." He shrugged, accepting the fact but not com-plaining.

Charlene enjoyed the misty rain and lighter snowfall in her new town. "It's too dark for me to think of it being an everyday kind of thing."

"Back then, they would have had lamps and under-ground lighting so it wouldn't be so dreary."

She glanced around at the shadows and jumped when a wood beam fell behind them. "This place is starting to freak me out. Let's hurry."

"We're fine."

They reached a crossroads beneath the city, and she could hear the road above them. "I sure hope this holds."

Kevin laughed. "It has for two hundred years—you're safe for the next ten minutes. This way." He strode away from the main street into a side corridor. There was no light at all except for what they had from their headlamps.

About five minutes passed and Kevin stopped. "Here we are."

Charlene looked around but didn't notice anything different about where they stood.

Kevin jabbed a thick finger to the stone timber and brick ceiling and brightened the light on his headlamp. "The Hawthorne."

Charlene scanned the walled-up doorways and brick arches above them. Light shone through one of the arches and dirt had been piled as if a rat had dug into the wall. She shivered with apprehension.

The structure wasn't as sturdy or well-kept as the earlier part of the tunnel, by his friend's storage space.

Stones and timber that had fallen from the ceiling were haphazard on the ground. The exit to their right was completely blocked. The left led into a dark, forbidding corridor.

She narrowed her eyes. "What's that?" she asked, pointing to the ground.

Kevin leaned forward. "Oh, hello . . ." He examined the gathering of dirt and debris at the floor. Prints.

"Rat?" Charlene asked.

"Too big for a rat." Kevin's tone held excitement. "Or a mole."

Charlene strode forward, taking off her headlamp to focus on the ground like a flashlight.

Rusty-colored drops created a splash against the wall. Six feet up was a hole wide enough to remind her of the crawl space under the hotel. For the first time since they'd started this underground adventure, she was truly afraid.

She dropped her gaze. Footprints smudged the dirt and it seemed like something had been pulled along the path. Something heavy.

Man-sized.

Charlene pressed her hand to her stomach.

Kevin reached down to pick up a white and pointy object from the ground. "What's this?"

He screeched and dropped it.

Charlene peered down. It looked like a part of a vampire costume. An eyetooth? Enamel rather than plastic. Asher had said he'd lost his teeth. She reeled backward.

"Don't touch anything," she said. "I think we've discovered where Alaric was killed. Asher said he'd lost his vampire teeth."

"Asher's the killer? You're sure?" Kevin pulled his phone from his pocket, accidentally dropping Patrick's book with a *thunk*. "No service."

"Pretty sure. I know he was involved. Asher was in sight the whole time that night. I bet he set up the stake with blood."

He'd been in sight, so had Orpheus, by the door. Elisabeta had been near Serenity. To make sure that Serenity did her part of the plan. Charlene went over everyone's position in her mind that she knew. Ticking off each person and their costume, accounting for their whereabouts. Lucas, Stephanos. Evelyn.

The pirate . . . where had Patrick been when the lights went out?

Patrick had said he'd been contacted by Orpheus wearing giant diamond earrings on Friday night, but that wasn't true.

Friday, Orpheus had worn thick platinum hoops with his zoot suit. Patrick was tall. Fit.

He definitely knew the tunnels.

It didn't make sense.

She paced back and forth between the wall and stones, searching the brick for anything that might help explain until her gaze snagged on a crumbled section.

"Kev." She smoothed her fingers over a hole in the wall. "Could this be a bullet hole?"

Kevin clicked a picture of it. "Yeah. We should go."

She wished she could talk to Kevin about the Night Shadows theft ring, but she'd promised Sam. She needed to talk to Sam, because Asher hadn't killed Alaric. Not with a gun. He'd been in sight the whole time. Orpheus's killer had seen him on Saturday. Killed him on Saturday and had been brilliant in trying to point the finger at Asher.

Brilliant.

Her stomach knotted. Her mouth dried. Orpheus would connect Patrick to the vampire scene.

"Kevin, somebody who knows the tunnels *very well* was down here."

"Dru? He wouldn't hurt anybody, not like that."

"I agree with you." She nodded at the book in his hand, not understanding *why.*

Kevin scowled.

"Who else knows them well enough to write about them? Knows the riches and history? Who is protective of the tunnels and said that the documentary falling through was for the best?" She brought her own book from her purse and tapped the author's name.

"Dr. Patrick Steel did not kill Alaric." Kevin dismissed this with a boot scuffle. "Sorry, Charlene. I just don't buy it. Why?"

"I don't know why. But he was very specific about me not being in the tunnels today. That he's been doing construction on them." She shook the paperback.

Charlene smelled a match, then a flare of light shone above her head as a stick of dynamite hit the ceiling. Dirt and wood and brick debris rained down, pelting her. She ducked and whirled.

Kevin stomped on the flickering end until it spluttered, then was at her side, peering into the dim tunnel. "What's going on? Who's there?"

Patrick ambled into their line of vision. He'd been the rat following them. She should have paid attention to her apprehension, but she'd foolishly explained it away.

"You're quite intelligent, Charlene, but your impatience makes you predictable. I've been watching you close enough to know." His white hair was tucked beneath his red wool cap, his jacket unzipped.

She straightened and reached into her purse for her pepper spray, feeling blindly around inside until she clasped the cool cylinder. She kept her hand on it, in her bag. Away from Patrick's view. "What do you want?"

Patrick lifted a heavy rock and aimed it directly at the loose beam with a solid throw. It connected, cracked, and more dirt and brick fell, creating a cloud of dust that made it difficult to see. "I'd set up the crime scene for the police to find, if they bothered." He rocked back on his heels.

Charlene realized he'd been the mastermind but still didn't understand why.

"They should be arresting Asher Torrance right about now, with the gun I planted in his bed of a coffin." Patrick scowled. "I can go house-to-house underground with nobody the wiser. I wasn't expecting you." He shifted toward Kevin. "Or you."

In the four-foot-wide corridor there was no place for them to hide. Nowhere to run. "Why did you kill Alaric? He was a vampire wannabe with no ties to you whatsoever."

"Wrong you are, my dear." Patrick's smile was grim, as if he took no joy in harming her. "He was head of a ring in Louisiana. A thief who planned on moving his gang here to Salem, to steal from us. He thought he was being so slick, asking about the tunnels and if they still led to the Peabody. Offered me a cut if I didn't turn him in. Not going to happen on my watch. Salem's treasures stay in Salem."

"Why didn't you just report him?" Charlene waved dust from her face. "You didn't have to kill him."

"He was sneaking around down here, that's why. I'd already warned him once—he had to die." Patrick winked. "Folks go missing in these tunnels all the time."

Bile rose up Charlene's throat. Had he killed others down here for trespassing? For getting too close to his secrets?

Patrick squinted in the light of their headlamps. "How did you realize that it was me?"

"Guess you got sloppy," she said tartly. Her fear made her voice sharp. "Orpheus's earrings. You said that he was wearing diamonds on Friday, but he'd been wearing platinum hoops."

Patrick slapped his palm to his thigh, never lowering the rock in his other hand. "You're right. I missed that important detail. As a writer, my job is to connect the dots. Huh."

Charlene gripped her pepper spray within her purse. "It was you in the closet at the hotel."

"I needed to get that book from Orpheus before he ruined everything. He was close to figuring out what I'd done." He clenched his fist and twisted like he held a chicken's neck. "I killed him quick."

She drummed up the image of the man racing away from Elisabeta's and compared it to Patrick. "Was that you running from Elisabeta's?"

"Yep." He grinned at her with a sort of pride. "You almost caught me upstairs casing the house. I grabbed a cloak from the coffin and booked it. That will make a great scene in the novel. I like that title, *Sordid Secrets*."

The man was delusional. "Why were you there?"

"Crafting my plan to set up Asher." Patrick raised the rock in his hand. His strength was that of a pirate, not a professor. "I'm a crack shot. Two more should knock it down and you and your friend here will disappear."

Kevin stayed by Charlene, glancing up at the eroding ceiling. "The police will look for us."

"I know! It will be with great sorrow that I find you and your friend in the tunnels, after everyone has expressly told you how dangerous they are. Collapsed tunnels happen down here often enough. When they uncover your dead bodies, they'll find the evidence that Asher had killed Alaric, and Asher killed Orpheus."

He tossed the rock where it smacked dead center. Debris floated down.

Patrick picked up the unlit dynamite and put it on a

pile of rubble behind him. "I'll save this for afterward. Give you a nice shrine." He chose a big round stone and aimed it at the teetering wood truss over their heads.

Crack.

"You don't have to do this." Charlene's mouth was as dry as sandpaper.

"I do. This will tie up all loose ends. I appreciate your support of *Salem Confidential*. Your story will definitely make the second book. What a way to kick off the tours! Book tours."

He aimed at the beam one more time. Charlene knew she and Kevin were going to be trapped in the tunnels. No cell service. No way of contacting anyone. Possibly dead, crushed by the ceiling of the tunnel.

While Patrick focused above them, Charlene raced forward, streaming pepper spray into his face.

Kevin grabbed her and hauled her to the side of the tunnel as the top dropped in large chunks, covering her body as the wood and brick fell on top of them, each with bruising force. A brick hit her on the head and she blacked out.

CHAPTER 25

When Charlene came to, she knew it couldn't have been too long that she'd been out because the dust motes were settling like gray snowflakes around them. Kevin was a heavy weight on top of her. "Kevin?"

He didn't answer. Brick. Stone. Wood.

She wished she had a light but was afraid of the dynamite. Where was it? Did Patrick have more? Where was he?

"Patrick?"

Neither man answered. She scooted out from under Kevin, finding his wrist. His pulse beat strong beneath her fingers.

He was alive.

She crawled carefully away, not wanting to dislodge anything. It was a gray dark. Her purse was still over her shoulder and she dug into the side pocket for the flash-light she'd put into it.

A groan sounded to her right. Her ankle hurt. Her tem-ple ached. She found the button for the flashlight and turned it in the direction of the noise. Patrick lay there, eyes closed, bleeding from the nose, his face sticky from the pepper spray and the brick dust congealing to it.

He was alive too. She'd dropped the can of pepper spray when Kevin had pulled her to safety. She rooted in her purse and found the umbrella—it was all she had left as a weapon. She prayed he would stay conked out.

Now, how to get them all out of here?

She returned to Kevin and started lifting the wood and brick off his body. His lashes fluttered. Somewhere she'd lost her headlamp and so she put the flashlight between her teeth to use both hands.

"It's me, Kevin. Charlene. We're okay. You have to wake up." She patted his cheeks—gently at first, then harder. At last his eyes opened.

"Stop hitting me," he said through a bloody lip. He tried to smile. "Guess the tunnels are dangerous."

"Especially when stalked by a crazy author." She helped Kevin sit up.

He winced and grabbed his rib. "Ouch."

She uncapped her water and gave him a drink.

He squinted at what she held in her hand. "How many pepper sprays did you bring? I know you're from Chicago, but still . . ."

Charlene showed him that it was her fold-up umbrella. "I'm ready if it starts to rain."

Patrick moaned and shifted.

"Will we run out of air?" Charlene asked. She kept her fear at bay by the skin of her teeth.

"No. This path will eventually go to the wharf, I think. And there are grates and holes. I think we should go back the way we came. Teresa will notice if we don't return."

"Okay. He thought he was so smart." Charlene rose gingerly, not putting her weight on her right foot to avoid the stabbing pain it caused. She glared down at Patrick Steel. "He became a character in his head. The pirate, the professor, the author. Tour guide. Guardian of the tunnels."

"Hope he likes the role of prisoner," Kevin said, sneering down at the man who'd tried to kill them.

"Should we tie him up?" Charlene asked.

Kevin undid his belt around his jeans, and they bound the author's hands together, though he remained out cold. "Just in case," Kevin said.

An hour later, Charlene and Kevin had minced their way toward Witch Tea, just as Sam, handsome Sam, burst through the door of the storage room from the street entrance, followed by two officers in Salem blue. Teresa was right behind them.

His face paled when he saw her standing there. "Charlene!"

At his voice, she forgot all about being strong enough for her and Kevin. All about her and Sam's rules. To hell with boundaries. They'd have to find a way to stay friends no matter what they were doing. She needed Sam in her life.

She launched herself into his open arms, and he buried his face in her dusty hair.

"How did you know to come here?" she whispered against his neck.

He kept his strong arms around her. "Brandy called and said she'd had a dream where you were in a tunnel and couldn't breathe. Dru is working security for the Peabody, and he knows about this tunnel entrance—it's a popular one because it's in such good shape. Teresa said you and Kevin had gone down here but hadn't returned. I had to come." He pulled back just an inch to look into her eyes. "You're bleeding."

She stayed in his arms, not caring about her injury—she had to clear Asher. He wasn't innocent in all this, but he wasn't the man who'd killed Alaric or Orpheus. "Did you arrest Asher?"

"He's being questioned about a gun found in his possession. He claims it isn't his. Why?"

"Sam, you are not going to believe what happened. Patrick Steel, the author, killed Alaric and Orpheus, and set up Asher to take the fall."

Kevin laughed but winced and tightened his hold on his ribs. "He views himself as the guardian of the tunnels. He may or may not have killed other people before now. I guess Alaric was part of a theft ring?"

Sam stiffly pushed back from Charlene, as if alarmed that she'd told Kevin what he'd told her.

She gave a slight negating shake of her head. "Patrick had warned Alaric to stay out of the tunnels. He had underground access from his basement. Alaric planned on robbing the PEM and foolishly offered Patrick a cut for his silence. Patrick shot him. The stake-sized hole was all part of the ruse to trap Asher."

Sam's shoulders sank. "Alaric was the leader? I'll be looking at those crates in the basement more closely now. Thank you."

He gave his officers orders on going into the tunnels. Armed and wary. They moved quickly. "Wait," Charlene called. "You'll need a flashlight." She handed hers over. Kevin offered the other policemen his headlamp.

"They have penlights already. Can we get you to a hospital now?" Sam's voice was deep with concern.

"I can call an ambulance," Teresa said.

"No!" Charlene and Kevin replied in unison.

"I can drive," Charlene said.

"How about I drive?" Sam countered. "That way I make sure you both go. Come on. I'm parked in front."

He reached for her hand and Charlene gladly let him take it. His worry turned to pointed questions once she had gotten into the passenger side of the SUV, and Kevin in the back. "Why didn't you tell me what you were up to?" Sam demanded.

"Would you have approved?"

He smoothed his mustache and clenched his jaw, answering honestly. "No."

She loved that about him. His integrity. "You would have told me to mind my own business—but this was my business. People I care about were in danger."

His brown eyes focused on hers and she squirmed. "Turns out that one of the old janitors at the Hawthorne Hotel knows of a trapdoor in the basement where you and Kevin were looking. Under a stack of chairs. He was shocked anybody had been down there. Usually people steer clear because of the ghost stories."

"How did you know it was us?"

He shook his head and started the car. "I am a detective. It's my job to follow anonymous phone calls and size eight women's sneaker prints."

"Oh."

"Tell me again how you put this all together."

She glanced back at Kevin, who gave her an encouraging nod. "I thought Asher had killed Alaric right until we were in the tunnel under the hotel. Patrick had warned me not to go there. He set up Asher as the scapegoat in the event the Salem PD went into the tunnels."

"You didn't listen to his warning." He drove toward the hospital, knuckles tight on the wheel.

"I thought he was an older author who liked to dress up as a pirate. Had no idea that he was a killer, Sam. Trust me. You said that Brandy called you?"

"Yes. Seems she had a dream that you were in the tunnel buried alive. She was quite adamant I do something. I know how interested you were in the tunnels, so I asked around, and Dru told me about Witch Tea and the entrance there."

"Brandy comes from a clan of powerful witches that include Serenity. That's why Alaric wanted her to perform the necromancer spell. Did you find the star sapphire?"

"Yes." They stopped at a light and he stared at her. "Among other jewels pertaining to the heist. I just don't understand how you can say all of this with a straight face."

"There are things in Salem you don't understand, Sam." She used to be just like him. Black-and-white. Logical explanations. And then she'd been blessed with Jack.

"Light's green," Kevin said, breaking the tension.

"I understand human nature." Sam stepped on the gas, calm and collected. "Alaric left New Orleans after his band of thieves was almost caught. He fled to Salem, thinking he could set up shop here. Cover his actions with his vampire ways—out at night, strange crowd, blood-drinking. Who's going to look closely?"

Charlene shrugged.

"He made plenty of people angry. Elisabeta, whom he'd replaced with Serenity, with Orpheus, his right-hand man, who he'd ditched to hold the rap in New Orleans when things got too hot for Night Shadows. You said he'd told Asher that the plan would go on—well, that meant the robbery of the PEM. Elisabeta is singing like a full church choir to try and get a deal. Those are the real connections I look for, not hocus-pocus about the witching hour."

Sam was very smart, very keen, very anti-paranormal.

"You know what, Sam? I hate to say this, but your unwillingness to believe in something more could hinder your ability to see what is right there before your eyes."

"Alaric was no vampire."

"Yet you came to save me on the word of a witch." She touched his hand. "Thank you."

Sam parked at the hospital in the emergency section. He turned off the car and got out, opening her door for her as Kevin stumbled out of the back.

Sam tipped her chin, emotions churning in his gaze. "Don't make me regret it."

CHAPTER 26

Within hours Kevin and Charlene were examined and released. Besides a few bumps and bruises, a couple of stitches here and there, they were fit to go. They decided to get their cars later and Kevin had a cab waiting when she finally walked through the exit doors. A thick bandage on her head hid her only wound, though her ankle was sore.

She'd take that as a win.

Kevin hugged her lightly and whistled a tune as he escorted her into the back of the cab. She grinned up at him, feeling like a champion who'd survived the great wars.

"You're a little worse for wear," he whispered, "but in Sam's eyes you still look mighty fine."

She punched him lightly. "Have you told Amy about our adventure today?"

"Yeah, briefly. She's going to meet me at the bar."

The cabdriver turned his head. "Excuse me, sir, but do you have an address?" Charlene chuckled and Kevin gave him the address for the bar, Brews and Broomsticks. "The lady will be dropped at Charlene's Bed-and-Breakfast after that."

The driver met her gaze through the rearview mirror. "Don't worry," she told him. "It's just right up the road."

Charlene felt a sudden chill. Under the cabbie hat, the driver's eyes reminded her of Callum's from the Pirate's Cove. *Nah! It was just a spooky night, that's all.*

She folded her arms on her lap and kept her focus on Kevin. It was a good thing she wasn't driving. "Guess Amy thinks you're quite the hero, right?"

"Well, *we* are. Helped Sam wrap up the case."

"Yes, we did."

She glanced out the window as Kevin began to text and let her mind wander. Fall was her favorite season. The end of summer, but the beginning of cozy winter. A few minutes later the cab turned into the parking lot of the bar. The sky had darkened; the overhead clouds grew ominous. Thunder cracked and she shuddered.

"Stormy weather," Kevin said. "It's our lucky day, Charlene. We didn't die, *and* we beat the rain."

"We are lucky." Her cell dinged and signaled a message. Sam wanted to video chat.

Kevin gave her a light kiss on the cheek and a cheery wave as he ran to the bar and pushed through the heavy front door.

The cabdriver turned around. "Where to?" She didn't make eye contact with him as she gave him the address.

Sam called and she answered, wincing as she saw the bandage on her temple reflected back at her.

"They let you go?" he asked, concern on his face. "What's that for?"

"I'm all right, Sam. They put a few stitches on my brow. Guess now I'm damaged goods."

He rumbled a low laugh. "Just the way I like my women." She couldn't even smile without something tightening. "If you're not feeling too badly, I'd love to take you to dinner."

"I'm pretty much wiped." She wanted her house, her bed, tea. Silva. Jack. "How about tomorrow?"

"It's a date since the case is over. Get some rest tonight. You've been through the wringer."

"I will." She didn't want to say goodbye until she was safely at her doorstep. "Did you wind everything up after I left?"

"Sure did. He's quite the storyteller. Giving us more than we need."

She felt a little sorry for Patrick, a gifted writer, a man whose mind had slipped away in his fight to save the city's buried treasures.

Patrick would have killed them both as he had Alaric and Orpheus, and who knew how many others were down there? Justice would be served and he'd have to spend the rest of his life in prison, but it was a sad ending to the professor's life.

"I'm glad it's over, Sam."

"Yup. Wanted to tell you that Alaric had that sun allergy, as well as an allergic reaction to garlic. In his medical records."

Poor Alaric.

"This is one of the top-ten strangest cases I've ever cracked. Elisabeta will be sent to Louisiana to face trial for her part of Night Shadows. Asher too. Couldn't have done it without you, Charlene."

"Thanks, Sam." Warmth flooded through her. Since moving to Salem, the cold, empty shell of her heart continued to open a little at a time. "What about Celeste?"

"She called her friend Tommy, in Jersey, and she's going home."

"That is the best news. See you tomorrow."

"Night."

The screen went dark.

"We're here, ma'am."

They were parked in front of her brightly-lit mansion—a sight for sore eyes. She touched her bandage above her brow.

"Nice place you've got here. Might invite my family to stay when they come for a visit from New York."

When she studied the cabbie's face under the glow of her porch light, she realized that he didn't resemble Callum at all. A good ten years older, a trimmed beard, and kind brown eyes.

"That will be twenty even," he said.

She added another five for a tip, then stepped out of the car, tucking her phone into her jacket pocket.

Minnie and Avery gasped as she strode through the door. "What happened to you?"

"Long story, my friends."

Minnie wiped her hands on her apron but didn't press—she knew Charlene would tell her everything in time.

Avery stepped forward and put a finger on the white gauze. "Are you hurt?" Her eyes misted with tears.

"No, barely at all." She gave them a brief explanation

of her day, knowing there would be many more questions she'd have to answer. But not now.

"I'm exhausted. Please tell the guests I won't be able to come to our happy hour, and I'm sorry to miss it."

She headed for her rooms and Jack. Another story to tell. If only Jack could read her mind, she could rest while he watched over her.

"Charlene! Where have you been?" He put a gust of air beneath her chin to peer into her eyes. "You've been hurt. Sit down. What happened?"

She tucked her feet under her on the love seat, snuggled in a comfy blanket, and slowly walked him through the events of the day just so she could put the ugliness behind her.

Jack was kind and sweet, listening, asking questions when needed, praising her for a job well done. "You're remarkable, Charlene. I couldn't be more proud of you."

"Well, Kevin deserves half the credit. We both got lucky, I guess."

"More than luck," Jack insisted. "We never suspected Patrick Steel as the killer."

"He wanted to collapse the tunnel over us."

"Using your pepper spray against him took a great deal of guts." Jack briefly closed his eyes. "I can't imagine what I'd do if this had ended badly."

"You'd put on your Superman cape and rescue me."

"I wish it was that easy." He chuckled. "You know what I'm going to research next?"

"No—but I can see that you're excited about it."

"There must be a way for me to escape the confines of the property. If I can fly around the widow's walk, why can't I just keep flying?"

"I haven't seen you do that lately." She put her arms around her knees, searching his face. "Do you want to leave?"

"Of course not. But if you were in trouble, I'd want the ability to save you."

She reached for him, stopping short of touching his cheek. "Let's start the research in the morning."

"You get a good night's sleep. It will be a busy day again tomorrow."

She remembered Sam had said almost the same words. A thought flickered through her mind. If she could choose, who would it be? Jack? Sam? Her eyes slowly closed, and she drifted off to dreamland.

Sam was sitting at the bar when she entered. She stood for a moment in the doorway just taking him in. A gorgeous man. Not just tall, but the whole muscular package topped with a strong face and thick chestnut hair. The way he'd held her yesterday?

He turned just in time to see her almost drooling over herself, and he gave her a welcoming smile.

She strutted over and plopped down on the stool next to him. "Hey there, good-looking. You need a date tonight?"

"No. Sorry. I'm booked with the sweetest girl in town."

"Ah. Why are you being so nice to me? It's disarming."

"You prefer it when I get mad?" Sam studied her face, the bandage at her brow, then skimmed down the rest of her. Nothing much to see since she was wearing a coat, but still she blushed and her insides warmed. "Come on, let's grab a booth." He put a ten-dollar bill on the counter and carried his imported beer.

She walked beside him, her hip brushing his to send tingles up and down her spine. Sam had reserved a table toward the back. He helped her remove her coat and handed it to a waiter standing nearby.

They both slid into the booth, heading for the middle, almost shoulder to shoulder. "What are you drinking?" He was so close that his mustache feathered her cheek as he asked the question.

"A glass of cabernet, please."

A waitress took their order and handed them menus, but they continued to stare at one another. Charlene was silent for a moment, taking in the beauty of this flesh-and-blood man. If only, she thought, not for the first time.

As long as she had a resident ghost living at the mansion, she couldn't date any man and risk hurting Jack. Especially not a detective who refused to believe in the paranormal.

She released a long breath.

"A penny for your thoughts?" Sam's hand found hers under the table.

"Oh, they are worth far more than that," she assured him.

"Tell me about them?" His deep brown eyes caressed her even as his thumb caressed her wrist.

"Not now. Let's order dinner, and then we can talk about serious things. It's nice just to be out with you."

His mouth softened with a smile. "We don't have to wait so long between dates. If you have the will, I have the way."

"Sam . . ."

They were interrupted by the girl who dropped off their drinks. "Are you ready to order?"

"I am if you are." Sam brought her knuckles to his mouth.

His mustache tickled her sensitive skin.

"I could give you a few minutes," the waitress said, backing away.

"Won't be necessary." He glanced at Charlene. "The usual?"

She nodded. Sam was a meat-and-potatoes man and had a French dip loaded with thinly sliced beef. She preferred something lighter and had shrimp over angel-hair.

After the waitress left, they raised their glasses and toasted as they gazed into each other's eyes. It was the most romantic moment she'd had in the past few years.

"What are we doing?" she asked softly, finding herself staring at his lower lip.

"Something we should have done a long time ago."

"I can't." She pulled away, but not too far.

"You can." He cupped her face and kissed her slowly. "If you don't like it, I'll stop."

She laughed and shook her head. "Not fair. We're almost like business partners," she said, hoping to set the tone for the next hour or two.

He clinked glasses once again. "Here's to partners, no matter what kind."

"What's gotten into you tonight?"

"You."

"Why?"

"Because as maddening as you are, the biggest thing about you is your heart."

She took a drink and he did too.

"I probably shouldn't have said that. I'm getting carried away." His voice deepened as he moved closer to her. "I want to be carried away." He abruptly turned his head.

She swallowed hard, wishing things could be different.

"No, you don't. You know I'm a real PIA."

"No arguing that."

Charlene put her drink down and cupped his face, gently placing a kiss on his mouth. When she was done, she said, "Sam. Now isn't the time for us. But some day, it might be. I can't promise more than that."

Connect with U s

Visit us online at
KensingtonBooks.com
to read more from your favorite authors, see books
by series, view reading group guides, and more.

Join us on social media

for sneak peeks, chances to win books and prize packs,
and to share your thoughts with other readers.

facebook.com/kensingtonpublishing
twitter.com/kensingtonbooks

Tell us what you think!

To share your thoughts, submit a review,
or sign up for our eNewsletters, please visit:
KensingtonBooks.com/TellUs.

Grab These Cozy Mysteries
from
Kensington Books